# ALL SPELL IS BREAKING LOOSE

## FATE WEAVER
### BOOK TWO

REGINA WELLING

ERIN LYNN

Willow Hill BOOKS

# CONTENTS

# ALL SPELL IS BREAKING LOOSE

CHAPTER

# ONE

L eather pants ought to come with warning labels.

An itchy tag reading: These pants will make you sweat and do nothing at all to increase your self-esteem might have made me choose my outfit for the night more wisely.

Instead, heat and friction produced a sheen of sweat that made my thighs chafe against the unforgiving hide, and I sent up a quick apology to the poor animal who had given up their skin so I could try to feel more comfortable in my own.

Magic coiled inside me like an adder waiting for a juicy mouse as I slid into and tried to blend with the crowd. Port Day festival transformed a six-block by six-block square ranging from the harbor all the way to the city center into one giant party. Foot traffic-clogged streets lined with food stands serving everything from deep-fried ice cream sandwiches to fish and chips. Dozens of artisans hawked their wares, pulling both the willing and the uninterested into the depths of their tents with the promise of treasures untold.

I passed by a makeshift stage where music, heavy on drums and bass, settled into my breastbone like a curse and enticed my heartbeat to a primitive rhythm. At least I was dressed halfway appropriately for this section of the venue.

The air smelled of booze, a jumble of different foods,

warm bodies, and desire. No, not the sexual kind, get your mind out of the gutter.

Okay, maybe there was an element of sexual tension, but I also sensed plenty of people looking for a love that lasts. That group was in luck because it's my job to make soul mates happen.

I'm Lexi Balefire. Witch. Matchmaker. Keeper of the Balefire Flame. Daughter of Cupid. A lot of titles to carry, but I try to make it work. Oh, and let's not forget Fate Weaver— whatever that means. I'm still trying to figure it out myself.

A restless hunger to ply my trade burned in me like a dark fire as I made my way through the crowd. So many matches so little time.

What I do doesn't require an algorithm for counting points of compatibility; it's both simpler and more complex than basic math. Before Awakening to my full complement of witch magic, I ran my business on a combination of instinct and the matchmaker's version of an internal GPS connected to my gut. Depending on the strength of the signal, I could pinpoint the location of a client's perfect match to within a few feet. I guess you could call me a divining rod for love.

In the weeks since my Awakening on Beltane, my process had changed significantly.

First of all, I no longer needed to get acquainted with clients before knowing exactly where to find their perfect match. I had always enjoyed the part of my job where information filtered in by bits and pieces as my clients talked a blue streak. Discovering the nuances of personalities helped create a connection between myself and the people I helped

—one I missed now that its absence left me struggling to feel engaged.

Since there was no one to ask—save for my half-brother, Jett, who hated me with a fiery passion (his input would most definitely fall into the "unhelpful" category)—I could only speculate that my witch magic impacted whatever love mojo I'd inherited from my father's side of the family. Finding out my dad was Cupid (yes, that Cupid), and that Cupid plus witch equaled Fate Weaver had answered fewer questions than it raised.

My heritage did explain my affinity for lovers, so that was a boon. The rest—the change in how my matchmaking skills worked—was not.

This day, though, the sweet desire to be helpful had given way to something slightly darker, more urgent. Something almost strong enough to be called a compulsion. I needed to be in control; to pluck the strings that turn a chance meeting into a fated encounter.

Port Day festival was one of Port Harbor's biggest yearly events and my all-time personal favorite. What's not to love? There's good food, dancing in the streets, great art, and best of all, a ton of people to watch. And to match.

The thread of giddy power coursing through my veins drove me among the crowd, into McGinty's pub where I intended to use a back exit that would drop me near the corner of Ballast and Westmoreland—that much closer to where my boyfriend was slated to play a set in half an hour. Plenty of time to do my matchmaking thing along the way.

On my way through the dark din of the pub, I grabbed the low back of a barstool and gave it a spin. The cute blond, who had been flirting with the brooding man to her left, now faced her one and only—the shy guy to her right. A kick to the leg of his chair pulled his attention away from the glass cradled in his hands. Their eyes met, and the match was a done deal.

"We'll be back in ten," the lead singer announced into the ringing silence left behind when the band stopped playing, and I corralled a thirty-something man with an earnest face before he could follow the wrong woman outside.

Biting the inside of my cheek to keep from smiling at his astonished expression, I covered by saying, "I can't believe how long it's been. You should have kept in touch." By the time he figured out we'd never met before, I'd maneuvered him across the floor and right into a knot of women waiting for their turn in the ladies room.

"Oh my God, it's like a crazy reunion." Keeping hold of the guy, I slung an arm around his perfect match. "How have you been? You two know each other, right?"

"I...uh..." He stammered.

I shoved the pair together while focusing my attention vaguely across the room.

"Hey, there's Sally, gotta run. You two catch up, I'm sure you have a lot to talk about," I said brightly, then raised my voice to no one, "Hey! Sally. Wait for me." I hurried out the back door, leaving the astonished beginnings of another match behind me.

Exiting McGinty's and zigging right, I made up a quick and dirty spell to make the middle-aged man ahead of me poke a bystander in the ribs. The sudden shock caused a chain reaction through the crowd.

While Mr. Poker went on his merry way, the innocent pokee jumped and stepped on the foot of the woman standing just behind him. She yelped in surprise and careened into the support pole holding up the canopy of a pottery maker's tent. It wobbled just enough to slip sideways and slap against the back of the man standing on the other side, who lurched into the street just as his perfect match happened by.

Boom. I gave myself a mental high five for using magic for good.

Three matches in a row. A decent result but not enough to tame the fidgety spirit still pulling my feet through the streets. I needed to find more, do more, bring more love into the world.

A force stronger than the intuition I'd relied on to make my business successful drove me forward. I hated the feeling of not being in perfect control and yet I craved the burst of adrenaline-like energy that came each time match met match.

Despite my best intentions, I felt myself becoming hooked on the seductive power of changing fates with almost no effort and the festival provided plenty of willing fodder. With each match, the craving grew.

Around the next corner, Mackintosh Clark stood near the stage he would occupy in a few short minutes. Our relationship was still new enough that the mere sight of him gave me the flutters. It might have been his rock star good looks— blond hair long enough to curl around a chiseled chin, hands that knew their way across a set of guitar strings—and a woman's body. We exchanged a hug made awkward by the

Gibson slung over his back and a kiss that lifted the top of my head to send it soaring.

"Are you going to stick around for my first set?"

The restless need to keep moving decided the answer for me. "I'll catch the second, if that's okay. There are so many matches here tonight it's an adrenaline rush." Gentle hands cupped my flushed face as Kin dropped a kiss on my nose. He leaned close to keep his next words for my ears only.

"Be careful, okay. Jett's probably hanging around if there's this much romantic energy in the air."

Having sworn to undo my life's work, my half-brother used his Cupid-given affinity to break apart couples before they could exchange true love's kiss, and I wondered if today's driving need to make matches had anything to do with his unmaking them. I hadn't seen him around, but after our last meeting I doubted he'd have the guts to face me.

"I'm on high alert. Don't worry; I can handle Jett." I gave Kin another kiss and walked away.

A woman possessed, I moved through the crowded street like a wraith. As though they sensed a higher purpose, people drifted out of my way as I ghosted among them, putting two more couples together with no regret for the dates they might have left behind. Those unfortunates would get their matches in due time.

No thought was spared for the ephemeral nature of the pairings, either. When a person visited FootSwept Matchmaking, my place of business, they could pretty much count on a *happily ever after.* That was my job, my credo, and I followed through until I was sure the couplings would stick. Due diligence went out the window today in favor of the *happily right now.*

Something about that bothered me, but not enough to stop. Or enough to think about the odds of having so many lonely hearts in such close proximity. Even crowded into a relatively small geographical area, there was usually much more distance between matches. What was up with that?

Logic should have warned me the chances were about as good as winning the lottery twice in the same day.

Logic was asleep at the wheel.

Otherwise, it would have been ringing the hinky bell in my brain long before that niggling feeling of being watched began to lift the hairs on the back of my neck.

The list of people interested enough in my actions to spend time spying on me only included two other names besides Jett's, and neither with the best intentions. My arch-enemy Serena hadn't the subtlety to pull off a surveillance mission on her own, and wherever she went, Jett followed. Or maybe it was the other way around—I didn't care enough about either of them to waste time trying to figure out the nuances of their relationship.

Then there was my mother, Sylvana Balefire. My innocent mother who'd been cut down in the prime of her life by my wicked grandmother. Or so I'd been led to believe.

Still, her intentions fell into the category of undefinable. Long-absent from my life for reasons I couldn't fathom, she'd popped up just long enough to disguise herself as a friendly shop owner, give me the key I needed to gain my full level of power, and then disappear again.

Poof.

The only thing missing was a cloud of purple smoke and any sort of explanation for why she had bothered coming back at all if she never meant to stay.

She had to know I'd eventually figure out her deception, and she should have been the one to tell me about my father. Instead, I'd learned about him from Jett during a showdown after he'd used Serena to cast a soul curse on my boyfriend. His bombshell explained a few things while leaving even larger gaps in my knowledge of my own family. Gaps my mother could likely fill if only she would come back around.

My inner Cupid rose up again and washed all other thoughts away. There were matches here, and it was my job to make them. You know what they say about ambition—it's blind, and I was living proof.

Every couple I put together fed the craving for more and more and still more. I knew I should stop while I still could, but I liked the rush too much. I liked it right up until the balance tipped and I knew I was about to tip over the edge of losing control.

Almost running, I dodged down a side street less clogged with bodies than the rest; the pull so strong I couldn't stop. I reached the outer edge of the festival, the sounds of music and laughter becoming quieter with each step. I heard the argument escalate before I found them. Jett's fingerprints were everywhere; if I didn't have a mess to clean up, I could have followed it straight to him and ended his reign of terror before he even laid eyes on me.

But I did have work to do, so I focused my attention on the couple in front of me. Honestly, I can't even tell you what either one looked like, but my nose filled with the stench of ill intentions and I had to take action, so I stepped into the middle of the fight.

Kids, don't try this at home.

Two things happened at once. The first was that their fury turned on me, and the second shocked me even more. It shouldn't have, though: this wasn't the first time a couple's life played out before my eyes in a powerful vision.

Not a still life in three dimensions, but a living, breathing representation of me standing behind the man and woman mid-fight, and I couldn't help noticing the back of my hair needed a trim. I resisted the temptation to reach out and see if I could touch the solid-looking figure because there was no scenario where the results wouldn't freak me out.

What if I did and the dream me flinched? Or if my hand went right through my body? Or even worse, what if I touched myself in the vision and the real me could feel it. Nope, not doing any of that.

Keeping my hands to myself I circled around so I could see my face, and that freaked me out more than touching myself would have. Shut up; I know how it sounds.

My eyes were lit with pink fire. Pink. And I was holding a bow and arrow in my hands. Okeydoke. Take me to the funny farm, because I've lost it. Me holding a bow and arrow would be like a baby trying to drive a race car. Not safe, not smart, and not effective.

Still, there I was, clutching the thing in my hand like I knew how to use it. Alternate universe much? The weapon seemed to be made of golden smoke and roiling shadow, its barb a heart-shaped tip.

I'm telling you, I almost peed my pants when my dream-self lifted that bow and nocked the arrow, because as she did she cocked an eyebrow at me.

A pounding heart and wobbly knees greeted me when my focus snapped back to the present and to the couple who'd been fighting so bitterly only moments before. Cute couple. I would have put them together myself if one or the other had asked for my help. And I would have felt good about doing it because every shred of my intuition insisted they were meant for one another. That this man and this woman, together, would make true love's kiss.

The bow and arrow from my vision had to be symbolic of my father's blood running through my veins, because no one in their right mind would turn me loose on the world with such a weapon. On a good day, my athletic skills are limited to running in heels.

I was not the hunter/gatherer type. Well, I might have hunted the shoe sales and gathered people together, but I don't really think that counts. Handing me a pointy object? No. Just no.

The dream or vision popped like a bubble, leaving me in the same place I'd been before it happened, right in the middle of an impending breakup. In other words, with my nose stuck in someone else's business.

Don't ask how I did it because I'm not even sure myself. The best way I can describe it is that Lexi moved aside and something else, something much larger than myself took over. Cold fire rushed through me to burn Jett's mark to a cinder, then to ash to waft away on the wind. The fight was over, the couple coming out of it like they'd been sleep-walking.

My job was done, but I couldn't pull back the fire. I needed help. I needed Kin. Turning, I raced back the way I had come.

Like a leviathan stirring in the deep, the power built inside me to the point of pain. My ears popped, then roared with sound and, certain everyone around me must be feeling the same pressure, I cringed. The crowd continued to party, unaffected. Dancing, drinking, eating, and shopping. Nausea dragged my stomach into my throat, weakened my knees.

Dizzy, I stumbled into a crowded pub where it seemed like the bathroom was moving away from me at a faster pace than I could walk. Stumbling forward, I smacked into a wall of tattooed arm and T-shirt clad chest.

"Sorry. I'm sorry," I shouted over the ringing in my ears.

"Are you okay?" T-shirt's companion, all teased hair and raccoon-dark makeup, grabbed my arm in a helpful gesture. "Had a few too many, Honey? Here, let Delta help you." The woman slung an arm around my waist and practically carried me toward the door marked *Chicks*.

"Thank you." My voice sounded tonelessly loud in the muffled quiet of the ladies room. "I just felt all funny for a minute; it's passing now." Marshaling my strength, I focused tightly on making my way to the sink with as close to a normal walk as I could muster. Water hitting porcelain rang through my head like thunder, but I managed to splash wet coolness on my face and felt marginally better for it.

When I lifted my head, I caught Delta's intense gaze in the mirror. The way she looked at me seemed to hold a little more concern than most people might feel about someone they met during a chance encounter in a bar.

"You're pale," Delta stated the obvious as I studied my face in the mirror over the sink. My eyes glittered oddly, at least two shades darker than their usual bright emerald green, and she was right, my skin looked pasty. Clucking quietly to herself, Delta pulled a blue bandanna from some hidden pocket, flipped the tap to warm water, and ran the cloth under the stream. Before I could protest, she cupped my chin gently and began to wipe at my cheeks.

Tingling heat, the kind I recognized from long experience of living among the Fae, rose from the point of contact and I knew Delta carried more than simple human blood. She was a supernatural of some type.

"What's your name, honey?"

"Lexi Balefire," I managed to stammer, and searched her eyes for signs of recognition. For all I knew, my mother had come to me in disguise again.

"Is there someone I can call for you? A friend, or maybe you have family nearby. I'm sure I've heard the name Balefire from somewhere. Are you related to Sylvana Balefire?" Something stronger than simple curiosity put a gleam in her eye and she leaned forward as she waited for me to answer.

Hearing that name coming from a stranger roused my suspicions and I searched her face for signs of familiarity. Not that I knew what to look for anyway. Burned out of all the family photos, my mother's true face was a mystery to me.

But she was good at putting on the glamour, since none of the witches at Beltane recognized her when she showed up as Athena. It still twisted my guts that she'd come back from the dead and chosen not to reveal herself to me.

"She was my mother, but she's long dead." I'll give her credit—if Delta really was Sylvana, her face betrayed nothing. Not even the slightest raise of an eyebrow.

"Oh, I'm sorry to hear that. Why don't you let me take you home?"

"Listen, my boyfriend's playing in…" I pulled my phone out of my pocket to check the time. An hour ago. "A few minutes," I lied. While I'd become lost in the matchmaking thrall, Kin had played his second set, and I'd missed it.

Several text messages from him attested to the fact that he'd noticed my absence. The final one in the series included a terse message that one of the acts had bailed, he'd been tapped to play the third set, and could I please answer this time.

"I'm just going to head over there. Thanks, really, for all your kindness."

With a single backward glance, she left me to the relative calm of the restroom, and I wobbled into a stall to sit for a moment and take stock of my condition.

The churning in my gut reminded me of stumbling off one of the big coasters when my faerie godmothers treated me to a day at Six Flags for my eleventh birthday. Motion sickness blended with a heady dose of adrenaline and made more potent by two kinds of strong magic turned my senses inside out.

"Breathe, Lexi. Slow and easy." I might have spoken out loud. In a moment, I was back to normal—or whatever passes for normal in my world, anyway.

Not trusting myself to the crowd again, I texted Kin that I was feeling a little under the weather and I'd see him later.

I blame television for most of my misconceptions about being a witch. Didn't Samantha wrinkle her nose and translocate herself to wherever she needed to be? Wouldn't that be convenient? I'd planned on riding home with Kin, and since that wasn't happening, I now faced a long walk back to my office where I'd left my scooter.

With no other option, I dodged down one of my patented shortcuts.

"Hello again, Miss Balefire." I recognized the gritty tones and tingle of power with a sinking feeling in the pit of my stomach. Delta.

"Are you following me?" I asked the first question that came to mind even though it rated a big, fat ten on the dumb-question scale.

"I need to talk to you in private, Miss Balefire. Make it easy on yourself and come with me." Gone was the fluffy quality from the bathroom, shed like a second skin to reveal a feral face and the honed body of a predator. Didn't jive with the bad movie dialog, and I wondered if she was about to make me choose between the red pill and the blue one.

"And if I don't?" What would she do when four angry faeries showed up? All I had to do was send out the distress signal. Not that I planned to do that; I'm a pretty powerful witch and half a God besides. Even under the weather, I should still be able to hold my own.

Talon-tipped fingers tightened around my bicep in response. She'd moved so fast I hadn't even seen a blur. I countered with a loosening curse that was meant for releasing knots, not for making someone let go of your arm. What can I say? I'm powerful but inexperienced.

Delta let out a strangled sound, and I yanked my arm away. Her fingers dangled like wet noodles, and the look she gave me was pure fury, but I didn't waste a lot of time waiting for her to regroup.

I bolted before the shock wore off and heard her voice faintly behind me. "You didn't have to do that; I only wanted to talk. You can't hide forever, *Lexi* Balefire."

Ignoring that for the load of horse manure it probably was, I gained a decent lead before I heard the pounding of her feet. If I haven't said it before, this is *my* town and I know her like no one else. A few well-planned turns and I increased my pace enough to make a strategic dash through the back door of Sinful and turn the lock behind me.

Very few people are familiar enough with Port Harbor's infrastructure to know about the warren-like system running through the oldest sections of town. According to what little documentation there is, the connections served as a way to move people and valuables to safety should the town be invaded by pirates. Scoff if you will; it was a hazard, apparently, of being a harbor town.

These days, most of the exits are locked or closed off to preserve privacy, but you can still get from Sinful to one of the suspended walkways crossing over Main Street and letting out into The Commons, an urban version of a mini-mall.

From there, I went up another level, cut through a second walkway, and came out in the next building down from my office at FootSwept Matchmaking. With every step the phrase *why me* reverberated in my head. Did getting my magic amount to slapping a giant Kick Me sign on my back?

First, my half-brother declares war on my business, and now this. I'm a nice person. I help people find love. Why are crazy supernaturals trying to burn down my life?

I had no answers to any of those questions by the time I navigated two basements and made my way back to my office where I peeked out the windows to ensure the coast was clear. I fired up the scooter parked in my vestibule and rode home, leaving Delta still searching for me somewhere in the city.

Correct me if I'm wrong, but people who only want to talk to you rarely leave finger-shaped bruises on your arm.

# TWO

My house appeared quiet as I tooled up on Pinky, my little bubble gum-colored scooter. The silence was unusual, especially with the scent of magic swirling from every window and door. Faerie godmothers fulfil the same role with witches as guardian angels do with humans, but mine had taken things a step further.

Upon finding me orphaned, Terra decided to raise me herself and drafted two of her three sisters to help. A witch raised by faeries. Yeah, nothing normal about that, but we made it work.

Until the fourth sister, Vaeta, had moved in and shifted the dynamic, and we had to readjust.

Still, tonight I wasn't in the headspace to face a house full of crazy

Besides, I owed Kin an explanation for bailing on him earlier, and he wouldn't smell Delta on me like my godmothers would. I wasn't sure I was ready to share everything that had happened with them until I had time to sort out my thoughts.

Luckily, Kin lived right around the corner. I tilted Pinky into a 180-degree turn and killed the ignition before coming to a complete stop next to his vintage Corvette.

I could have magicked the door open, but if I were going to stoop to that low, I would at least like to be wearing a sexy negligee to soften the whole breaking-and-entering blow. Instead, I was faced with a humorous image of trying to wiggle sensuously out of the skin-tight leather pants that were now glued to my legs by a layer of sweat. Neither my body nor my pride was on board for a beating tonight.

What I needed was a refuge. And a big glass of wine. Fortunately, Kin paid attention, so I knew he was well-stocked for a big girlfriend meltdown.

Knocking once, I let myself in, and heard Kin's smooth song rise over the strumming of his guitar before I stumbled into the living room.

His chocolate brown eyes widened as he took in my disheveled appearance and pink-stained cheeks. The black leather guitar strap became tangled in his haste remove the instrument and envelop me in a warm, concerned hug. As it always did, the touch of him sent a thrill up my spine.

"What happened to you? You ditched me and then your text had me worried." A little annoyed, too, by the sound of his voice, but he settled me on the sofa and kept an arm around me for support. "Are you feeling better now?"

I described what had happened to me but kept the part about holding a magical bow to myself.

"Kin, you should have seen how many matches there were there. I was a tornado, whipping through and pushing people together. It was so much stronger than before my Awakening and more immediate, too. Like those people might never be happy if I didn't help them find their match."

Now that the nausea had passed, I could only remember the high that had preceded it; the intense feeling of purpose I simultaneously craved more of and yet wished would never return.

"Isn't that a bit out of the ordinary?" To have that many matches in one place, I mean? Are you positive that there's nothing else behind it? Did Jett have anything to do with it?" Questions tumbled out of Kin's mouth in a rush.

Jett. Blaming it all on him was the safest course of action, and I could understand why Kin's mind would settle there since he'd nearly died when my half-brother cursed his guitar.

"Well, he did put a whammy on that one couple, but I can't see him tossing matches at me willy-nilly like that— not when it's the exact opposite of his intentions. He's more concerned with *breaking up* fated couples in the hopes Cupid will swoop in and save the day."

Shifting positions, Kin pulled my feet across his lap and eased my boot zipper down and I got distracted for a moment wondering if a spell to ward off foot odor would be considered personal gain or if I could get a pass since it would be to Kin's benefit.

Since our relationship had gone from zero to ninety in record time, we weren't at the *comfortable with each other's funk* stage yet. Truth be told, I wasn't sure that was even a thing. I'd never been in a serious relationship before and the rules were still a little foggy.

My second boot landed on the floor next to the first, and I chanced the spell, just for a little peace of mind.

His fingers playing along my instep, Kin said, "I'm having trouble wrapping my head around that piece of logic. Wouldn't Cu....um...your father be upset at having his work undone?"

"How should I know? I've never met the man. God. I'm not even sure what the naming protocol would be. Honestly, it's a lot to take in, and I haven't let myself think about why he's out of the picture with no contact."

"Well, it's his loss, but I think you're more than capable of handling Jett Striker."

The thought was like a warm, snuggly blanket and I was fully prepared to cuddle up underneath it and hope for the best. Personally, I didn't much care where Cupid was, or why he hadn't made contact with Jett or me for the past 25 years, but my brother certainly did, and he'd do anything to get his daddy back.

What I did care about was keeping Kin safe and off Jett's radar, and that meant making sure Jett didn't find out Kin and I had shared true love's kiss. Screwing with *my* love life would certainly jump to number one on his master to-do list if he was aware Kin was more than just a passing fancy.

"You're probably right." I still wasn't ready to tell him about the vision just yet, especially since I had no idea whether what I had seen was real or caused by Jett's meddling. I needed to sort through that experience for myself first. If the couple whose future I'd seen was uncertain, that meant my future with Kin might also be, and I cared about him too much to cause him any more pain—especially if it wasn't necessary.

"Then why do you look like you've still got something on your mind?" Kin prodded gently. I had to tell him *something*, and since I still hadn't told him about my mother being alive, it seemed like a good idea to absolve myself of one sin before committing another. He deserved some explanation.

"There's something I haven't told you—haven't told anyone. Not the faeries, not Salem, not even Flix."

Kin kept his face free of surprise and concern, though he must have been worried about what could have kept me from confiding in my family, my familiar, and my very best friend, and it occurred to me that he probably figured nothing I would tell him could top the big secret of exactly *what* I was, and we had cruised past that easily enough.

"What is it?" He asked.

I broke away from his embrace with what I hoped was a comforting kiss and began to pace around the room. I do my best thinking on my feet, and Kin was familiar enough with this particular trait that he simply poured me a glass of wine and kept quiet until I began to speak.

"My mother isn't dead." I paused, and Kin's eyes went wide, but he waited to hear what I had to say. He had never badgered me for more information on my status as an orphan raised by faeries, which, now that I thought about it must have been difficult to swallow with no details. And so, I laid it out for him, starting at the beginning, with the one thing I had always known to be true: the witches in my family were wicked.

"When a witch kills another witch, she turns to stone. You know that statue across the street from my house? It's my grandmother. Not *of* my grandmother, it's actually her, Clara Balefire. I'm sure you've noticed the resemblance; we look almost exactly alike."

He must have had a million questions, but Kin didn't press me for details. Or maybe he thought he was better off not knowing.

"When Terra heard my cries, she rushed in and found Clara turned to stone, me swaddled in a basket nearby, and nothing left of my mother, Sylvana, but a black smear on the ground. She assumed the scorched earth my grandmother was pointing toward was where my mother had been standing, and that Clara had killed her."

"Any idea why?"

I shook my head. "Nope. Just one more mystery."

He didn't ask why I'd kept quiet, and for that, I only loved him more.

"So how do you know she's still alive?"

"You remember the first night we met? Out on the street after Salem broke into your house?" I asked, taking a big gulp of the oaky cabernet and willing the wine to work its own kind of magic.

Kin smiled. "Of course, how could I forget?"

"Well, I was on my way home from work, and I stopped at this magic shop near Sinful. And when I say magic shop, I mean it was a place to buy magical supplies, but it was also a *magic* shop. I had never seen it before, and when I went back later, it was gone—like it had never existed." My brow furrowed and Kin's quirked as he motioned for me to continue.

"Anyway, this woman—this witch—Athena, helped me

find the supplies I needed for the Awakening spell and gave me this." I fingered the pendant around my neck, a priceless family heirloom, the missing piece of the puzzle I had needed to Awaken my inner witch.

"Then, after we detached your soul from Skip Stark's guitar, I went back to the sanctum, found the original copy of the Awakening spell, and realized that the only way I could have attained my magic was with the Stone of Blood, and only if it had been passed *directly to me by a family member*. I could just feel it in my gut—that woman in the magic shop was my mother, in disguise."

"You mean she got a glamour spell past you?" Kin interrupted, "Even the faeries can't do that."

I nodded. "I don't know how she fooled me, but she did. I've been looking for her ever since, and then tonight I ran into this woman, Delta—well, actually, she's more than that. She was definitely a supernatural, and at first, I thought she might be Sylvana in disguise. It turns out, she knows my mother, and something tells me they're not on good terms. My mom might be in trouble." I showed Kin the mark Delta left on my arm.

His eyes flashed, "You're positive one of your godmothers would be there in a hot second if you were in danger?" He looked slightly mollified by my reassurance and heaved a big sigh. "Why didn't you tell me about your mother before now? I could have at least been there for you..."

"I haven't told anyone else, if that's any consolation, and I'd prefer if you don't spill the beans to the godmothers. About Delta or my mother. At least until I can sort out my thoughts."

Kin's face changed. "I'm sorry, but I can't make that promise. I think they need to know everything. Especially if this Delta poses a threat. Forewarned, and all that jazz."

Were we about to have our first fight?

"Trust me, you don't want to crack the top on that can of worms, because it could turn out to have been packed by Pandora herself. Nothing good will come of the faeries knowing anything until I have concrete proof."

A motorcycle roared past the house, and Kin waited until the noise died down before pointing at my arm. "Proof of what, Lexi? That Delta is bad news? Those bruises look pretty concrete to me, and what do you think is going to happen when they find out about Sylvana? If you don't tell them, I will."

All things considered, his stubborn face was sort of cute. I wanted to slap it off his head, but it was still cute.

"Give me a few days, at least. Delta will give up and leave once she knows she's chasing the wild goose and if my mother has managed to stay gone for this long, I doubt I'll ever see her again. Clearly, she didn't want me enough to stick around."

That right there was the bitter gall I had been trying to swallow since I'd learned who Athena really was.

"Unless she left to protect you. Don't discount her motives, okay?"

He had a point, and I let him think I was convinced in order to get him to give me the time I needed to think things through. Plus, whatever happened next, annoying as it might be, was up to Sylvana.

"I think family is one of the most important things in the

world. I can't imagine a life without mine, even with all their faults they're everything to me. Don't forget, Sylvana gave you the necklace to help you. Doesn't that give her any points at all?"

Poor, sweet, unassuming Kin. That's the thought that scrolled like a ticker tape through my mind. He still believed people were inherently good, but I wasn't dealing with people here. I was dealing with a witch. Not that witches aren't people. It was all very confusing because some were good and some were wicked and with some it was hard to tell the difference.

"Yeah, she gets a few points, I guess. Can we just talk about something else for now? I'm sorry to dump on you, but I've been over and over all this in my head a bajillion times, and I came here for a slice of normal. Is that okay?"

Kin stood up and wrapped his arms around me, stopping me from further pacing and calming my mind with his hypnotic gaze. "Of course, whatever you want."

Maybe he'd forget about tattling to the godmothers if I distracted him with my natural talents.

"What I want is to get out of these pants." Because they were itchy, but I left that part out.

"Your wish is my command." Kin waggled an eyebrow suggestively, and suddenly there was only one thing on my mind.

I pressed my body closer to his and tangling my fingers in his hair, let the rush of emotion, the festival's carnal energy—all undulating bodies and desperation roiling beneath the surface—guide my desire, pulling Kin tighter a bit more roughly than normal. He responded in kind, his lips (and other things) surging beneath my touch until we were both gasping for air. I pulled Kin out of the living room and down the hall toward his bedroom, and it turns out you don't need to look sexy getting out of leather pants if you've got a hot boyfriend who's willing to peel them off for you.

# THREE

Dressed in a pair of Kin's sweatpants, I avoided the fashion faux pas of wearing my walk-of-shame leather pants out in the broad morning daylight. Somehow, that wasn't enough to spare me the histrionics waiting on the other side of my front door.

"There you are, I was worried sick about you." Evian, in her mini form, flitted in like Tinkerbell and then grew nearly six feet. She had on one of the Donna Reed outfits she thought most appropriate when taking on a motherly role, but in her haste to chastise me, she'd forgotten to put on her face. I don't mean her makeup, I mean her human disguise.

Hair, the bright blue-green of a tropical ocean, spilled over her shoulders and softly framed a face of flawless beauty. Lips to match the hair, eyes the color of an angry sea, and skin like pearls looked plain silly paired with the attire of a fifties housewife.

The dramatic exclamation elicited no more than a raised eyebrow from me. She wasn't fooling anyone with her act. As my official faerie godmother, Evian's sister, Terra, had an inborn ability to track my whereabouts. All four of the elemental faeries had known where I spent the night well enough, but they just couldn't let it alone. Sleeping over with my boyfriend was a new and rare enough occurrence to become a topic of conversation.

"Where have you been? We checked your room, and you weren't there. You know how we worry when you're not in your bed at night." Soleil popped into the doorway behind Evian, trying hard to suppress a grin and I had to smile.

"I lost track of time and Kin was just so dreamy I couldn't help myself."

"Fine. Don't take our feelings seriously. You could have called. It's the polite thing to do." I ignored Evian's fake pouty face and headed toward the kitchen.

"Is there breakfast?" I asked nonchalantly.

"Not for you, Missy. You want pancakes; you sleep in your own bed."

Other than the half-hearted attempt at teasing me, things seemed fairly quiet, which only served to rouse suspicion. If you've ever spent any time around a toddler, you know they are too quiet when they're into something dangerous. Same thing with elemental faeries, except on a much larger scale.

"Lexi's here," Evian spoke loudly enough to command attention, but it seemed more like a warning to stop all suspicious activity.

The kitchen looked like a party goods store had barfed all over it. Several of those dry erase boards on easels ranged around the room, color-coded notes covering their faces. Garlands of flowers draped over half the long trestle table and Terra, elemental faerie of earth, was busy making more of them. The process reminded me of a conductor skillfully directing an orchestra.

A graceful gesture with her right hand sent out a vine to snake along the ceiling. When Terra judged the vine to be long enough, the drawing motion altered to a series of flicks with the fingers of both hands and buds burst forth to festoon the swag. When there were enough of those, and she had placed them to her liking, Terra stepped back and let Evian, mistress of water, and Soleil, whose element was the sun, take her place.

A burst of concentration from each and another floral garland was born in a wash of scent and color that reminded me of a film shown at faster-than-normal speed. Vaeta, wielder of air, directed a blast of wind that wafted the piece onto the top of the pile. A magical assembly line.

I like flowers just as much as the next person, but this seemed an odd activity. "What's going on?"

"We're getting ready for the wedding, of course." For a split second, I thought Vaeta meant *my* wedding, and a full-blown panic attack threatened. Parts of my body lost the ability to communicate with the rest, and even my lips went numb.

"The wedding?" Words barely squeaked out of my closed throat and the rush of my heartbeat drove away all thoughts of confessing about my mother's status among the living.

"It's not a wedding, Vaeta, it's a 25th wedding anniversary," Evian corrected her sister, and I breathed a sigh of relief before I realized the explanation hadn't actually explained anything.

"What's the difference?" Vaeta's silvery eyebrows beetled in a frown. On her, the color gray would never appear drab or neutral, every tone and shade represented a shimmer of the sun at the edge of a cloud, or the sparkle of moonlight on still water. Lips the color of a dove's feathers contrasted with slate gray eyes over cheekbones sharp enough to cut.

"Twenty-five years of marriage, you twit."

"Ladies, please," I begged. Name calling is how almost every faerie fight I have ever witnessed got started. Nipping this one in the bud seemed prudent. I had visions of those garlands turning into Technicolor snakes. Shiver. "Explain, please."

"We've been getting calls ever since Harry and Lemon Tart got married here." Terra looked back at me over one shoulder as she knelt and buried her fingers in a planter full of soil. "Putting on that wedding was so much fun; we decided to make a go of it."

Earth mother in every sense of the word, Terra's hair coloring mimicked the rich, russet shades of fertile soil, her cheeks and lips as soft as the berries they resembled. It's a good thing I have a healthy ego of my own, otherwise living among such stunning women might have given me a complex.

"A go of what?" Why I bothered to ask was beyond me, the evidence was clear enough that when Vaeta gave me a look her sisters generally reserved for her, the one that accused her of being an airhead, I clued in. "Party Planning? Like a business?"

"Would that be so bad? We won't be hosting the parties here, just planning them. So it won't disrupt your life, or anything. What's wrong with that?" Terra withdrew her hands from the pot, brushed them together until not a speck of soil remained, and moved on to the next while the first shoots broke the soil. There were six in all and by the time she thrust a hand into the last pot, the first one had sprouted a four-foot tall orange tree covered in fragrant blossoms.

Miracles like this happened every day in a house with four elementals and a witch, but the four of them working in harmony did not.

Sending another vine twining across the ceiling, Terra repeated her question, "We pulled off Lemon's party without a hitch, what do you think is going to happen?"

Several scenarios of things going haywire leaped to mind, each one worse than the last. At least two of them had me bailing the faeries out of jail, and those were the most benign of the bunch. "You'll fight."

"We won't; we made a pact." Vaeta's assurance carried weight. Pacts among faeries involved blood oaths and catastrophic consequences if broken. Too bad I couldn't get them to make one about not fighting at home. Then again, the alternative of them taking it to the streets was worse.

"How are you going to transport all this stuff? You can't just pop in and out of places without someone catching you."

"Give us a little credit, Lexi. We're not stupid." Evian glared at me and a little rain cloud formed over my head. I needed to practice my summoning spells for just such situations. An umbrella would come in handy right now.

"We bought a van." Soleil clapped her hands and did a little two-step across the tile. "The nice salesman is going to deliver it this afternoon." Her short cap of fire-bright hair lifted in the breeze she made as she danced.

"You can't just buy a van and start a business," I countered. "There's paperwork involved; you need an accountant, an insurance agent, and a bank account. Identification papers, birth certificates, tax documents." Just for starters.

"Done, done, and done." There's a bit of irony involved when a water being speaks in dry tones. "We're not idiots, Lexi. It's not that hard to get a birth certificate." The rain cloud spat a mini cloudburst over me, then dissipated leaving me slightly damp, but not drenched. Evian was feeling merciful.

"Well, you'd need to be *born*." We've never talked about how new faeries come into the world. I've always assumed they're born like humans, but for all I know, they drift down out of the clouds on a puff of dandelion fluff like the Whos in Whoville.

Sometimes Terra's dirty looks really are dirty. This was one of those times, and suddenly, I felt sand and grime itching away under clothes now caked in mud due to Terra's ire combining with Evian's tender mercy. Taking a shower climbed to the top of my to-do list and arguing over their new endeavor dropped to the bottom.

"Or you can just buy them on the Internet," Vaeta practically chirped.

"You bought fake IDs from the black market so you could run a party planning business out of my house?" I just wanted to get the sequence of events straight in my head, but frankly, it wasn't the worst thing they'd ever done.

There had been the time they'd raised half a dozen pink ponies and put them on Craigslist for free. Money has never been the motivating force behind the quest for faerie entertainment. That catastrophe landed them on the news and required a widespread memory charm before the dust settled.

"Take a chill pill, Mrs. Fuddy Duddy, we only got driver's licenses, and we put the van on your insurance." Vaeta shushed my protests, "and we're not even charging for the parties, so we won't need all that other stuff."

"Nobody says *chill pill* anymore, and are you kidding me? If you do the parties for free, people will take advantage of you." Sad but true.

"Oh, people pay," She said reassuringly, "they just don't pay *us*. We have them give the cost of the party to charity. It's philanthropic."

Terra chimed in, "Plus, we only buy from local businesses. We've got Kin in mind for entertainment, have already ordered a couple of cakes from your friend Mona who works at Crumb, and we've even tapped your friend Sinclair Fuller for some top-of-the-line chocolates. Relax, it's all under control."

On the pro side of the list, they'd be too busy to muck around in my life. The con side was too long to contemplate and had words like death and dismemberment on it.

Shaking my head and leaving them to it, I went upstairs for that shower. There hadn't been a good opening for my revelation about Sylvana, and Kin would just have to understand. I hadn't chickened out, it was just a matter of finding the proper time.

"Look what the cat dragged in." My familiar cracked up at his bad joke. Even in human form, Salem was still a cat, which meant his sense of humor tended toward more juvenile levels. "Who'd you piss off this morning?"

"Evian and Terra, hence the mud bath. Did you know..."

"About the party planning?" Salem raised an eyebrow and stared at me as if I were a complete dolt. "For days now, naturally."

I glared back at him, "And you didn't think this was information I needed to know?"

Rolling over, he arched his back to stretch out the kinks. "What? And take away the surprise factor? Let them have their fun. You know it won't last." He changed the subject, "You smell like magic."

"I can't imagine why," was my sarcastic reply.

"You've been using some serious mojo." Salem rose gracefully from under the covers of my bed. For once, he wasn't naked, although I'm not sure if boxers in a fish-patterned silk was that much of an improvement. At least he was trying.

He circled me, inky black skin brushing against my filthy clothes as he sniffed my skin.

I batted at him. "Cut that out."

"Tell me about it." He ordered.

"Shower first, then I'll give you the rundown." On just the parts having to do with the matchmaking and vision.

"With the lag you're having at work lately, you have the time to get serious about your training. The stud muffin can do without you for a few hours so we can get you up to speed." The unspoken implication was that I needed a finer level of control over my abilities.

He was right; this was something I needed to do. With Delta gunning for me and the changes in how my match-making skills worked, I could use the extra edge. I'd just have to make sure I didn't let too much slip; until I knew my mother was back for good, I'd be keeping her lack of deadness to myself, or I'd never be let out of the house alone again. That meant also keeping mum on the subject of Delta and everything her presence entailed. Jett, however, was already a known issue, and I could use Salem's help getting him off my back.

"Pick a time and put it in my schedule. Work has gone from feast to famine over the last couple weeks, not that I'm complaining, mind you. I could use the break with everything else that's going on." I tossed Salem my phone, so he could access the calendar app.

"What's wrong with today? You have the day off, right?"

"Plans with Kin, and don't give me that look. I'm entitled to a life."

I ignored Salem's rolling eyes and paired a pink and yellow flowered sundress with strappy white sandals and a matching belt. Mahogany curls cascaded down my back, and I'd applied nothing but a bit of mascara to my already thick lashes and a dab of lip gloss. Beauty was one thing that didn't run in short supply for the Balefire witches, but I was realizing it didn't solve as many problems as one might think. And if given the choice, I'd rather look like a harpy than turn into a wicked witch. "Try to keep the faeries out of trouble while I'm gone."

"I'm a familiar, not a miracle worker."

# FOUR

Cool air hit my face, and I inhaled the heady scent of summer night like I'd been on a year-long diet and someone just offered me a chocolate cake. Looking back, I can't understand how I could have missed the metallic taste of magic on my tongue, or why it didn't register that a breeze of any kind—especially one running through a city alley smack dab in the middle of a record-setting heat wave—wasn't normal. Maybe I was just too green for words, or maybe I was distracted by the back flips my stomach had been nailing with perfect form for the past fifteen minutes.

Nevertheless, I should have known trouble when I smelled it. Then again, the stench of my own deceit was strong. I'd left Kin's after dinner, telling him I needed some things from the drugstore on my way home when, instead, I'd followed my personal rabbit down the hole and detoured back to the place where I'd first laid eyes on Sylvana: Athena's Attic.

It was all his fault I was here; he'd spent the day talking about his family dynamic, specifically the way his relation-ship with his own mother had evolved over the years. It was an attempt at reassurance, which I appreciated even if I had no frame of reference for such a conversation.

Comparing his stories of her to what little I knew of Sylvana sparked a restless desire for more information. The spark kindled a burning need to revisit the one place I no longer doubted she had been and I knew I had to come alone.

I pressed my face against the front window and flicked on the penlight from my key chain, hoping its meager light would pick out some clue to finding my mysteriously-disappearing mother. Dust shrouded the fixtures and floors, the same as they had the last time I'd peered through this window in vain.

If I wasn't wearing the amulet she had placed around my neck with her own two hands, I might be able to talk myself into thinking the whole experience had been nothing more than a wishful dream. That and the butterfly squad zipping around in my gut. The little buggers had been coming and going frequently since the day I learned my mother had not, as I had always believed, died shortly after I was born.

Yes, I had taken to scanning every female face in every room I entered, hoping she would turn up again. My biggest sin was not telling the faeries about Sylvana masquerading as Athena. The woman had been in our house at Beltane, for goddess sake. That fact alone would be enough to send them looking for payback.

It didn't help that dear old mum was the only person I had ever met who could get a glamour spell past what I thought were my infallible detection skills. For all I knew, Sylvana Balefire could have been standing right next to me, disguised as a man, or a dog, or even a mote of dust. Her powers were yet another mystery to me, and another thing to lament on and curse the stars for.

The stars, not the gods; I now intentionally avoided blaspheming anyone who might be considered a *God*, lest I insult some random family member currently lounging on a cloud and tallying up all of my mistakes.

You don't know, it could be a thing.

Just add my uncertain heritage to the list of things I didn't understand. Speaking of the incomprehensible: had Sylvana been following me around for my entire life, watching from the sidelines? And why now, and not during the confusing teen years when I had wished and prayed for a connection to someone like me, had she found me, only to disappear *again*?

See how I circled back around to that one big question? It had been happening for days.

Don't get me wrong, my faerie godmothers filled most of the gap—most witches never even come face-to-face with their one godmother, and I was lucky enough to have been raised by mine, plus two of her faerie sisters. I often wondered why Soleil and Evian didn't have charges of their own but had never summoned the courage to inquire on that subject. Now that I think about it, avoiding certain subjects with them was sort of a theme.

Still, they were Fae, and I was a blood witch with no blood relatives to guide me. Well, not until Sylvana, disguised as Athena, magic shop proprietress, and sporting a look that was almost the complete opposite of my own—blond hair, crystal blue eyes, and a gentle face—popped up to give me some crucial guidance. Scratched or cut out of every photo in the house, I still had no idea what my mother looked like which, needless to say, was making it quite difficult to find her. My grandmother and I could have been twins, but Sylvana was an unknown quantity.

I'd tried every variation of location spell in the Book of Shadows but was loathe to ask for help. When Terra, Evian, and Soleil found out I had come into my powers, their fear I no longer needed them had sparked a truly epic enchanted backyard faerie fight—boulders with teeth, sprites dancing in the trees, and a foul-mouthed chickadee.

I was still washing swamp slime out of my clothes, and figured if that was the molehill, I sure as Hades didn't want to see what happened when they had to face the mountain. I could only imagine what kind of catastrophe would ensue if they knew my "real" mother was alive and well. Which didn't matter much at the moment; I realized this whole trip was an exercise in futility and turned back to Pinky, the matching helmet still clutched in one hand.

With the myriad of thoughts rolling around inside my head, you can see why I might have let my guard down momentarily. I realized my mistake in an instant, as magic, intuition, and biology culminated to set my arm hair on end and send a chill up my spine. Talk about being fashionably late to the party.

Every muscle tightened; even ones I didn't know I had, and a fleeting resolution to kick my geriatric-style workout of power walking around town into high gear ASAP flitted across my subconscious, not to be revisited until New Year's Day, approximately 337 years later.

If I were a wolf—or a dog, or a raccoon, even—I would

have bared my teeth and growled out a warning. Instead, I allowed the warm and fluffy thought that I was *Lexi Balefire, powerful witch, demigod* inflate my self-confidence, and spun toward the source of the wonky vibes with a hip and an eyebrow cocked, my arms akimbo and the pink helmet dangling at my side.

"Nice ride." The supernatural who had chased me through town and identified herself as Delta (I'll save my diatribe about people who refer to themselves in the third person for another time)—stepped out of the shadows and insulted my scooter with her sarcastic remark.

Away from the dim lighting that had enveloped her during our last encounter, her face had softened to a large degree, lulling me into a false sense of security for a moment longer than it should have.

"Nice hair," I retorted, "I didn't know they still made level 5 Aquanet. You know, chlorofluorocarbons are a really big deal nowadays. Haven't you heard?"

Delta's brow wrinkled into a frown, and she fingered a crunchy curl with a confused expression. I realized then that the lines I had taken as a demarcation of age were streaks of caked-on concealer, and that she wasn't much older than my 25 years.

"Cut the trash talk and hand it over, Sylvana," Delta commanded. Her voice was suddenly much stronger and lacked the lilting southern drawl.

Her question made me stop and refocus my attention. I looked down at my hands and Pinky's helmet, and then back at her. She couldn't possibly want to steal my scooter when there were so many better options available. Two spaces over, a sleek black Harley seemed more her speed.

"No, I don't want that hunk of junk." Delta rolled her eyes and calmly strode in my direction. Maybe calmly isn't the right word; the fluid quality of her movements flipped a switch in my brain, and I suddenly held no illusions that, given even a moderately good reason, she would uncoil like a snake and strike with razor-sharp precision.

"Don't make me ask you again." I heard the warning in her words, and while part of me wanted to run, I still held out hope that half witch, half god would trump supernatural whatsis.

Relying solely on nature and ignoring the nurture side of things is always a risky bet. Not that it appeared this woman had ever been treated with tender loving care; what I mean is, I may have been inherently stronger, but I was untrained and would be of little use in a physical battle.

I felt adrenaline and power course through my veins and began gathering the loose strands of magic into a tight ball at the center of my chest. It flowed down through my fingers, which sparked with electricity as I tapped the tips together in warning. But Delta had a plan, a purpose.

She wasn't caught off guard and had come prepared. I, on the other hand, only had a moderate amount of control over my witchy abilities, and even less over whatever powers came with my inherent godhood. So far, they'd been a ton of help when there was a couple for me to match, and none at all when I was in danger.

Also, I hadn't been expecting her to pull a rapier with a 4-foot long blade out of her jacket, Mary Poppins style. She pointed it right at my neck, causing me to take a step back-ward, trip over the helmet that had fallen near my feet, and land on my sundress-clad butt, hard.

"What part of me telling you I'm *Lexi* Balefire didn't you understand? My mother is dead."

"You are Sylvana Balefire, daughter of Clara, defiler of that which I am sworn to retrieve." Delta turned up the palm not holding the sword and produced a near holographic quality image of me that floated above her outstretched hand.

"I am Alexis Balefire, and I haven't defiled anything." Unless she was counting Kin, but what went on between two consenting adults should be private, right?

"Enough of this. Where is the Bow of Destiny?" Delta ignored my protests and began to snarl, just as I was preparing to send a rescue wish to Terra. Her words stopped me in my tracks.

"The what of what, now?" I managed to choke out, the image of me carrying a glowing golden bow with a heart-shaped arrowhead flitted through my head. It couldn't be a coincidence that I'd seen a bow in my vision, and now here someone was, asking me about a similar item.

Eyes narrowing to slits, Delta dispelled the image and pulled a leather pouch from her pants pocket. Using her teeth so as to keep the sword pointed firmly, she tugged the string closure open and tossed the contents toward me.

Some kind of dust, I assumed based on the sneezing. When my eyes finally cleared, Delta was staring down at me with a funny look on her face.

"Sorry, my mistake. Look, I'll lower my sword if you

promise not to try anything stupid." I nodded, and she took a slightly less homicidal stance. "You might not believe this given my actions, but I was sent here to help you."

"Who sent you? Was it my father?" The last great family mystery in my life, who else could it be?

All the bluster and aggression gone now, she seemed like she wasn't sure where to start. "No. Not him."

It is possible to feel relieved and dismayed at the same time, but it's not fun.

"You're a Fate Weaver—of that much you are aware, I presume," she didn't wait for my response, "Your mother was among the last to see your birthright, so we assumed it was in her possession. I'm here to secure the bow and return it to its rightful owner—you. No one told me you were a dead ringer for your mother, though."

Dead ringer? No wonder Sylvana had disguised herself to look nothing like me; because she looked *exactly* like me, and there would have been no way I'd have missed the resemblance. Of course the thought had crossed my mind, but it had seemed unlikely that three generations would be nearly identical. Perhaps all the Balefires in history were doppelgangers.

The part about me being the rightful owner of Cupid's Bow of Destiny—now that was a twist that made sense, since I'd already seen myself using it. Mind blown.

"What exactly are you expecting me to do with the bow?"

Delta stared at me like I'd grown a second head, "Weave fate, obviously. Isn't that what you do? Or are you just a common neighborhood matchmaker?"

Well, how was I supposed to know when I had no definition for the term Fate Weaver?

"I guess not," was my wishy-washy answer.

"I didn't think so. You can't have missed what's going on out there—you can't tell me you haven't noticed how love has been seeping out of your world. Do you think that doesn't have consequences? It's Cupid's job to maintain the balance, but he's MIA, and the gauntlet now falls to you. At all costs, you must—"

And then she was abruptly silent, frozen in mid-sentence like a stone statue, the blade of her rapier still gleaming in the moonlight. I carefully backed away and scrambled to my feet, looking around for my godmother; I must have called out to Terra subconsciously during Delta's diatribe.

"Wow, T, that was cl—" I stopped short of rushing into the soothing embrace of one of my foster mommies because the figure moving toward me wasn't Terra at all—it was my real mother closing in on Delta with a ball of witchfire in her hand, and a look of feral rage on her face.

And just like that, one of the biggest questions in my life had a definitive answer. Sylvana did indeed look exactly like me.

Three generations, one face. It was uncanny and unsettling.

"No!" I shouted to stay her arm.

This Delta person had seemed perfectly willing to carve me into itty bitty pieces when she thought I was my mother and I didn't know whether she deserved to die or not, but I definitely didn't want to be part of it. Not, at least, before I found out what in the Sam Hill was going on between the two of them. Who the heck is Sam Hill, anyway?

My mother stopped in her tracks, lowered her arms, and squared her shoulders. "Hello, Alexis."

"Hello, Athena." An ice cube would have shivered under the cool breeze from my tone. "Or would you rather I call you Sylvana?"

"How about Mom?"

"How about no." I couldn't believe I was having this conversation in front of the ninja Popsicle, but there was no way around it now.

"How long have you known?" The question was so devoid of emotion; I couldn't tell if she cared or was just making idle conversation. Half of me wanted to run into the arms that should have been my safe place and the other half violently opposed the impulse. Talk about fight or flight.

My blood pressure, already high from being attacked, shot up into dangerous territory. Of all the emotions I expected to feel if ever confronted with the chance to talk to my dead mother, fury hadn't ever made the list. But there it was, anyhow.

"We're not having a personal conversation right now," I warned. Processing the fact that someone had just threatened me at the point of a sword was about all I could handle. "If I hadn't stopped you, you would have killed Delta."

"Don't be ridiculous." My mother snapped. "Go home, Lexi. I'll take care of the...of *Delta*. Don't worry; she won't bother you again."

"Why? Because you're going to do something horrible to her?" A buzzing street lamp turned the alley into a cubist's dreamscape and even with the shadows falling over her face, looking at my mother was like looking in a mirror—a funhouse mirror that adds a decade to your age.

"She just tried to kill you." Gritted teeth bit the words out.

"Only when she thought I was you. After that, she was trying to talk to me. To give me the information no one else has bothered to give. If she wanted to hurt me, she had the opportunity."

"No one points a sword at my daughter and lives to tell the tale." My mother's voice carried none of the soothing safety I'd dreamed of hearing since I was a child. Instead, it dripped like tainted honey, dark and vile. Her insistence seemed too vehement to carry the ring of truth.

"You're the reason she's here at all." Sylvana flinched when I hit squarely upon the crux of the matter.

"No, I'm not." A two-year-old caught with one hand in the cookie jar could lie better than that.

"Yes, you are. She thought I was you. When she realized I wasn't, all she wanted to do was talk. She was about to tell me something about the Bow of Destiny, which she thinks you stole, by the way. Take the spell off, Mother. Let Delta tell me her side of things."

Here I was defending the person who just attacked me. Remind me again why I wished for family all those years. "It wouldn't be self-defense. Not like this."

"For Hecate's sake, I'm not the one who stole the bow. If I was going to steal it, don't you think I'd had plenty of chances while your father was with me? And I'm not planning to kill anyone. What is wrong with you? It's a temporary stasis spell, and it's going to wear off any minute, so unless you're somehow hiding a weapon under your clothes-_"

She flicked a glance at my floral ensemble, "We'd probably both be better off somewhere else when it does. She won't be happy to see me, and I don't want you getting caught in the crossfire."

A grunt followed by a twitch from Delta verified Sylvana's declaration, and I decided to listen, for the first time ever, to my mother.

"Fine." I slapped my helmet on my head with short, angry movements. "See you around, Mom." I didn't care if I sounded like a snot-nosed brat, or if I did, I couldn't seem to stop myself.

Resisting the temptation to gun the engine and roar off —I'd had the last word, after all, and why ruin the effect by being even more childish?—I spared only a short sideways glance at my mother as I pulled past. Imagine my surprise when she landed on the seat behind me and gripped my waist.

"Go," she ordered, and I did by pushing the pink Vespa to her limits for half a dozen city blocks, my back ramrod straight so as to avoid any sense of cuddling into the warm weight of my mother at my back. She hadn't earned the right to touch me so intimately, no matter how much I craved the contact.

Judging we'd traveled a safe enough distance, I slowed to a more sedate pace; getting a traffic ticket wasn't on my agenda for the evening.

"Where do you live? I'll drop you off." Anger pinked my

cheeks again. She'd probably been living nearby my entire life. That thought provoked a vivid mental picture of me shoving her off the scooter without bothering to slow down.

"Go left at the next light." I followed her directions and ended up on the edge of the seedier part of town. "Stop here." I pulled up in front of an all-night diner. "My place is upstairs, but can we go inside? I'll buy us some pie, and we can get to know each other better. I've missed you, Alexis. Please."

Sailors tell epic stories of the Siren's call—oh, so beautiful, and deadly enough that men dashed their ships upon the rocks just to hear more, be closer. I understood the impulse. This was the mother I had mourned for a lifetime, whose loss had shaped me in more ways than her presence might have done. This was the woman who had been murdered in a family tragedy, leaving me orphaned and stigmatized by the wickedness of my grandmother. Except none of that was true. Sylvana hadn't been taken from me; she had simply walked away.

Which is what I did, too. Okay, I rode away, but it's the same thing, right?

# CHAPTER
# FIVE

Fury carried me right up to Kin's front door and then deserted me like its pants were on fire. I couldn't go home with the stench of my mother and another supernatural all over me. No doubt someone would have smelled it, and then I'd have had to answer a bunch of questions. Two nights in a row spent with my boyfriend was sure to get the faeries' panties in a bunch, but I needed sympathy, not a fight.

By the time he pulled open the front door, I wasn't sure what I was feeling. The aftereffects of an adrenaline rush or a complete emotional breakdown. Either way, I plastered myself to him and let him guide me inside.

One look at my face, and he skipped my customary wine in favor of something a little stronger. Soon he had me settled on the sofa with brandy burning away some of the shock.

He took my hand. "Tell me what happened. Was the drug store out of your favorite color of nail polish?"

Kin's attempt to lighten the mood made him sound like a total jerk and earned him a glare from me, but I needed to unload, so I let it pass.

"If there was any doubt about my mother's status among

the living, it's gone now. I ran into her in town. Or rather, she ran into me just as Delta had a sword pointed at my throat."

Okay, so maybe I meant to shock him. Served him right for the jerky nail polish remark.

"Are you okay?" Grabbing my arm, he started to check me all over for signs of injury.

I shook him off. "I'm fine. Delta didn't hurt me. In fact, she wasn't looking for me at all. She was looking for my mother. Turns out we share a face."

"It's time to tell the faeries about this." He jumped up and would have gone to them right then if I hadn't yanked him back down beside me.

"Just listen to the whole story first."

I filled him in on all the details.

"So apparently I'm supposed to use the Bow of Destiny to weave fates—whatever that entails. All those Valentine's Day cards depicting a plump baby with a toy bow and arrow are cute and all, but Cupid is not a toddler, and the barb on that bow is not made out of stuffing. It's the real thing; I can't be expected to shoot people with it. How is that going to help?"

"Maybe the tip of the arrow is symbolic." Leave it to a singer/songwriter to look for the more esoteric explanation. "Love's pointed barb, or piercing the heart with love." His next song title? "Or, there's something dangerous about it, and your job is about to get far more complicated than ever."

"It won't matter anyway, considering I have no clue where the stupid thing is hidden. Sylvana claims she doesn't know, but it's not like she's been forthright and honest up to now. I regretted running off on her the second

I left, but I couldn't help myself. It's a lot to deal with, you know?"

I tried to justify my actions, but my reasoning felt a little like a cop-out. "It's so tempting just to go back and knock on her door, but I'm not sure I could take it if I found the place deserted. Not that I expect anything different, that seems to be her pattern."

Ten years agonizing over whether I'd ever get my magic paled in comparison to the angst I felt now. As much as I craved her presence, knowing my mother had not been dead this whole time was a bitter pill.

"If she's turned up twice now, it's safe to say she's probably interested in seeing you again." Kin seemed to have more he wanted to say on the subject, but was choosing his words wisely.

In the span of a few short weeks, my life had gone from unusual to downright absurd, and we were still new enough as a couple for him to not understand all the dynamics.

Whether Kin was concerned more for my well-being or his own, I couldn't be sure, but either way, his trepidation was understandable. "Unfortunately, I think the same is probably true for Jett and Delta. Of the three, she's the person—or whatever—whose intentions are most unclear. At least with Jett, you know what to expect: cheesy melodrama worthy of a comic book character. I couldn't get a good read on Delta's, well, *species* isn't the best word, but you know what I mean."

Poor Kin. What would happen once he delved all the way into his new reality? Better to ease him into it considering the look on his face.

"The faeries have brought some of their friends around —mostly nymphs and dryads, a few elves, and a giantess with an interest in horticulture, but I have no idea who or what Delta might be. Nothing much surprises me these days, though."

One more question Sylvana could answer. My mother had a long way to go before she could earn my trust, but I'd ask her before I went to the faeries or Salem for help.

Kin must have read my mind. "Can't you ask the godmothers?"

Guilt must have showed on my face.

"You didn't tell them yet, did you?"

I avoided a direct answer. "Terra is at my beck and call in any emergency. Worst case scenario, I call for help and explain later. Hopefully, it won't come to that; as soon as I have more information—or they're in a spectacularly good mood—I'll break the news."

Kin raised an eyebrow, and I knew he was all for going over there and dropping the bomb right now, but he decided to let the subject drop.

It would be nice to be able to go home at the end of the day and not worry about keeping secrets. Outright lying has never been tolerated in my household; one of the faeries would know I wasn't speaking the truth before I could get the words out, and I'd been walking a fine line by simply withholding information. But I wasn't ready, and if Sylvana never showed her face again, it was a moot point anyway.

Once again, there I was, burying my head in the sand. Way to go, Lexi.

"...actually coming into town in a few days and would

love to meet you." I faded back into awareness in time to hear the end of Kin's sentence. Apparently, the conversation had shifted while I'd been in la-la land, and I was caught completely off guard.

"My dad won't be with her; she's just coming to shop, but that's probably better anyway. Less pressure. Unless you don't want to meet her..."

His mother. Kin was asking me if I wanted to meet his mother. As if I didn't have enough issues with maternal figures, and I'd never been in a long-term enough relationship to bother getting to know a boyfriend's family in the past. But, there was no way I'd cause Kin any pain, even a cut this shallow, so I pasted a smile on my face.

"Of course I do. I'm sorry, but the idea of meeting your mother is more scary to me than meeting Delta in a dark alley. What if she doesn't like me? What if she thinks I'm not good enough for you? And what if she figures out I'm not normal?"

Kin grinned. "See, that's the beauty of it. My mom doesn't hate anyone. There's not a mean bone in her body, and she's quite thrilled that I'm dating someone I actually want to introduce her to. So stop worrying, and just say yes." He treated me to a kiss that would have convinced me to agree to meet the hairy scary monster under his bed, and when he pulled away, I nodded my head, grinning what could only have been a disgustingly mushy grin.

"I already said yes, silly. Just tell me where to be. Oh, and what to wear, and what to say."

"You'll be fine, I promise."

# CHAPTER
# SIX

As soon as I walked into the office the next morning, Flix appeared out of nowhere, as faeries—even half-faeries—often do. I hadn't even had time to press the button mounted beneath my desk to summon him, so he must have been waiting for me. It's difficult to hide things from any halfway decent best friend, but when he's the best kind of best friend and also your business partner, it's impossible.

I hadn't been at the top of my BFF game lately, for obvious reasons, and I figured he was ticked off at me for not filling him in on everything that had gone down since my half-brother revealed a few family secrets to me.

It turns out; I was dead wrong. Call me self-centered if you must—you'd probably be right. What can I say, I'm an only child. The second Flix turned one hundred percent solid, I could tell there was something different about his energy, and it had nothing whatsoever to do with me.

Today, his platinum mane hung in long curls and tumbled over one shimmering violet eye in a haphazard manner I knew was completely contrived. Flix never left the house without transforming himself into a walking sex symbol. High cheekbones, a chiseled jawline, and six feet something of lean muscle appealed to both men and women alike. He preferred the former, and I'd seen more than one woman's face crumble at the realization.

What did concern me were the leather loafers on his feet and the button-down shirt on his back. I knew the leather was of the finest quality Italian variety, and I'm sure the shirt cost more than I made in a month. Flix worked with me for fun; any paycheck I could have cut him would have been like tossing two pennies into Scrooge McDuck's vault. But I'd been privy to several of his diatribes on plaid before, and had I not noticed the subtle signs of a person in a new, exciting relationship I would have thought he was late to a costume party.

Now, while I've never been able to get a read on the status of Flix's soul mate—I assumed this was due to the Fae half of his heritage—I had also never exactly been asked to try. My impressions were that he preferred a series of one-night stands. The Fae usually avoid getting into long-term relationships; I'm sure you can guess why.

"*Son of a witch*, you've met someone. Spill, now." I demanded, flicking a fingertip to coax a pair of armchairs into a cozier position (this was getting easier by the day), and grabbing Flix's perfectly-manicured hand from where it was jammed into the back pocket of a pair of designer jeans to pull him into sitting position.

He fixed me with a cold stare for all of two seconds before his face dissolved into a smile. "Yes." Flix confirmed, "But it's too soon for glowing phrases and a tell-all session. All I'm going to say is that he makes me happy. I don't know if it's serious yet."

"Which means it is," I retorted. "What's his name?

Where did you meet him? Do you have a pic? Is he...human? Have you...*you know*...yet?”

“I’m not answering any of that. Except that his name is Carl.”

“Carl? His name is Carl? I’m assuming that means he’s human. What Fae would name their kid Carl?” Oops, that came out snarkier than I’d intended.

“Whatever, you’re dating a guy named after either a raincoat or a type of apple. What human names their kid *Mackintosh*?”

“It’s a family name,” I sniffed, “and I think it’s cute.”

“I’ll introduce you when and if it goes anywhere. Now it’s your turn. You haven’t come into the office for days now, and it’s been a ghost town as far as business is concerned.”

Once addicted to his hands in their hair, a number of my former matchmaking clients refused to let anyone else near them again. Whether he liked it or not, Flix was Port Harbor’s most sought-after stylist. His elusively-kept business hours increased the demand. What can I say, the man has amazing hands, and he gives good hair. Word gets around.

“I was taking a much-needed break. The decline in business is coincidental but appreciated. I actually wanted to talk to you about some things. Things I can’t tell Terra and the others because they already don’t understand what I do. But you’re with me all the time, and you know how this stuff works.”

What I didn’t say, but what I meant was that Flix understood because that’s just what he did. It was part of his faerie magic. Some Fae are elemental, like my godmothers, and others have different abilities. Flix's special talent was empathy. He could gauge a person's feelings on sight. That's why he was always able to be whatever I needed—whatever our clients needed.

Sometimes, though, it made it difficult to know what kind of person was under the calm demeanor. For all I knew, there was an anguished soul screaming for release. Mostly, the insight into others seemed to make him happy, even though he didn't like to talk about it. I left it alone. I was beginning to realize I'd done that with all the Fae in my life. What does that say about *me*?

Flix shifted in his seat, settling in for a long conversation. "Lay it on me."

"Well, for one thing, Sylvana is back."

"Sylvana? You mean your mother?" Rarely ever surprised, Flix was taken aback. "Why didn't you lead with that? How long have you known? Have you talked to her?" It was his turn to rattle off a list of questions.

"Don't be mad at me; I've known since right after we released Kin's soul from Skip Stark's guitar, and I only talked to Kin about it the day before yesterday. And only because I was so shaken up after what happened at the Port Day Festival and it all came out." I walked him through the experience I'd had that night, my encounter with the enigmatic Delta, and how I had left Sylvana without so much as even attempting a conversation. Flix sat back in silence for a moment too long when I was finished.

"Wow, that's insane. So what happened to your grandmother then? Maybe she's the one who hid this Bow of Destiny."

I hadn't thought of that angle.

"No clue. I mean, it did occur to me that Clara didn't kill Sylvana, but she's still standing in the same place, stoned as always. She must have killed another witch, and I should probably ask one of the coven who it might have been, but I'm still on the outside of that circle."

When my magic took ten years to show up, I'd felt like a pariah among the local witches. Not entirely their fault, since I avoided them all like the plague. Well, except for Serena Snodgrass who, after some imagined slight, had become my nemesis and to make matters worse, was the skanky witch who was dating my half-brother, Jett.

Serena's mother, Calypso, had taken over coven leadership after Clara's stoning, and while I had no proof, I suspected the mother/daughter team did anything they could to maintain friction between the coven and me.

At this point, I wasn't sure which witch to ask, anyway, but Flix had sparked my curiosity.

"Just a couple of the questions I intend to ask when I work up the guts to talk to Sylvana again. If I ever do, I mean. I can't believe I just walked away like that. I've been wondering about her for weeks now, and then when she shows up I scamper off like my butt's fire. What an idiot."

Flix patted my arm, "It's not like you wind up face-to-face with your presumed-dead mother every day. You've dealt with more than enough life-changing curve balls over the last couple of months; cut yourself some slack."

"I know, and I will." I promised. "For now, I need to focus on beefing up my magic defenses. If Delta was telling the truth, it sounds like my job is about to get even more complicated. Kin thinks the matches were Jett causing trouble for me, but I'm not buying it. It's not in his wheelhouse to help me make matches; he's more concerned with ripping them apart—and, he was busy doing just that during the festival."

"Unless he knew you'd get all hopped up on power, and was trying to goad you into making a mistake." Flix played devil's advocate. "That's the only way it fits, and even then it's a bit thin."

I raised an eyebrow, "You might be right. He probably thinks making me mess up is an easier way to accomplish his ridiculous goal."

Leaning forward as if he was about to hear some juicy gossip, Flix said, "Do tell."

"Weren't you there that day? When he trotted out his insane theory that our father will return to save the day if he senses there's not enough love left in the world."

When Flix snorted out a laugh, I had to smile along with him. Jett had not hatched the most brilliant of diabolical schemes.

"Nope, I showed up in time to pick up the pieces after he'd done his level best to break you." Every now and then, I'm reminded that the Fae are formidable and that Flix was one of them. Under the façade of normalcy, his face fined down to a series of sharp planes and angles that were still beautiful, but also terrifying. I'd hate to be on his bad side. Jett was already there, and had no idea. I pitied him for that while I explained the whole situation.

"Well, it seems to me that the world has been going to hell in a handbasket for quite some time, and if Cupid were really the big shot Jett thinks he is, he'd be here already."

I'd been thinking along those same lines, so I nodded my agreement.

"What I do know is, if Jett finds out Sylvana is back in the picture, it's only going to fuel his fire. The one thing we had in common was that both our mothers were dead."

"Lexi…" Flix's voice carried a warning, and I quickly realized why.

"Hey, guys!" Mona Katz burst through the door and flopped into a chair.

Still dressed in work clothes—I could tell by the dusting of flour on her pants—the petite blond, perky to the point of annoyance most of the time, wasn't smiling today. A former client, Mona should have been tangled in her new man's bedsheets right now, and my stomach lurched at the thought of a possible failed match. It had been hard enough to set her up with Kin's friend Mark in the first place.

"Well, hello, Mona," I said, my eyes wide with more surprise than necessary; I'd already pegged Mona as someone with limited respect for boundaries, and had figured our paths would cross again. "Everything working out okay with Mark?"

"Oh, definitely." Mona grinned, blue eyes sparkling over high cheekbones. "I'm so happy, I can't stand it. You're my hero. In fact, that's why I'm here. I need your help."

Flix caught my eye with his own and turned his lip up in a small smile. I knew he was mocking me for getting too involved with a client, and I crinkled my nose in response before mouthing *bite me* at him the second Mona glanced away.

Mona continued without waiting for my response. "It's

my mom. She's lonely now that all us kids are out of the house. I don't think she's dated since my dad passed almost ten years ago. I'm happy, and I want her to be happy too. I tried to do what you do, but it didn't work out like it does for you."

Now that wasn't what I was expecting to hear.

"What do you mean, you tried to do what Lexi does?" Flix asked with a raised eyebrow. I held my breath as I waited for her response.

"Well, I got her dressed up and took her out—introduced her to some men I thought seemed like her type. She's really pretty—look." Mona flicked through some photos on her phone and flashed a picture of an attractive woman in her early fifties, with the same heart-shaped face as her daughter, and a head of loosely curled strawberry blond waves that complemented a spattering of freckles across her nose and cheekbones. "But that didn't work, so I signed her up for Lifelong, that online dating site for *mature adults*." Mona rolled her eyes and used air quotes in the description, but it was clear she had been desperate enough to give it a shot despite her better judgment. Too bad she hadn't listened to good sense.

"Mona, that's not really how it works. Why didn't you just call me and send her into the office? I'm more than happy to lend a hand." And I was. I couldn't help liking Mona; when she had come through my door the first time, I had seen through the frumpy outfit and drab haircut to the smart but self-deprecating woman underneath. I wanted to take credit for bringing her out of her shell, but all I had done was offer her a blowout and listen to her insecurities until the fuel allowing them to burn had been exhausted. She was responsible for the rest.

"Well, now she's determined never to date again." Mona chattered on. "There's no way she'd come down here of her own free will. I could trick her to get her into the office, but I think that might make it worse."

"Don't do that." I warned.

"Why?" Over the hand that lifted to cover her mouth, Mona's eyes were wide. "Oh, maybe it's too late. I mean, my parents were so happy together I always thought of them as soul mates, so maybe she's not meant to find someone else. Like, he was the one for her, and now I'm butting in and wasting your time, too. I'm sorry, I should have thought of that before I came here."

"No, that's not what I meant," I called after Mona, who was on her way to the door. "Come back and let me explain." The woman could be exhausting, and I didn't want to delve into the complexities of making matches with her, mainly because most of what I knew was a three-quarters assumption and the rest speculation. If there was a manual that came with my God-given (literally) powers, someone had forgotten to hand it along to me.

"This is my inexpert opinion based on what I've seen over the years," I ignored Mona's raised eyebrow and cocked head. "Nothing in this life is set in stone." Well, except for a murdering witch, but let's not have *that* conversation. "Books and movies rely heavily on the notion of preordained fate being the definition of a soul mate. It's more romantic to think there is only one person in the entire world you could be happy with and if you never get together with him or her, your life will be loveless and tragic."

"People do love a good tragedy." Flix commented. "Romeo and Juliet could have spared themselves a lot of angst if they'd been a bit more sensible."

"Love isn't supposed to be sensible," I chided.

"Are you telling me Mark might not be the love of my life?"

See, I knew she was going to leap to that conclusion, and that's why I don't talk about these things in polite society.

"Not at all. I'm telling you that if something tragic happened like it did for your mother, the person you would become as a result of that loss would have a perfect match out there somewhere." Give me a break, I know it sounded ridiculous and inept and a hundred other words that meant the same thing.

"I think I see what you're saying, and it gives me hope. Can I confess something to you? As much as I wanted to see my mom happy and not have her be lonely, I was feeling bad for the man who tried to fill my father's shoes." Brightened, she continued, "Now, how are we going to pull it off?"

"Does she know you hired me?" I hadn't cashed Mona's check and never planned to, so technically, I wasn't sure she had.

"Not at first, no. When I came to see you, I was in a bad place, and I didn't want her to worry. So, I told her I met Mark at a wedding, which is the truth, and I talked to her about my new friend Lexi. I finally told her the whole story when I thought I could use your method to help her and that failed dismally, so here we are." Mona shrugged.

"Okay, we'll keep it loose for now. Off the books. She'll be more comfortable in a social setting, so get your mother to meet you for lunch as soon as possible. Text me the details. I'll talk to her, see if I get the vibe, and how she responds, then we'll take it from there."

"Thank you, Lexi, seriously; you're the best." Mona gushed, squeezing me into a hug that nearly knocked the wind out of me before prancing out the door.

"That girl is a hurricane, and you are the coast of Florida. You might be able to see her coming, but there's not a damned thing you can do to stop her. I think you'd better find a bomb shelter to huddle up in." Flix ribbed.

"She's sweet, but we'll need to be a bit more careful if she's going to make a habit of these spontaneous visits. She's eventually bound to see something we can't explain away."

Oh, if only I had known just how accurate that statement was going to turn out to be.

CHAPTER
# SEVEN

To me, *soon* meant in a day or two, to Mona it meant *right freaking now*. She wasted no time setting up the lunch and texted me within ten minutes of leaving my office. She requested I meet her in half an hour at a small café a couple of blocks away. I bade goodbye to Flix, promising him a movie and catch up night ASAP.

He looked a little forlorn about being passed over for Mona, but I was used to him putting on the occasional show of jealousy by now and didn't let it bother me too much. I'm allowed to have other friends, sheesh.

I was a bit annoyed about the fact that even though her mother was mad at her, she still agreed to meet Mona for lunch at the drop of a hat. The reasons why this might bother me are pretty obvious, and once again my mind dived into thoughts of my own mother.

I was just approaching the cafe when my lunch companions stepped out of a cab. We spent several minutes with introductions right there on the street.

If I hadn't been busy chatting with Mona and her mother, I might have caught the scent of overpowering perfume and flop sweat coming off Serena Snodgrass before she materialized in front of us.

Formerly lank and blond, Serena must have decided the

goth look was more suited to her new bad girl persona because she now sported a still lank, but decidedly darker do. Black actually, and clearly a home dye job since her scalp still bore the evidence of her inexperience.

An encounter with the skanky witch ranked right up there with getting a root canal and a bikini wax at the same time.

"Lexi Balefire." Ninety-eight pounds of bobble-headed, stick-figure ugly marched right up to me and stuck her huge beak in my face.

"Serena Swampgrass." I ignored Mona's questioning look for the time being.

"Maybe you should try to get my name right since we're about to become sisters-in-law." She attempted a purr that sounded more like dying cats to me.

"Oh, I'm sorry Serena *Snotass*, then. I wouldn't start posing for the wedding photos quite yet. Jett's just not that into you."

Lucky for me, I wasn't interested in a family relationship with my half-brother. If anything, he hated me more than Serena did—in that respect, they made the perfect couple. That she couldn't see how deftly he was using her to get on my nerves only proved her level of social ineptitude.

"Who's your little friend?" Serena turned beady eyes on Mona.

The last thing I wanted to do was expose Mona or her mother to the vile witch, so I turned to them and said, "If you ladies could go in and get us a table, I'll deal with this... *person*, and join you in a few minutes."

Only too happy to take herself out of an awkward situation, Mona gave my arm a squeeze and pulled her mother into the café.

"Does that singer know you're stepping out with a skirt these days?" Serena's barb failed to score.

"Is there a reason you crawled out of the gutter to annoy me? Or maybe it's Friday the 13th, and I walked under a ladder."

I missed whatever dull-witted retort she came up with when I noticed a familiar face halfway down the block. My relationship with Serena was based on insults and the occasional curse being tossed around as the result of some childhood transgression buried so deep in the past I can't even remember what it was.

I gave her credit for one thing; the witch knows how to carry a grudge. It wouldn't surprise me if trying to stick it to me over some ancient slight was her sole reason for hanging around with Jett. I hadn't been lying when I said he wasn't into her. Anyone could see that after two minutes in their presence.

While I was distracted by the sight of Delta strolling casually toward me, old Swampy actually thought she'd gained the upper hand because I quit trading insults with her.

"What? No snappy comeback?" She half-whined.

"Sorry, I'm just not up for a battle of the wits right now." I shot back. "Besides, it wouldn't break fair, what with you being unarmed and all."

Sizzling magic arced toward me. "We're in public, you idiot," I hissed as Serena loosed something green and glowing in my direction. A quickly-whispered spell deflected the curse skyward where it burst harmlessly. Or almost. One area birdwatcher would go on to create a panic among his peers with a report of having seen a raven covered with green spots, sparking rumors of some new version of bird flu.

"Lexi, is everything okay?" Mona chose that moment to reappear next to me, and I glanced over to see her mother's curious face peering through the café window. Of course, they'd chosen a ringside window seat, and now she was looking up toward where Serena's ill-advised curse had gone. "Did you see something strange? I thought I saw..." Mona shook her head to dispel the image. "...Something odd."

Outing myself to her before she discovered my true nature on her own moved up a few places on my to-do list. Friendships are complicated enough; hoping your new friend won't look at you in awestruck horror adds another kink.

"It's fine. Serena was just leaving. She has places to be, small children to scare."

The rule for not displaying magic out in the open might be unspoken, but it's one that every witch with a lick of common sense follows. Even Serena. Visibly shaken by her own stupidity, she carried her gangly self away down the street with nothing more than a furious backward glance. I watched her go and only rolled my eyes once. I'd like to think I'm growing more tolerant as I get older. The rude hand gesture I couldn't hold back proved me wrong on that count.

As I turned to follow Mona inside, I searched the street for signs of threat, but Delta had vanished again.

"Lexi." Mona's voice broke through my reverie. "You're

scaring me. Come inside and have lunch, you're acting sort of spacey; I think your blood sugar must be low."

Delta was long gone now, and Mona was right, I needed a moment to process the possibilities. Poor Mona seemed to land herself right in the middle of a new existential crisis every time we went out in public together.

"Sorry. My mind was somewhere else. You must be wondering how I manage to crawl out of bed every morning." Linking my arms in hers, I let her lead me to her mother and the table they'd chosen near the café window. "I haven't been at my best lately, and you keep scoring a front row seat for some of my worst moments."

"If you need to talk about anything, I'm happy to listen."

Run, Mona. Before I take you up on that generous offer and tell you things that would scare the legs off a spider.

"Thank you, I...things are complicated. For now, why don't we look at a menu? I'm starved." Total lie, but accepting my reluctance to divulge personal information, Mona did as I asked.

"Have a seat, Lexi." Vivienne welcomed me to the table. "My daughter thinks you're some kind of miracle worker." A warm smile under eyes that searched me for evidence of sainthood. Vivienne was either skeptical or even less interested in my help than Mona thought.

"I wouldn't say a miracle worker, but I do try my best to put happy couples together, and Mona deserves every happiness. She's a lovely woman; you must be proud of her." The genuine praise and my smile drew some of the tension from Vivienne's shoulders, relaxed her spine. I would have to go slowly with this one.

"I am." Mona and her mother exchanged fond looks while I battled the jealousy that roiled up inside me. "And Mona's had such a run of bad boyfriend luck that I had begun to wonder if she'd ever find someone who made her happy."

"It wasn't that bad. You make it sound like I was three steps away from spinsterhood."

The mildly defensive edge to Mona's tone tensed me up. In my house, a statement like that would be followed by a challenge that escalated the discussion to an argument and next thing I knew, we'd be on the road to faerie Armageddon. I so did not want to be a spectator for the human version.

Instead, Vivienne fixed twinkling eyes on her daughter and said, "I only want you to be happy...and give me grandchildren."

Mona's grin matched her mother's even if her face blushed prettily. "Mom. It's only been a few weeks, let's not start painting the nursery just yet."

That was the end of it. No screeching. No flying spells. And they were still smiling. Is that how normal mothers and daughters act toward each other? With no frame of reference for normal, I just listened while Mona led her mother into telling me all the details I needed to know to find the older woman's perfect match.

Vivienne was a lot like her daughter: sweetly steadfast, caring, and gentle, but with enough fire and steel below the surface to carry her through the tragic loss of her husband. As the two of them spoke, a vision of their happy little family played gently in my mind's eye. Lovers parted by death make my job harder.

Once a person has experienced the true merging of hearts, it can be difficult for them to accept there might be more than one person in the world to suit them. But a mere two seconds after meeting her, I knew there was a new man for Vivienne. A nice man who would treat her kindly and with whom she would make more good memories and a lovely life.

Nudging Mona's ankle with my toe, I flashed her a subtle wink, and when her mother made noises about being late for a hair appointment, Mona walked her out and returned to the table. Watching them exchange hugs before parting ways touched the raw, motherless being inside me.

For someone who tends to move first and think second, Mona could be surprisingly perceptive at times. This was one of them. One look at my face and she dropped into the chair with a concerned look. "What's wrong? You look so sad." I could tell she was wondering what had happened in the last two minutes to put that expression on my face.

Choosing my words carefully, I laid out the bare bones version of my life. "My mother left when I was an infant, and based on the way it all went down, no one ever expected to see her again. I was raised by," no mundane description of the faeries leaped to mind, "my aunts."

The faeries would be mortified by the moniker.

"A few weeks ago, my mother came back as if from the dead, and all I can think is how she didn't love me enough to stay when I was born." A truth I'd been struggling with since the moment I realized Sylvana lived. Tears burned my eyes, and I blinked hard to clear them while my stomach twisted into knots.

Mona's hand closed over mine and squeezed. The simple show of friendship and support unlocked the torrent of conflicting emotions I only thought I'd managed to bury deep. I don't cry often. I think it's a witch thing. We're supposed to be powerful and stoic. And I guess you can add dramatic to the list, because I made a small scene once the first sob escaped. It turns out I'm not a quiet crier. The noises I made sounded like someone stepping on a duck.

Bless her little heart; Mona took it all in like a saint. Any time another café patron slid a curious glance my way, she glared back at them like a she-bear defending a helpless cub.

Helpless is a good word to describe how I felt as the onslaught of painful memories flowed. Mommies would come to school to celebrate birthdays with cupcakes and ice cream. Mine, because Terra had no idea what was expected, passed unmarked.

The faeries made up for the lack of classroom cupcakes by putting on elaborate mini galas in my honor. It's not every eight-year-old who gets to ride a unicorn for her birthday, but I would have happily traded the experience for a single hug from my mother.

The greeting card industry has made a killing over the years trying to convince people that time erases grief and given enough of it, the pain and fear will fade. No offense to the card companies, but what a fat load of hooey, and that's nothing compared to knowing your mother could have ended that pain by coming back around at any time, but chose not to do so.

Nothing else ever cut me as deeply. Nothing.

Mercifully, the crying jag lasted only long enough to

leave me feeling awkward and keep the waitress from bringing the check. When it all was over, I felt hollowed out, and clean. A feeling that died in flames at the sight of Delta slithering past the plate glass window. Again.

"Excuse me, Mona. I hate to dump a load of angst on you and run, but there's something I need to take care of. I'll explain later." Dashing away from the table, I tossed an I'm sorry over my shoulder, noted the astonished look on Mona's face and knew I'd removed all doubt from her mind.

Lexi Balefire is a flake. The flakiest flake in the whole stinking snowstorm.

CHAPTER

# EIGHT

Ducking into doorways and behind other pedestrians, even though she never once turned to look behind her, I carried on an argument in my head the entire time I trailed Delta. I already knew supernatural abilities lurked underneath her very convincing disguise, and there was a better-than-average chance she was leading me into a trap. She'd wanted to talk during our previous encounter, but I wondered if whatever warm and fuzzy feelings she'd had toward me evaporated the instant Sylvana had shown up and frozen her solid.

More importantly, she thought Sylvana had the Bow of Destiny, which meant she had information about my mother that could be useful to me. Once I started thinking about Sylvana, it was hard to concentrate on anything else.

What would I say to her after dumping her off without a word? For the hundredth time since making the connection between Athena and Sylvana, I replayed the memory of our first encounter in my head and parsed it for clues to her state of mind. Each glance, the nuances in her speech, the way the touch of her hand felt warm on my neck—all fodder for speculation. The debater inside played both the pro and con side.

Pro:

My mother gave me what I needed to bring me to the fullness of my power. Without her, my chance for Awakening would have passed me by forever. Plus, she had wanted to protect me from Delta. My mother was good. Innocent and pure.

Con:

In the process of giving me what I needed, my mother used a glamour even I couldn't penetrate and worse, she'd manipulated me and clouded my mind. If Delta was to be believed, she was in possession of a magical bow that was supposed to belong to me and was lying to me about it. My mother was bad. Wicked to the bone.

Delta had poofed. While I'd been busy daydreaming I'd missed the fact that my quarry was no longer ahead of me. Son of a witch, I'd lost her.

Fuming, I hurried to the next intersection and looked in both directions hoping to spot which way she'd gone. Nothing. She could be in any one of a dozen buildings by now or skulking somewhere close by, waiting to do something. What that might be, I wasn't sure, but it probably wouldn't involve tea and cookies.

Tempted to stomp my feet all the way back to my office, I resolved to do the adult thing and merely mutter a few phrases under my breath that would have made Terra turn my saliva to soap—the faerie method of washing your mouth out for cussing. For once, my beloved city failed to lift my spirits, and I paid little attention to her as my feet ate two blocks of concrete sidewalk.

That was as far as I made it before annoyed resentment gave way to the dark caress of the same compulsion I'd felt at the festival. A whisper at first. My gut said I needed to go, to follow the call only I could hear.

Time and reason fled as I mindlessly sought the source of the piper's tune. Right, then left, then right again, my feet carried me to Tidewater Park before the driving need left me and I reeled at its sudden loss.

Quivering tension tingled through my limbs, and I felt like I'd just come out of an extended sleep with only a faint memory of how long it had been since I closed my eyes. My internal GPS—or rather my LPS (Love Positioning System) kicked in hard, and the force of it nearly drove me to my knees.

While I stood there ignoring the voice in my head that talked like Yoda and blathered on about the force, the pull intensified and focused on a young couple strolling toward the picnic area. Little hearts and birdies could have been circling the pair, they looked that deeply in love, so what did they need me for?

The answer came quickly and in the form of my half-brother, who dodged out from behind a tree. He tossed a sardonic smile my way and hit the lovebirds with some kind of whammy. The couple turned on each other so fast it was hard to believe they'd been in lockstep only moments before.

Torn between going after Jett or fixing things with the young couple, I made a split-second decision and took off after the ill-fated lovers as fast as I could without calling attention to myself.

The idea of busting up possible soul mates made me sick inside. It went against everything I'd built my life and business around, on top of making me wonder just how many more times Jett had botched up the works with me being none the wiser. Shoving the weight of that burden aside as best I could, I knew I had to do something to fix this—and fast.

"...ever saw in you, to begin with."

"Right back at you. And by the way, that pot roast you're so proud of always comes out dry."

You can criticize a lot of things, but a woman's pot roast is sacred, so I tried to diffuse the tension.

"Excuse me, but I couldn't help overhearing your discussion, and I wanted to say..."

"Butt out, lady." Waves of negative emotion poured off the man like black smoke. Jett had certainly done his job well. I sensed Serena's hand in whatever spell he'd tossed. Talking reason wasn't going to cut it, and I had no real experience as a mediator anyway.

What would Cupid do? WWCD. My life reduced to an acronym and a question I had no idea how to answer. Hell, I could barely process the concept of my male parentage, much less predict with certainty the reality of what he might expect from me in any given situation.

Add that to the list of conversations I needed to have with my mother. It would go somewhere after *where have you been* and *what were you thinking*. Probably repeated a couple times for good measure.

His face a furious mask, the guy turned on me, reaching out to give me a shove while the woman, who still retained some shred of dignity, grabbed his arm to stop him. When his hand made contact with my arm, darkness blanketed my sight for a split second, then cleared to shock me with a vision.

Technically, it was two visions. One where the couple lived a happy life with a passel of kids and all the ups and downs that true love can weather. The second was quite different; sadly, I watched them go their separate ways and spend the rest of their lives in search of the love they had lost. I couldn't let that happen.

I took a step back, and they promptly forgot all about me and went back to screaming insults at each other.

*Thanks for the useless visual*, I said to no one.

There wasn't time to contemplate any hidden meanings in the vision, and with no other recourse, I'd have to go all witchy on the situation. I ransacked my memory for anything useful and hit on a love spell I remembered from one of the books in the sanctum. Another moment to make some adjustments, and then I whispered:

> *Wind, water, earth, and fire*
> *Hear my call; know my desire*
> *May two hearts beat in time once more*
> *And hate return to its consort*
> *As I command, so mote it be!*

Hushed words, rippling power, and a final intake of breath before the spell slid through me; a reckless rush of energy tinged with the darkness born of a negative working. Three times power would return to show me the truth of this making. I could only hope my desire to help would balance the scales, or I was in for a world of hurt. But, it had to be done.

Twinkling motes carried my intent across the air toward the man and woman walking a few feet ahead of me, and I wished I knew their names. It seemed like the least I could do given the havoc my brother had created in their lives. The spell hit with a shiver and the faint scent of ozone.

It took about two seconds before all hell broke loose.

As though they were Stepford families out on furlough, every person within shouting distance turned on the unwitting victims of my spell. Instead of pitchforks and torches, the crowd wielded whatever they had at hand. The poor couple went down in a hail of Frisbees, softballs, and even a picnic basket. It wasn't just people who went berserk. A squirrel leaped onto the man's back as he tried his best to protect his woman.

What had I done? I turned my concentration on the couple and pointed directly at them, hoping nobody in the vicinity noticed I was acting like a complete lunatic and tried to undo whatever mistake I had just made:

> *Reverse my spell, cleanse the slate*
> *Return the love of true soul mates.*

The spell dissipated, but not before a baying beagle lifted his leg and loosed a stream all over the prone woman. My plan to handle this with magic collapsed like a house of cards and, hoping guilt was not written plainly over my face, I rushed to help.

"Are you all right?" With the spell lifted, the crowd

wandered off, most shaking their heads as if to dispel an unbidden daydream.

"Did you see what just happened?" The man helped the woman to her feet and began searching her for signs of injury while brushing bits of grass and dirt from her clothes. She had a Frisbee welt on her arm, a purpling raw mark on one knee, and a look of disgust over the wet dog stain on her Capri pants. "Grace, are you hurt?"

"I'm fine. Just a bit winded from when you landed on me, and a little wet. What happened? One minute we were walking along and the next..." Grace turned her head, luminous brown eyes scanning the area for signs of threat, "...you landed on me."

At least the fight was forgotten.

"My name is Lexi, and I was right behind you." I tried to lay my spin on things. "It looked like you were in the wrong place at the right time. A total coincidence."

"Are you kidding me? You call it a coincidence when someone tosses a picnic basket at you? That's pretty specific, if you ask me. Those people were throwing things on purpose. I saw their faces, and they meant to hurt us." The hand not wrapped around Grace's arm gestured wildly toward the rest of the people in the park. "I ought to call the cops."

"James!" Grace injected enough heat to pull his focus back to her. "Whatever started this, it's over now, and there's dog pee dripping into my shoe. Just take me home." When he stubbornly stood in place, she tugged on his hand, "Please."

With great reluctance and an annoyed glance back at me,

James allowed Grace to pull him away from the scene of the incident. I watched them walk away before turning my own feet toward home. Not only did I have the worry of how the spell's energy would return to me, but I had to go back and describe the debacle to my familiar, Salem. I was not looking forward to that.

By now, Jett was long gone, and if he'd meant this to be a show of power, he'd come out on the losing side, but only just. I was going to have to step up my game.

## CHAPTER
# NINE

Kin was the first to arrive at my house for dinner. Flix was also slated to make an appearance, bringing the head count to a comfortable eight including Salem and the godmothers, who needed no excuse to throw a soiree but were also using us as guinea pigs for their next party planning endeavor. We were expected to taste test their menu, and they demanded nothing less than brutal honesty, which we hoped would not be used against us at a later date.

The Balefire, crackling loudly from its hearth in the parlor, was visible through the open adjoining door to the dining room, but every bit of heat it produced got sucked right up the chimney during warmer months thanks to an effective faerie charm.

Since Vaeta let it slip that as the fire's mistress, I could change the color of the flame with nothing more than my will, I'd been experimenting. Tonight, I'd gone for shades of purple to complement the current color scheme in the dining room. Storing up points with the faeries never hurt.

Lavender linen so soft it felt like silk draped the expanse of the dining table, illuminated by a series of twinkle bulbs suspended from the ceiling by an invisible thread. Golden light danced off hand-blown glass goblets rimmed with a strip of silver inlay and matching cutlery. The entire center of the table was a tangle of multi-colored orchids and some exotic greenery I couldn't name.

"Hello dear!" the four of them chorused as Kin entered the kitchen which was, for once, pristine even though they had been cooking and preparing for dinner in there all afternoon. Terra rushed forward to envelop Kin in a hug that prompted a blush (having your head crammed into a faerie's voluptuous bosom will do that to any guy) and accepted the jar of homemade caramelized onion jam he offered with a puzzled expression.

As rarely as we had guests, no one had ever brought her a gift.

"My mom sent me a couple of these; it's always a big hit at parties so I thought maybe you could recreate the recipe..." Kin trailed off as though just now realizing onion jam was an odd hostess gift but was treated to a wide, sincere smile that wiped the embarrassment right off his face. "It's really tasty on top of steak, or with those little slices of toasted baguette," he finished, his cheeks finally returning to their normal color.

"That sounds fantastic," Soleil piped up, "Thank you, Kin, that was very thoughtful." And he blushed again.

Evian and Vaeta nodded in agreement from behind the kitchen island where they were placing edible flowers on top of individual ramekins. I couldn't tell if it was cheesecake or some kind of custard, but suddenly I couldn't wait for dessert.

Just then, the air between where the faeries and Kin and I stood shimmered, and Flix shivered into view carrying a bottle wrapped in twine. Twinkleberry wine; there was no doubt in my mind, and I could have slapped him. I'm not exactly human and can only handle one glass; any more, and I'll wake up with a headache the size of Texas and just enough bits of embarrassing memories to make me swear off drinking for a year. I never followed through, but the sentiment was the same.

A single sip was sure to knock Kin on his butt for a week, and Flix knew better. "You're a pain in my rear," I whispered into his ear as he reached over to envelop me in a tight hug. "We've got a whole cellar full of that stuff, and you know it."

Flix just laughed, ignored my protests, and took his turn hugging the godmothers. The Fae side of his family treated him as though his mixed blood was tainted. But mine accepted him with open arms.

Everyone was part something and part something else nowadays. At least, that's the philosophy I had been raised to uphold, and I knew it meant a lot to Flix to be included in a family environment devoid of open hostility. Just one more reason I loved my godmothers unconditionally.

Salem came flying down the stairs at top kitty speed just then, whooshing into his human form as he stepped into the kitchen to complete the guest list. Kin shook his head, and I figured he was wondering how he'd managed to get caught up in this very strange household.

The wide grin he shot me over Salem's shoulder went a long way toward easing any worry over how well he had assimilated. Four and a half faeries, a witch, and her familiar is a lot to take all at once. Who am I kidding, one of my godmothers is a lot to take. All four of them in a room is a tsunami.

"Sing for your supper, Mackintosh," Terra ordered Kin while I observed her closely for signs of early inebriation. Finding none, I let a small sigh slip past my lips. Even-tempered and with a mile-wide open mind he might be, but a bout of full-on Faerie hilarity was more of a six-month anniversary thing.

Not only did Kin comply with her wishes by launching into the bawdy song he knew she liked best, but he also pulled me into a little two-step around the kitchen while his voice soared to the accompaniment of a set of reed pipes Vaeta plucked out of the air. For all I knew, they were made of the wind.

The song ended with a dip and a kiss that left me wanting more. And hooting noises from the peanut gallery.

"The first course is ready." Vaeta chirped, sent a platter sailing on a cushion of air to land gently on the table, and winked at Salem. "Strawberries stuffed with salmon mousse and drizzled with balsamic glaze." My mouth watered; the juxtaposition of perfectly-ripened, slightly firm berry and delicate, tangy whipped fish was so satisfying it could have been described as orgasmic.

"Wine?" Flix offered Kin with a wicked grin. I've never actually seen the effects of too much Twinkleberry wine on a true human, and I didn't want to spend the rest of the night watching my boyfriend frolicking naked through the back yard and jumping at invisible lightning bugs.

"We'll be having the red, thank you very much." I snatched the wineglass back before Flix could pour.

"Party pooper. I was hoping to get you tanked up and pry some secrets out of you."

My hot glare failed to burn Flix to a crisp and I couldn't even protest that I didn't have any secrets because that would be exactly the kind of lie the faeries would spot.

"What's in that stuff anyway?" Kin gave the bottle a narrow-eyed glance as though it might turn into a snake and bite him. Not out of the realm of possibility in our house.

"It's Terra's special blend of death by embarrassment— fun while it lasts, but packs a punch and the hangovers are epic. If you're planning on working at all this week, I'd pass."

Kin gave Terra raised eyebrow which she returned with a shrug. "A sip wouldn't hurt you."

He eyed the bottle again and I could see the temptation, but he shook his head. "I'll stick with the red, but maybe Lexi will want a glass or two."

"One's my limit, but not today, thanks." This was not the time to lose my inhibitions. Who knew what I might let slip, so I filled Kin's glass and then my own with the safer option.

He'd managed the first swallow and a bite of the second course (tender lamb chops in a delicate mustard sauce) when the doorbell rang. I can count on the fingers of one hand the number of times the doorbell has rung on a day that wasn't Beltane. There's a powerful spell on the place to ward off traveling salesmen and even Girl Scouts selling cookies. That last one I lobbied to have lifted because I do love my Samoas, but the faeries refused.

"I'll get it." I rushed to press my eye to the peephole. Mona stood on the porch looking slightly nervous.

"Just a minute," I hollered through the door and returned

to the dining room. "Red alert, folks. It's Mona, you remember her from Harry and Lemon's wedding? Get your game faces on and make like normals. Sorry, Salem. And check for anything weird. Hurry"

I left the faeries scrambling to stash food back into the oven rather than leaving it out under a few of Soleil's miniature suns. Pots stopped stirring themselves.

"I'm letting her in now." I went to the door and hoped all four faeries would look like humans before I got back.

The last thing I did was set the Balefire to orange and yellow on my way past the parlor door.

"Mona, won't you come in?" I crossed my fingers behind my back.

"Oh, Lexi, I'm sorry for just showing up like this, but I was worried about you. You took off so fast, and you looked… I don't know, upset. I just had to come by and make sure you were okay."

Once she got started, it took Mona some time to run down. She followed me toward the dining room. "It smells incredible in here. Oh, I'm sorry, I'm disturbing your dinner." Her cheery smile took in the whole room.

"Nonsense, I'll get you a plate." Evian rose gracefully to set another place at the table, and I grabbed the bottle of Twinkleberry wine before Flix could offer her some. He waggled his eyebrows at me, and I refrained from thumping him on the back of the head. There are times when his sense of humor runs on the mean side.

"You're going to help her, right?" Mona said somewhere between the second and third course of exquisite food. For a moment, I couldn't think who she meant.

"Oh, your mom? Yes, of course. Don't worry, I've got it under cont..."

Vaeta bobbled the platter she was carrying and used a whiff of power to right it. Mona caught the motion out of the corner of her eye, but before she could get a full view, Kin jumped up to take the platter from Vaeta courteously.

"That looks heavy. Let me carry it for you." The man was so getting lucky tonight.

"Urrrrgh!" I hollered, thankful that my silencing charm was working nearly as well as Terra's did, and that my grunts and moans of annoyance couldn't be heard throughout the house. Apparently, the charm had no effect on my familiar, because Salem tripped the handle on the parlor side of the fireplace, reverted from his sleek black cat form into his sleek black human one, and was now standing with his arms folded, glaring at me.

When I reached my hand into the Balefire the first time and watched the fireplace rotate to reveal a secret room, I had no idea what to expect within the depths beyond the entrance. A treasure trove of magical paraphernalia had come as a welcome surprise, even if I had barely spent any time exploring the plethora of supplies at my disposal.

I hadn't had enough magic to keep the Balefire alive on my own before coming into my full powers, but now it was roaring with bright, licking flames. Every year on Beltane (which happens to be my birthday) all the witches from miles around tromp through my parlor, light their torches, and transmit a bit of the Balefire's power from coven to coven.

The women in my family have acted as Keepers of the Flame for centuries, and even though it was my most sacred duty, the revelation that I was also a demigod had thrown me for enough of a loop that I had all but ignored the magical training sessions Salem kept scheduling for us.

"What exactly are you trying to accomplish?" He raised a sardonic eyebrow beneath a shock of pure white hair, and his eyes—one green and one blue—twinkled with feline mischief.

I must have looked a sight, standing in the middle of the casting circle—a raised area with an etched pentacle at least eight or ten feet in diameter—wielding a wand I'd found during my search of the cavernous space beyond the dais.

"I'm trying to transfigure this ceramic garden gnome into a real one." I scrunched my nose in concentration and flicked the wand. It did nothing to focus my power, and the gnome sprouted ceramic butterfly wings. "What am I doing wrong?" I wailed.

"Well, first off, that's not a wand, it's the broken handle of an old cauldron stirrer. Wands aren't effective if you don't properly prepare and cleanse them, anyway. Secondly, you're holding it in the wrong hand. And thirdly, you're expecting the wand to do the work and it's only meant to focus your magic. This is exactly why I keep hounding you about training. Now tell me what you're really trying to accomplish."

I sighed and tossed the gnarled stick into the fireplace. "I'm trying to figure out what parts of me are God and what parts of me are witch. I cast a love spell—or more accurately, tried to remove a hate spell yesterday, and the result was...well, not good. I'm actually a little scared of the repercussions." I carefully told Salem all about the poor couple in the park. "There, are you happy now?" I shot him a dirty look.

I give him credit for keeping a straight face. "This little debacle is probably all the backlash you'll get; your intentions were good, and it doesn't sound like it was a terribly powerful spell. No offense. Now, if I tell you everything I do know about demigods, will you agree to follow my instructions and get serious about your training?"

"You mean you've been holding out on me?" As if I had any room to talk. I still hadn't told Salem that Sylvana was back in the picture. Given the good fortune he currently enjoyed at the hands of four faerie godmothers who were cooking and baking delectable goodies for a half dozen parties they had agreed to coordinate, it seemed a safe bet that he'd turn into a tattletale and I'd wind up in some kind of magical time out for lying. To faeries, the difference between being five years old and twenty-five is not significant.

Salem leveled my gaze. "Do you promise?" He repeated.

"Yes, yes. I promise."

"Okay." Salem settled onto one of the tufted sofas, curling his legs up underneath himself and resting his chin on top of his folded hands, proving to me once again that he was always a cat, regardless of whether he had arms and legs, or paws and a tail.

"Gods have been consorting with humans for an eternity —that's pretty much common knowledge, so it's not surprising that there are a few of you hybrids walking around out there."

There went my feeling of being unique.

Hesitating as if choosing his words carefully, Salem continued. "In order to get the full experience, though, most gods who play at being human don't reveal their nature to their consorts. Nor do they have anything to do with the children who are born as a result of the union."

"Someone should explain that to Jett. Might clear up his obvious daddy issues."

But it explained a lot about why my father might have gone MIA all this time. Circling a hand, I indicated for Salem to finish.

"The gifts bestowed on these children show up in unexpected ways: charisma, power, beauty; they all come naturally to demigods. Some of the most powerful people in history descended from one deity or another." Salem sounded like a college professor, and I could tell he was thoroughly enjoying himself.

"So, you're telling me that these people don't ever have to deal with the supernatural world, but they get to just be beautiful and famous and powerful? And I get—what? All this responsibility? That doesn't seem fair." I may have whined a tiny bit during that last part.

"I agree, it doesn't. It seems to me that you've got an edge; your awareness gives you a higher purpose. But you're also a witch, and every witch has strengths and weaknesses." Salem attempted to comfort me. "We need to discern what yours are, and that should help us figure out which of your abilities stem from either side of your heritage. For the time being, I wouldn't go casting any more spells on people, or you might overcompensate and find yourself on the whammy end of a karma grenade."

"But Salem, what about Jett and Serena? If they're going to try and screw with my livelihood and my life's work, I've got to do something to stop them. Are you saying I should have just let them tear that couple apart?"

"No. I'm not. You have a lot of power at your disposal, but it's raw and untrained. You can't go tossing around spells you sort of remember from a book and altering them on the fly. We need to get through the basics, and then we'll figure out how to apply active magic to matchmaking. Agreed?"

I grudgingly agreed, because what choice did I have? Salem had a point. I was beginning to learn he always had a point and didn't mind sharing. If you could call shoving it down my throat *sharing*.

Shouting out instructions, Salem had me gather materials and put them in neat piles on the tables lining the walls of the main room. I have never been a mathematical genius, but even I could tell that the proportions of the cavern behind the fireplace didn't remotely match the available space. The only explanation was magic —or an entirely separate plane of existence. I vehemently hoped for the former.

The raised central platform took up only a portion of the space below a glass domed roof that provided a clear view of the sky overhead. Across from the entrance, a wrought iron staircase spiraled up to a balcony section lined with shelf after shelf of old, leather-bound volumes. A wealth of information that would take a normal human lifespan to read.

Unless I did something stupid, I would have plenty of time to peruse them all.

Shelves of preserved ingredients lined the workshop area of the room where Salem would prepare me for my first guided foray into taking control of my powers.

"Lesson number one. There are several different types of magic. You're already familiar with elemental magic; it's essentially what Terra, Evian, Soleil, and Vaeta do. But, they're tapped into the earth, water, fire, and air in a way that you're not. You'll still have to call on, or invoke, each of the elemental spirits for certain spells and rituals."

In full-on teaching mode, the only things Salem needed were a pair of horn-rimmed glasses and a jacket with elbow patches. Oh, and a chalkboard with one of those pull-down maps over it.

"The same kind of invocation is used to bring forth the essence of the gods, depending on what you're trying to accomplish. That part is probably going to be a piece of cake for you since presumably, you're already connected to the gods."

My eyebrows went north at an alarming speed. "Presumably? Sure, we have lunch three times a week."

Ignoring my sarcasm, Salem continued, "This is the first thing a young witch usually learns. As you become more advanced, you'll only call the corners for healing or protection, and for ceremonial reasons, like to celebrate a solstice or commune with a specific deity."

"You don't think there's been enough deity communing in the family as it is?"

Salem's shut up and get serious look made me giggle. On the inside, anyway.

"Witchcraft is not just about making things happen with the wave of your hand—that's why my last couple of charges got blown up; they didn't care about living in harmony with the world around them. Don't make the same mistake." Salem narrowed his eyes and gave me a reproachful look.

"I'll give it my best shot."

Enough of his former charges had blown themselves up that I might be forgiven for harboring a little worry about Salem's abilities as a familiar. Not that I'd ever say that to him because I was his ninth witch and when I died, he would die for the last time. Talk about an added weight on my shoulders.

Sure, I could live for centuries, but I could also self-destruct if I chose the wrong path. Sometimes I hoped I'd never have to deal with all of the pain and loss that comes with an extended life span, and I'd already decided to ignore the possibility—and all of the implications that could make my head spin. Ignorance isn't bliss, but it can keep a person from going off the rails.

While I'd been contemplating Salem's history, he'd continued with his litany of instruction.

"Alchemy also falls under elemental magic, and that's where I think we ought to start. You've proved yourself able to successfully call the corners, as evidenced by our little brush with the near-destruction of Kin's soul. Clearly, the gods were willing to answer you, or he'd be dead. Most healing and protection spells require some degree of alchemical skill, especially at this early stage."

"So we're talking about potions?" I interrupted.

"Not just potions; powders, salves, anything that combines ingredients to create a desired effect. Modern pharmaceutical methods are actually closer to the alchemy witches have been practicing for thousands of years—not that today's doctors would ever recognize or admit to the similarity. Your concoctions will be much stronger and imbued with your own energy and intentions—that's what differentiates them from those mixed by a layman or a regular human."

*Blah, blah*, I thought. *Let's just get on with it.*

"Okay, so what do I do?" I had always tuned out during my classes in school when the teachers began lecturing, and I could feel my attention wandering. Hands-on was my preferred method of learning.

He handed me a sheet of paper yellowed from age and covered with elaborate script and motioned toward the table covered with ingredients.

"I've gathered the ingredients for a basic luck potion. Now, I want you to follow this recipe as closely as possible. This isn't like cooking, where you can just throw some herbs and spices into a pot and—unless you're a complete dolt—get something edible; it's more like baking, where you have to measure your ingredients precisely and add them at the right time. Let's see how you do." Salem stepped back and watched my every move.

I set to work, lighting a small fire to heat a medium-sized cauldron and roughly chopping some ginger, then thinly slicing a whole preserved lemon and grinding the mixture into a paste.

The recipe called for a significant amount of grain alcohol, a few drops of cinnamon bark essential oil, and a half-dozen four-leaf clovers. Lastly, Salem instructed me to choose a tiger eye stone from one of the many labeled boxes of gems and minerals spread over a large table perpendicular to the alchemy station.

"Now, first you'll need to cleanse that tiger eye, to get rid of any previous user's energy," Salem warned. "Who knows what nefarious purposes your grandmother might have had for these tools. Better safe than sorry."

"I know how to do this part." I hushed Salem, clasped the stone in my hands and focused on funneling my own will into its molecules. Heat swirled from my elbows to the tips of my fingers, and I could see all of the veins along the back of my hand standing out against the pale golden glow radiating from beneath my skin.

The tiger eye rose to eye level, and then by no intention of my own, plunged itself into the bubbling cauldron. A fountain of steam erupted from the mouth of the vessel, which abruptly quieted and turned a lovely shade of shimmering emerald.

"Holy sh—" I shouted, just as Salem exclaimed, "Tuna biscuits!"

"Did it work?"

"It definitely worked. That's exactly what it's supposed to look like. It's perfect. And on your first try! I thought you'd surely find some way to screw it up." The incredulity in his voice made me want to smack him on the back of his furry little head.

"Salem!"

"Er, I mean, well, you know, it's not like you have the best track record."

I stuck my tongue out in his direction and made a mental note to buy the chicken flavored kibble I knew he hated next time I went shopping. "So can we try something else? This is easy."

Salem nodded, refusing to take my bait. "Let's try something a little different. We're going to move on from the Elemental school of witchcraft, and into the Arcane branch. A very simplified definition would be that Arcane magic has to do with dark energy."

Now he was getting to the interesting stuff. Not that I wanted to fool around with dark energy. My grandmother was enough of a warning on that topic.

"I'm not sure if I should...you know--" I waved a hand to indicate the casting of spells. "fool around with anything evil. There's a track record in my family I'd rather not uphold."

"No, I don't mean evil energy per se, but dark meaning mysterious and unquantifiable, even after thousands of years of research and study across the field. Intention makes all the difference, so if you don't intend to do evil, you won't."

He made it sound so simple, but I had to wonder if, being a cat, his understanding of human nature might be lacking. Sometimes evil happens even when people have the best intentions.

"It's important to know and understand all the facets of your power lest you make a mistake and accidentally blow yourself to smithereens. Eventually, you'll learn how get results without using totems to focus your power. Mastering the arcane takes some witches years of training, and even then there are caveats."

Maybe he had a point. "No one uses the word lest anymore, but I'll take your word for it. So where do we start?" I was eager to get this lesson over with, and not interested in another long explanation.

"Summoning. You're going to call forth a cuddly woodland creature of your own choosing. I only hope that you avoid squirrels and birds." At least he had the presence of mind to look ashamed of himself for needing to ask.

I suppressed a grin. How bad could arcane magic be if you could use it to summon a squirrel?

"Sure thing, boss. How about a nice chipmunk or opossum."

"Not exactly what I had in mind. Could you make it a bunny? They're not so bad."

I agreed and began prepping the spell. Once I had all the ingredients laid out, I lit a couple of candles and followed Salem's instructions.

"Oryctolagus cuniculus sylvilagus floridanus leporidae pronolagus paprolagus." I chanted, over and over. Somewhere around the third time through, I felt my focus begin to waver and through closed lids sensed the presence of another being in the room.

When I opened my eyes, it wasn't to see a fluffy little bunny hopping across the center of the pentacle, but a giant animal of indeterminate breed—part leopard and yet somehow wolf-like, and entirely pissed off at being dragged away from whatever it had been doing when I so rudely interrupted it. A scrap of bloody flesh fell from its mouth, and when it turned its fangs in my direction, I could swear it was smiling.

But that wasn't even the concerning part; what turned my arms to gooseflesh and sucked all of the air from my lungs was the unmistakable scent of magic roiling off the thing. It let loose a growl so terrifying I would probably need to shower twice and change my underwear, provided it didn't eat me alive before I got the chance.

"Terra!" I screeched, slamming my eyes shut and raising my arms in front of my face as if blocking a predator twice my own weight would actually do me any good. It concerned me that I didn't even try to put up a magical shield, or use my powers in any way; those reflexes had yet to set in deep enough to replace the regular human ones I'd been using all my life, and even though it was probably completely normal, I felt ashamed.

Thankfully, I wasn't exaggerating when I said that Terra could hear my call and come to my aid inside a shallow breath, and she dispatched the beast with little more than a flick of her finger while keeping her eyes trained on my terrified expression.

"What the hell are you thinking, summoning an Eaflock to this house? How did you even do that?" Terra demanded. "That thing is the Fae equivalent to a hellhound, and he could have taken your head off and dragged you into the Unseelie dimension. Salem, have you lost your ever-loving mind?"

Soleil, Evian, and Vaeta, who had appeared within a tenth of a second of Terra's arrival, were huddled together near the fireplace exit, glaring at Salem with fury in their eyes.

"Just for the record," Terra continued to rant, "I'm the only one of us who can do that, so you're damned lucky I'm the one who hears your calls. These three would have been about as useful as an ashtray on a motorcycle, and you'd be dead right now. Off to bed, both of you. And tomorrow, you're going to clean up this mess and buff out those claw marks, Mister." I had a feeling Salem wouldn't be sampling any of the godmother's party treats tomorrow.

"Terra, I was trying to summon..." I began, my voice reaching a pitch it hadn't touched since I was a teenager.

"It was supposed to be a bunny!" Salem shouted, "She must have made a mistake with the wording, and she's still using a hand grenade in place of a hammer when it comes to magic. I should have known better. I'm sorry."

"I don't want to hear it right now." Terra insisted, but I could feel her softening already. "Out."

CHAPTER

# ELEVEN

"Salem, have you seen my…" Have you ever seen a cat make one of those gravity-defying leaps when it hears a sharp sound? Well, picture that same reflex on a man, and you'll know why I tried not to snort out a laugh.

Salem's body landed back on the bed, his eyes shot wide and then made exaggerated sideways motions accompanied by the merest nod to my right.

To my credit, I didn't jump or drop my coffee when my mother spoke into the sudden silence.

"Hello again, Lexi. We need to talk." Okay, so my mouth dropped open a little.

My *mother* was in my *bedroom*. A million wishes had just come true, every one of them turning to ashes in my mouth.

Arms wide, she stood in the center of the space. The pink light of impending sunset filtering through the sheer curtain created an angelic halo effect around her and lit the tips of her dark hair to golden fire.

My mother was in my bedroom with arms open wide, and all I wanted to do was run to them, but I couldn't force myself to take that first step.

My mother was in my bedroom, and now Salem knew this wasn't the first time we'd met.

Great.

A hundred questions crowded my head, but only one popped out.

"How did you get in here?"

As far as I knew, the place was warded against any intrusion. She should have been covered with festering pustules or caught in a quicksand trap or something worse—not standing here all cool confidence and without a mark on her.

"Please." Her arms inched down her sides and Sylvana snorted at the half question, half accusation. "There are four secret ways in and out of this house that your precious faeries don't even know about." She thought about it for a minute, then pronounced, "Wait, make that five."

Information I could have used during my unfortunate infatuation with Buddy Crenshaw during senior year. His idea of living wild had not included *camping* out under the stars and had I been able to sneak out and join him, I too might have racked up a police record before graduation. Hecate knows I wanted to run with the bad boys. They just didn't want to run with me. It was probably for the best, though, because explaining Buddy's disappearance would have been tricky.

Most parents aren't ready to accept that their darling delinquent would be spending the rest of his formative years as a pink-eyed toad with yellow skin and purple warts. Terra likes pretty things.

Thinking of her triggered a wisp of imagination featuring Terra and Sylvana squaring off against each other with a sports announcer giving color commentary until I shook the visual out of my head.

But I couldn't shake the hopeful look on my mother's face as she took a tentative step toward me. "Lexi, please. Let me just look at you for a minute. I've missed so much time." The intensity of her gaze made me squirm. But no matter how much I yearned for her touch, something in me held back from closing the distance between us.

She took one more step and reached out as if to lay her hand on my cheek and I let her. I even leaned in to make the most of the moment of contact. Slim and smooth, her hand felt like a hundred things. Like warm mittens on a cold day, like a kitten's nose, like home, and like everything I'd yearned for my entire life.

The sensation stole my breath, and sent my heart lurching into my toes as an unexpected emotion flashed through me.

Turns out, I was mad at her. At least I was at that moment. I'd swung back and forth between anger and longing so many times I felt dizzy just thinking about her.

Flinching away from her touch, I launched off the bed and put some distance between us.

"How many times..."

"Never. Not until today. Not without me knowing about it, and I would have found a way to warn you even before you got your magic." Salem leaped to Sylvana's defense and earned himself a dirty look for his troubles. Actually, a pair of them. Identical but for the shadow of a line or two betraying my mother's additional years.

"Regardless of what you might think of me, it was never my intention to leave you. That's something you can blame on your grandmother." Bitter words. "I'd like to tell you the whole story if you're ready to hear it."

Was I? Was there anything she could say to banish the hurt gnawing at my bones? Sylvana's version of the story might be worse than the one I'd built up in my imagination. Some part of me—the part that would lead the way with a banner and parade should I ever decide to give in to my baser nature and turn wicked—felt a burst of satisfaction when she saw I wasn't going to bend that easily. I wanted her to grovel, expected her to beg for my forgiveness. Neither of those things was happening.

Crestfallen, Sylvana said, "Don't you want to hear what I have to say? Maybe I misjudged the situation; I thought you'd be happy to see me."

Well, so had I, right up until it happened. Now that we were face to face again, I couldn't get past being angry. What kind of mother dumps her kid and runs? What had she done to deserve a hero's welcome?

Other than helping me with my Awakening.

Trust never comes easy to those who have been abandoned, and I was no exception to the rule. So what if she had helped me that one time; it wasn't enough to make up for years of neglect. There's no rhyme or reason to the way I yearned for her and burned to reject my mother at the same time.

"Why now?" Of all the questions that needed answers, this was the one that bubbled up inside me. Not why did you leave, because that was already done and over with.

"It's complicated." Her eyes slid away from mine then

back, the expression in them pleading. "I'm here because I'm in trouble and I need your help."

Great, my mother finally shows up and instead of *I'm sorry, Lexi,* or *I've missed you,* all I get is a chance to do her a favor. Whoop-de-do, it's just like Christmas. The sound of my heart and mind slamming shut against her was nearly audible.

Every tick of my bedside clock sounded louder than the last as silence stretched out between us and grew until I wanted to scream it away. Questions crowded against the back of my lips, but I would not let them pass and make it easy on her. If she was in trouble, she could just...oh, who was I kidding?

"What kind of help do you need? And how much trouble are you in?" The stand-off suddenly felt foolish, so I plunked down in the edge of the bed and indicated Sylvana should make herself comfortable in my desk chair. She declined to sit and paced back and forth between the bathroom door and my closet for a minute or two. A family trait, apparently, that I also possessed. At least now I knew which parent it originated with.

"Those..." words failed Sylvana, "...jerks from Olympus sent a Fiach after me because they think I took the Bow of Destiny. I don't have it, Lexi. I swear to you." Earnest words, an expression to match. It felt like the truth.

"A Fiach?"

Sylvana gave me a funny look. "A Fiach," she repeated more loudly, in that way that signifies the person either thinks you're an idiot, hard of hearing, or don't speak the language. In my case, it was the latter.

"You can keep repeating it, but I'm not getting the reference."

"Delta. She's a Fiach. A type of bounty hunter, and I'm the bounty. Stupid faeries. Didn't they teach her anything?" I caught the muttered words as I'm sure my mother intended.

"Don't even think about disparaging my family like that. They showed up when you couldn't be bothered and maybe the sisters aren't remotely close to normal, but they were here for me. Every day. When I fell and skinned my knee, Terra wiped away my tears. When the boy I liked in fifth grade called me weird, Soleil made fireworks in the backyard to cheer me up. I took my first steps into Evian's arms. If I'm not familiar with every single being you might have pissed off in your day, then that's on you, isn't it?"

Magic gathered in the dense pool at my center, its energy trickling along my arms like a wave of electricity. Salem, lapsed into his catly form, dropped the pretense of sleeping, arched his back, and puffed out his tail.

"Sorry. I didn't mean..." Sylvana ran her hands through her hair in a frustrated gesture. "I'm handling this all wrong, and I don't blame you for being angry with me. You have every right to hate me, I just hoped..." She looked away for a second or two, "even if you didn't need me as a mother, maybe we could be friends."

Springing off the bed, I opened the closet doors and busied myself sorting shoes from the pile on the floor back into their cubbies. Anything to avoid eye contact until I got my face under control.

"I can't remember the last time hanging out with any of

my friends ended with a lunatic launching a sword at me." I tossed the words over my shoulder.

"There was that time with Kin when..." I spared Salem a withering glance and was just happy he'd thought to add clothes when he morphed back into human form. His company manners were getting better, but still needed work. He hadn't flashed any of the godmothers in over a week. We were calling that a victory.

Sylvana fell quiet while I wrestled with my decision. *Mother* is only a word; one easily defined by a biological process and function. The deeper meaning of the term cannot be parsed by logic or even by memory. This woman's loss had burned my soul to ash more times than I could count. Each time, I rose from the fine dust of her death and, phoenix-like, soared on with the knowledge that her absence was unwilling. A twist of fate had left me motherless, not a choice. That had been a bitter lie.

Every fairytale has an inconvenient truth at the heart of it—most times it's as simple as *be careful what you wish for*—and I railed at fate for subjecting me to the moral of the story. *I* was the victim here, and yet it seemed like I was the one being asked to take the biggest step.

*Send her away, she's trouble*—logic screamed in my head.

*Hold tight, she's your mother*—my heart lurched with the need.

"No more deception. I need there to be truth between us. Tell me everything: why you left, where you've been, and if you're not the one who took the bow, why is Delta chasing you? I want to believe you, so I will listen. It's the best I can offer." I took a deep breath and waited for her to begin.

# TWELVE

Several tense moments passed while I pulled my head out of the closet and tried to read my mother's face for clues to what might happen next. I wanted to trust her. I wanted to hear an epic tale of danger and intrigue, because anything less would not have been enough of a reason for abandoning a baby. I wanted this moment to be special and heartrending.

Now that her chance to speak had come, Sylvana's eyes darted away from mine. Tension set lines around her mouth and lifted her shoulders. Was she going to back out now? To tell me her story or not, it was her choice, and even if it gutted me, there would be no begging.

Without the truth between us, I would be forced to make a hard decision. Letting her go would bookend our relationship quite nicely, and I was prepared to do just that. Nothing owed, nothing changed. Just an *hasta la vista, baby* and I'd roll right along as if my deepest wish hadn't come true only to be snatched away again.

Can we not talk about the fact that she had been the one asking to tell her story from the beginning and only when I actually wanted to hear it did she waffle? Maybe our faces weren't the only thing my mother and I had in common. Just call us the yo-yo twins.

"I'd like a few minutes alone with my daughter." Sylvana made eye contact with Salem, then nodded toward the door. "This is a private conversation."

"Fine," I snapped, and then threw her under the bus. Okay, not the bus, the faerie van of party planning. "Salem, please go down and tell the godmothers I've decided to take a nap. Ask Terra, and do it nicely, to put her favorite silencing charm on my room. I'd do it myself, but we both know how *inept* I've been at spells lately."

Flipping off the bed in a graceful motion only a cat should be able to accomplish, Salem shot me the subtlest hint of a raised eyebrow indicating he understood the message.

The door closed behind Salem with a soft click and Sylvana turned to me. "Delta and I have history, and she's convinced I know where Bow of Destiny is hidden." I'd meant for her to talk about our briefly-shared history and what she wanted from our relationship going forward, not explain her current predicament. With a sinking feeling, I listened to her skirt the issue of the past in favor of the problem she was facing now.

"Delta's after the bow, and she won't leave either of us alone until she has it in her possession. I know what she told you, but the truth is she's ruthless, and she'll do anything to get what she wants. She has no intention of handing something so valuable over to a novitiate, regardless of your heritage. She'd spin any story to get you to lead her to what she's after. If we work together, we have a better shot of finding the bow, and once you have it in your possession, taking out Delta won't be a problem. I get the Fiach off my back, and you get the bow—we both win."

I wanted to trust her, needed to. She was my mother. The one person who was supposed to love me no matter what; who was supposed to have my best interests in mind. I'm not so naive that I think the act of giving birth is some kind of magic that makes a person into something she's not. Perhaps I'd built up a fantasy that *no* woman could have fulfilled.

"I'm going to want more than just your help. I want answers to all my questions—truthful answers. If you're not ready to talk about why you left, then start by telling me exactly how you expect us to find the Bow of Destiny in the first place."

"You want the truth?" Sylvana shot back. "It was your grandmother who took the bow."

"Clara?" It seemed like something a murdering witch would do, but I had no doubt there was more to the story; recognizing subtle untruths is a skill I exercise on a daily basis in my work life. People almost always try to show themselves in the most flattering light, it's basic human nature, and I would never presume to cast aspersions since I'm as guilty of it as anyone else.

"Yes, and there are only a couple of places she'd have considered hiding it. I can take you there. We'll find the bow first, remove Delta from the equation, and then we're both in the clear. I also promise I'll answer any question you have. We can check the first place on my list tonight—right now if you want."

Following along with her change of moods was like

trying to catch the wind. It spun me around in circles until I was dizzy.

"Define removing Delta from the equation. You're not talking about..." I drew a finger across my throat and as if that weren't enough, tipped my head to the side with my tongue out.

"Of course not. What do you take me for? I have no intention of ending up like my mother," Sylvana spat.

Did that mean Delta was part witch? As far as I know, committing witchicide is the only crime that results in stoning.

"Can I have a minute to think about it?" The brief flash of annoyance smoothed out so quickly I wasn't entirely sure I'd seen it at all.

"Take all the time you need." I sensed sarcasm lingering behind the seemingly genial response.

A short battle raged in my head, but desire won out over common sense. I wanted answers more than I wanted the satisfaction of turning her away.

"Okay, I agree. Just let me go down and tell Terra I'm leaving." An action that was completely unnecessary. I knew Salem had taken my hint and my faerie godmothers had been listening the whole time. It wasn't permission I was seeking or the simple act of courtesy in telling them my plans. I wanted their take on the conversation because if there was one thing a faerie could recognize, it was a lie.

Sylvana wasn't the only one I'd put in jeopardy today. Sending Salem to drop the mother bomb on my godmothers put his already precarious relationship with them on the fast track to Nowheresville, and didn't take me off the naughty list, either. We would both pay the price for this, but I hoped by cluing them now, the cost would be lower. Maybe a small scale freak-out instead of a full-on apocalypse. Apocalypse being their default, I might have indulged in some wishful thinking.

After a lifetime of practice, I can smell an irate godmother from fifty paces. Terra takes on the scent of dry leaves; Evian reeks of dead fish and Soleil of brimstone. The degree of scent strengthens in direct proportion to the annoyance level and Vaeta's influence spreads the love into every nook and cranny.

Today, the combined stench of all three squatted at the foot of the stairs like a foul gargoyle waiting to pounce. I followed it through to the kitchen and out into the backyard where the presence of poisonous-looking knee-high toadstools signaled they were at DEF CON 3. Maybe higher. I probably should have mentioned something to them about Sylvana not being dead before she showed up on our doorstep (understatement of the year). Now I owed Salem at least a pound of prime Ahi tuna for handling the situation.

Silence lay heavy on the air as I walked through the garden located in the lee of the L-shaped addition where the four faeries lived. As much as I love them, my godmothers can be a double handful. The quieter they are, the scarier their reaction. A knock on the sliding door netted me nothing—not a hello or a come in, but I slid it open and went in anyway. A grim-faced Salem met me before I got more than a few steps inside.

"It's bad. I'm not sure you should be here right now. Go! I'll handle it," He hissed.

"Tell them I wasn't keeping secrets, I wasn't even sure she was back until she showed up right when Delta....Oh, the Fiach. I guess I should have said something about her before. I'm in big trouble."

"If they ever calm down enough to listen to reason, I'll tell them." Salem promised. "It's best if you just go, but Lexi, do you trust her to keep you safe?"

"I trust them to be there if I need help," I nodded to indicate the faeries. "Even if they're furious with me, I know they have my back, and I trust you. She hasn't come close to earning that right. I'd like to hear what she has to say, though, and if she can help me get the bow, it's worth a shot. All my instincts tell me I'm supposed to find that bow. I have to do this, and I know they're not going to be happy. Just remind them it was my idea for the listening spell, okay?"

Salem rubbed his cheek against mine, and I returned the caress.

"It's going to cost you at least a gallon of seafood chowder for this. With lobster." Salem got in a parting shot as I headed out the door and into the car with my waiting mother.

"You growing up in a house full of faeries instead of with me was all your grandmother's fault." Sylvana spun the wheel on a '77 El Dorado. A car so big it practically needed a docking permit to park anywhere. Comfy ride, though.

My grandmother. There was a topic I'd like to explore.

"What did she do?" Trying not to arouse suspicion, I scanned the familiar spot as we drove past. For as long as I could remember, my grandmother's stoned body dominated a clearing just far enough from the house that if I leaned left, I could see it from my bedroom window.

Any witch who killed another suffered the instant punishment of turning to stone. Self-defense, murder, accidental death all ended up the same. One of the reasons I remained a solitary practitioner was the stigma from having a stone-cold wicked witch in my family. My grandmother, Clara, upon killing her own daughter, so the rumors went, suffered the ultimate punishment on the spot.

You'd believe the rumor, too, if you saw Clara's statue. Wild hair blowing in a magical wind, a fierce expression on a face that could have doubled for my own, arms raised in the act of her final casting. A quick glance was enough to send shivers up your spine. Looking at her longer made the blood run cold with knowing this had been one badass witch.

Except for the minor detail of her supposedly dead daughter sitting next to me, very much alive and breathing, so what was up with that? If not Sylvana, then who had my grandmother killed the day I became an orphan?

"My mother was a miserable old witch. Wicked to the bone and mean as a snake. I worked hard to master every spell, to make her proud, but the harder I tried, the worse she treated me. Nothing I did ever pleased her. She hated my hair and my clothes and my friends. Most of all, she hated your father."

Sylvana pounded on the steering wheel. "If you keep dating him, you'll end up with a broken heart," she said in a mimicry of Clara. "My happiness was never as important to her as being right. Probably because she wasn't pretty enough to keep a man of her own. Goddess knows your grandfather dumped her in a hot minute—before I was born."

I fought to keep from raising a brow at that one. I've read the dozens of love letters from prospective suitors Clara had stashed in her bedroom, and seen enough photos of her—not to mention, I have mirrors in the house—to know how attractive she had been. Three peas in a pod didn't even come close to describing the resemblance between us, and I'm no slouch in the looks department. Neither was Sylvana, but I've heard that hatred can be blind.

"Is she the one who cut your face out of every photo I could find?"

"Yep, that was her handiwork." Sylvana shook her head in disgust.

"Where have you been all this time?" I blurted out of nowhere. The hum of the tires, even in a car this quiet, almost drowned out my voice. This question had burned in me for so long that I wasn't sure I would survive the answer.

"Hell."

Did she mean literally or figuratively? I think my reply went something like, *ahum*.

"No, really. Your grandmother, in her infinite wisdom, imprisoned me in a nexus on the edge of the underworld."

The comment sent my body into red alert, my stomach lurched, my heart skipped a beat then raced into a gallop, and my fingertips tingled. Several months ago, the faerie godmothers had teamed up with an earthbound angel to rescue Vaeta and a guardian angel from a nexus on the edge of the underworld. I'd tagged along, and during the excitement, I'd fallen against the shrouded cage rumored to hold a legendary villain known as The Darkest Heart and banged my head. I remembered the sharp pain, the trickle of blood, seeing stars, and the feeling of great energy rushing past me.

"How did you get out?" I asked even though my gut told me I already knew the answer. I stared straight ahead and braced myself.

"Time turns back on itself inside a nexus, and it felt like I'd been in that cage for an eternity at times and then at others, only a minute. Mist surrounded my prison walls, so I'm not exactly sure what happened. I heard the sounds of a battle and called out for help, but no one came. When everything went quiet again, I figured I'd lost my chance, and then I was free."

Maybe it hadn't been me.

"You didn't see who let you out?" I hedged.

"No. The second the walls went down, I blew out of there. I wasn't about to take a chance of being caught again. I hit the edge of the nexus and just kept going. If I'd had enough magic left, I would have closed it behind me to make sure nothing and no one would come along to drag me back, but I was running on fumes by then. Cost me months of time getting back to full strength."

The impulse to confess my part in her grand escape died on the tip of my tongue. Given a chance, she would have trapped me in that portal without a second thought. More evidence of my wicked heritage. A whisper from my inner voice cautioned against trusting her with this particular piece of information. For once, I listened.

Whipping the wheel, Sylvana guided the car into a parallel parking spot under a flickering street light and popped the trunk. Judging by the contents, this witch traveled with a portable sanctum. A medium-sized cauldron squatted in one corner and the rest of the space was crammed with spellcrafting supplies. Carefully sorting through the contents, she selected a few items which she tossed into a black messenger bag and slung over her shoulder.

"You ever been to the Fringe?" The question drifted back to me as I followed my mother down a dead end alley not too far from my office.

"What? That pop-up club? No, that's Binge. I keep mixing up the names." How had I never noticed this alley before? I'd passed this spot thousands of times. Must be magic of some kind.

The shadow slicing across her face hid half of a shocked expression when she abruptly turned back toward me. "The Fringe. The place where worlds meet."

"Oh, *that* Fringe. Sorry, I wasn't thinking." Cut me some slack, this was all a little weird for me.

"Follow me and stay close." With that order, Sylvana took a step forward and vanished into the solid brick wall. If the train to Hogwarts was on the other side of that wall, I was out of here. Odd place for a portal between worlds, but this wouldn't be the weirdest thing I'd ever done, so I took a deep breath and stepped forward.

Magic shivered across my skin, teased every fine hair to taut attention with a prickling whisper of power. I didn't even realize I'd closed my eyes until they popped open and I faced my mother, silhouetted against a line of flashing bulbs riding past on the canopy of a carousel.

That the place where my world overlapped with the next was a carnival should have surprised me, but in retrospect, it seemed appropriate. I'd probably fit right in.

Sylvana led me through the crowded midway where I tried to take in all the sights without seeming overly interested. Some species of supernaturals take great offense to being noticed. Others flat out require it. The trick is knowing one from the other.

As much as I wanted to linger and explore, Sylvana set a blistering pace that took us diagonally across one corner of the Midway and dumped us into a no man's land of a cart track across a short field.

Unfamiliar birdsong and the swishing sound of grass brushing against our legs punctuated the silence between us as we trudged down a narrow dirt trail leading into a forest right out of a fairytale nightmare. Gnarled, curse-blasted trees arched high overhead, their branches resembling arthritic fingers against the dusk-laden sky.

"Don't you think it's time to tell me where you're taking me and what I have to do when we get there?" I hoped talking would lighten the atmosphere and drive back the heebie-jeebies.

"We're going to case the Mudwitch's house." Again that tone like I should be familiar with her every reference.

"Okay. Is she dangerous?"

"You'll be perfectly safe." For some reason, I didn't feel reassured. "She was a *friend* of your grandmother's."

"So what am I supposed to do? Just knock on the door and ask her if she's hiding Cupid's bow and if she is, can I have it back? Pretty please."

"Don't be ridiculous," Sylvana laughed, "she'd skin you alive."

"Literally or figuratively?" My feet slowed to a stop. Just how much danger were we in here?

"I've got it covered." Sylvana swung the pack off her back and rummaged around until she found a large potion bottle and slugged down half the contents before handing it to me.

"What is it?" I sniffed cautiously at the rim. The contents of the bottle smelled like smoky vomit.

"Transparency potion." Sylvana nudged my hand. "Hurry up, we'll have five minutes before it takes effect and then an hour before it wears off."

I could think of at least fifty things I'd rather do than drink the sludge, but I'd given my word, so I tipped the bottle up and let the contents drain down my throat. It tasted worse than it smelled if that was even possible, and it burned like fire in my belly.

"At least you didn't hand me an invisibility cloak. Do I want to know what was in that?"

"Who on earth would enchant a cloak? Too easy to trip over." The reference went right over my mother's head.

"Guess you didn't keep up on popular literature during your time in the underworld."

"I'm glad you can find humor in my situation." She said dryly.

"Sorry." I wasn't, not really.

While we walked, a full moon rose to spill soft light through barren branches and cast shadows that writhed along the ground like living things.

"Hurry now. I want to be within spitting distance of the

house before that potion takes effect. If Mag catches sight of you, we're in trouble." Sylvana took off at a brisk walk, and I followed behind, an obedient puppy, while the fire in my belly spread slowly throughout my entire body.

Ahead of me, my mother began to fade around the edges. Don't tell her I said this, but I thought it was the coolest thing I'd ever seen. Before she turned completely transparent, she reached into her pack again, pulled out a jar, unscrewed the top, and tossed some powder over me.

"Perambula."

Both spells took hold at once. The potion's fire turned to ice in my veins right before the adrenaline kicked in and the top of my head flew off. Okay, it didn't really fly off, but it felt like it could. What a rush. Not only was I invisible, but I could walk through obstacles unimpeded; as evidenced by the rock I would have stubbed a toe on had my shoe not kicked straight through it.

"Hey, where are you?" For a split second, I panicked. There I was, in the scary woods with an invisible companion. How's that for feeling totally alone? Sylvana didn't answer right away, and the volume on my panic button went right up to eleven.

"Sorry. I thought you were following me." Her voice came from twenty feet down the track.

"How am I supposed to follow you when I can't even see you?" Clearly, there were a few holes in her plan.

"Follow the trail, you can't miss the place. Trust me."

Trust me. I say that to my clients all the time. Hearing the phrase come out of my mother's mouth made me feel just a little closer to her and slightly annoyed for some reason.

"And when we get there, what are we supposed to do?"

"We aren't going to do anything, you're going to walk through the wall and see if you pick up on anything."

"Me? Why me?" My voice reached a pitch that could have cut glass.

"Because you're the one who should have a biological affinity for her father's tools." Sylvana's voice drifted back from ahead of me.

"Oh. What are you going to be doing?"

"I'm the rear guard. Enough chatter, we're getting close."

Just ahead a moss-roofed cottage rose up from the forest floor as though it had grown there. Mud daubed in all the cracks between twisted branches let flickering pinpricks of candlelight shine through in a few spots. Unforgiving cold stole over my limbs and turned my guts to ice.

"Exactly how mean is this witch?" I whispered.

"You'll be fine. Now go, and remember to get out before the potion wears off." The *or else* hung in the air, unspoken but clearly implied.

Heart in my throat, I made for the nearest wall and began by thrusting a single hand through the wood and mud. The wall felt cold where my hand passed through, as though the house were the ghost and I the solid entity. Thankful Sylvana couldn't see the terror on my face, I stuck my head through next, just to get the lay of the land. Old Muddy wasn't shopping at Ikea, that's for certain.

The entire place was kitted out like a Victorian parlor. Gilt glittered around a fireplace I estimated at three times larger than what should have fit in the room given the outside dimensions. A long-haired white cat sprawled across an oval-backed Louis XVI armchair while just about the cutest little old lady I'd ever seen knitted away on its twin. Hair that matched the cat's in hue and fluffy texture haloed pink cheeks tracked with gentle reminders of her advanced age. How dangerous could this old granny be?

Shoulders followed head and soon the rest of me was birthed inside the Mudwitch's house. With no useful instructions for the next part of this mission, I stood in the center of the room and sent out my Spidey senses to see if I could feel anything remotely Cupid-like. As if that was even a thing.

Five minutes stretched to ten and then to fifteen. The potion would wear off soon. There was nothing here, or if there was, I was going to be useless in finding it, because I couldn't feel the bow. I turned to leave the way I had come in when a quiet question slapped me in the back of the head.

"Did you find what you were looking for, my dear?" The voice did not go with her looks. It creaked out of her like a rusty hinge on an old barn door and turned my legs to noodles. "It would have been more polite to knock on the door. Now come into the light and let me get a good look at you."

I felt Sylvana's spell run off me like water and turned to face the Mudwitch.

Dead black eyes burned in that gentle face, and I got the same feeling I'd had the time the faeries took me to the zoo, and I had gazed into the eyes of a python. Totally creeped out.

"Sylvana Balefire. Back to cause more trouble, I assume." She crowed.

"No. I'm not. Sylvana, I mean. I'm Lexi, her daughter, and I don't want to cause any trouble." I also didn't want to pee my pants, but I wasn't ruling it out. "I'm sorry for sneaking in here; it's just my mother thought you might have...that my grandmother might have sent something to you to keep for me." Mentioning the bow was probably a bad idea since, as far I could tell, it wasn't there.

Lightning flashed in her eyes.

Fight or flight kicked in, and I chose flight. Tossing another sorry over my shoulder, I made a dash for the door. The spell hit me in the back before I managed three steps. Tendril-like branches shot up through the floor to coil around my legs and effectively cut off all chance of escape.

"Not so fast, Dearie. If you're in cahoots with Sylvana, that's enough for me." Cahoots? Was I in cahoots? Who says that anymore? "Tell me the truth about why you showed up on my doorstep this fine night."

Words tumbled from my lips no matter how hard I tried to stop them.

"The Bow of Destiny? Here? Ridiculous. If Clara hid that bow, you're going to have to try a lot harder than this to find it, and even if you do, she'll have put up safeguards to keep Sylvana from touching it. Safer for you all around if I keep you here with me. You look like a sturdy one; I could use a little help around the place. These old bones aren't as spry as they used to be."

"No. You have to let me go." I wasn't about to wind up in a burlap sack, sweeping her fireplace for the rest of my life.

"Mayhaps I will." Mag moved close enough to rest one of her claw-like hands on mine and pierce my soul with those eyes. Her lips peeled back as she tasted my magical essence, turned it around and around on her tongue. "Strong magic and a pure heart. Be careful where you place your trust. I don't have your bow, but I do have something that belonged to your grandmother." Mag turned one hand palm up, and a ring appeared out of the ether. "She would have wanted you to have this, don't show it to anyone."

The ring, warm from her grasp, dropped into my hand.

"Hide it. Quickly now, child."

"Why?"

Before the old witch could reply, the front door blew off its hinges and framed my mother in the opening.

"Now Mag, you know I'm not going to let you keep my daughter. The question is how ugly do you want things to get. Let her go, and we'll leave quietly." Sylvana's wide-legged stance, defiantly raised chin, and level gaze spoke eloquently of steely determination.

Mag backed down, though I knew her reluctance was just for show. She was going to let me go anyway. Tendrils snaked away from my calves, and suddenly I was free again. "You didn't have to knock the door down. I'm just a lonely old woman trying to defend her home."

"Save it for someone who cares." Sylvana dragged me out of there.

CHAPTER

# THIRTEEN

I was still flying high from my visit with Mag and actually found the ride home enjoyable. It was as if the adrenaline running through me burned the anger and sadness from my veins. One thing was for sure; the term blood witch was certainly accurate. Every power-laced drop sang a song of vitality whenever I practiced magic. Whether that was an indication of good or evil, I couldn't tell, but it felt more like joy than pain, so I was willing to figure out the nuances at a later date. Procrastination was my middle name.

Sylvana seemed slightly more relaxed, and conversation strayed to my relationship with Kin.

"Do you love him?" She didn't pull any punches, did she?

"Yes."

"I sense a *but* coming..."

"No but. Only crippling fear and self-doubt." I wouldn't pull any then, either. It's not as though I expected any decent motherly advice; Sylvana ended up trapped in the nexus when she was about the same age I was, and she might as well have been frozen in time for all the experience she gained sitting in a cell. We were more equals than mother and daughter—a thought so achingly sad I locked it up tight in that box in my mind and buried it beneath a half-ton boulder.

"You're Alexis Balefire; there is no room for self-doubt. And no need. You're far more than his equal."

"I'm not scared of getting my heart broken. There are plenty of other reasons why relationships don't work out." Maybe there weren't for her; after all, how many relationships could she have had? I was starting to realize my mother was, quite possibly, more of a child than I'd ever been. "I'm worried that he'll get hurt and it will be my fault. And then there's the whole lifespan problem. Watching him grow old and die before I do just means more pain and loss."

Sylvana was quiet long enough to carefully frame her response, and when she finally spoke, it was with more grief in her voice than I had heard so far. "You've had to deal with a lot of that, haven't you?"

I started to get choked up and felt the high I'd been riding quickly begin to deflate. "I can handle it. I'm sure things will work out the way they're supposed to. What I'd really like to talk about is my magic. You're the only person who has knowledge of both sides of my heritage. I don't fully understand what it is to be a Fate Weaver."

Sylvana sighed, "I figured it would only be a matter of time before you asked me that. I wish I could answer your question, but the truth is, I can't. Your father would have taken over your training if you showed potential in that area."

I detected notes of longing, sadness, and pain in Sylvana's tone. Almost enough for me to believe that she had wanted to make us a family—and certainly enough to allow the hatred toward my grandmother to turn from a constant, almost subconscious simmer into a full, rolling boil.

Early dawn paled the sky as we turned onto my street. "Pull over," I instructed Sylvana who, to my astonishment, obeyed and parked us right in front of Clara's statue. She killed the engine and beckoned me to join her on one of the ivy-covered benches bordering the park. I didn't think letting her roll up in front of the house was a good idea, and she seemed keen to keep her distance for the time being.

"So he was planning on teaching me? Being there for me? Becoming a family?" I nearly whispered the questions.

"Yes, of course. What would make you think we weren't going to be a family?"

"Um, I don't know, maybe the fact that I've grown up without either of you?" Duh.

"I've already apologized for that. I was trapped in hell, Alexis, not partying in Cancun." Frustration colored her words, and I tamped down the part of me that suddenly reared up and wanted to scream in her face.

"Doesn't feel that different to me," I mumbled, knowing she could hear me just fine, but Sylvana didn't take the bait. In fact, she remained unexpectedly calm as she responded.

"I would assume that you've done your own research on your father; at least, I expect you've typed his name into one of those blasted electronic devices you're all carrying around these days. If so, you'd know that Cupid didn't have it much easier than either of us when it came to the family department. It's well known that his mother was Aphrodite, Goddess of Love and Beauty; but you've probably noticed that his paternity has been attributed to several different gods. The truth is; Cupid isn't even sure who his own father is. You're dealing with the same thing he had to deal with; wondering just exactly who you are and what you came from. Cut him some slack."

The very idea that I would be expected to feel sorry for my long-absent father made my head spin, but before I could formulate a response we were rudely interrupted.

"Well lookee what we have here." A voice spilled out of the darkness; one I had only heard a handful of times but would recognize anywhere: Jett.

Before I could whip around Sylvana was on her feet in a fighter's stance, magic crackling between her palms, ready to be unleashed at a moment's notice. Part of me wanted to see her in action, and another part wanted to wipe the smile off Jett's face using my bare hands. He brings out my primitive side.

"Watch it; he's never alone." As if on cue, Serena stepped out from the shadows and tried to snake her pasty white arm around Jett's waist in a seductive manner. The attempt failed utterly as Jett edged away from her and toward us; Serena looked like a succubus deprived of her next meal but pasted a smug look on her pointy face anyway.

"Well, aren't you just two peas in a pod?" Her pointy chin popped up a notch as she glanced at Clara's statue. "Spending a little quality time mourning over the dead with Mummy?" She condescended.

"Shut up, Swampgrass or my Mummy might show you what a real witch can do."

"So it's true? Sylvana Balefire is back." I hadn't noticed the expression on Jett's face—he always appeared to have just eaten an entire lemon, anyway, but if looks could kill, I'd be ashes on the wind.

"Isn't that just lovely—isn't everything just lovely for perfect little Lexi. You were supposed to be dead," he turned and pointed at Sylvana who, recognizing the threat before he could articulate it, winged a spell in his direction and sent him flying into a stone pillar where he crumpled into a heap.

"Don't you dare threaten me, you little brat!" She yelled. "Yeah, I know who you are. I know you've been causing trouble for my daughter, and whatever it is you think is keeping your father away, you're wrong. He won't come back for you, and he won't thank you for screwing with his work."

Keeping her finger pointed directly at his nose, Sylvana walked slowly toward Jett with enough intimidation factor to keep him from trying to get up. Jett might be a complete idiot, but he could recognize power when it was two inches in front of his face.

Serena, on the other hand, seemed to have little sense of self-preservation and lunged toward me, flinging a lightning bolt that grazed my calf and left me with a deep but cauterized cut spanning from my ankle to my knee.

Anger flooded my senses and magic welled into my chest from some deep, dark place inside my bones. For a split second, I let it flow through me until it coalesced at my fingertips and swelled with the intent to inflict pain upon whoever stepped into my path.

I flung a curse in Serena's direction, aiming for the tree behind her, but Jett still had a trick or two up his sleeve. He took advantage of Sylvana's distraction—she hadn't taken her eyes off me since Serena had struck—and loosed a gust of wind that knocked Serena out of the way just in time.

The tree I had been aiming for broke in half with a burst of sparks and thundered to the ground at my feet. Amazed, I looked from my outstretched hand to the scorched wood and let out a cackle that would probably have made all eighteen of Salem's toes curl.

I admit it; I reveled in the sensation for more than a few moments, enjoying the comfort of knowing I could hold my own. It never even occurred to me that I was walking a very dangerous line.

"Get out of here, both of you." I spat at Jett and Serena. "And leave me alone from now on, or next time I'll be sure to hit my target," I spoke quietly, and even Sylvana stepped back and allowed them safe passage out of the park.

It seemed I'd wandered into irony's grand territory once again; on the spot where Clara had cursed Sylvana into the underworld, I had just allowed my anger to cloud my better judgment. I've heard that dark magic leaves a trace; perhaps the ground I was standing on had been tainted with Clara's ill-intentions all those years ago.

Or maybe I really was just as wicked as I'd always feared.

# FOURTEEN

I knew it was going to be bad as soon as we approached the front yard. The rising sun—we'd sat in the park until the first rays of light speared over the horizon—cast the house into a different silhouette than normal. Tooth-shaped spikes decorated the peak of the roof. For all I knew, the spikes could be birds, or gargoyles, or maybe even actual teeth. I'd known the faeries were upset when I left, and now my disregard for their feelings was coming home to roost, possibly literally.

We skirted a border of lilac bushes, peeking through the branches surreptitiously to survey the yard. Greasy brown mushrooms with yellow underbellies—an entire lawn full of them—provided cover for some type of creature with big eyes and a barbed tail. If they'd lost control enough for the madness to make it to the front of the house, what was waiting for me inside must be absolutely horrendous.

If not for the Balefire in my hearth requiring my presence, I'd have been tempted to run and never look back. I'm sure my escape would have lasted about ten minutes since Terra could find me anywhere, but it's the thought that counts, right?

"You should probably leave before things get ugly," I warned Sylvana in case those really were teeth on the roof.

"Define ugly." Her seeming to want to jump to my defense warmed a cold place inside me. "I can stick around to make sure it's safe."

"No, this is a family thing." The words slipped out before I thought them through. Way to go, Lexi—how does that shoe leather taste? "Wait, that came out wrong. It's just that adding you to the mix would be like pouring gas on a firecracker. Both stupid and dangerous. They're just blowing off steam."

"I understand." Just like that, the momentary harmony was gone, and we were back to circling each other warily. "Well, I guess I'll see you..." Sylvana faced forward and waited for me to exit the car, which I did reluctantly.

The Caddy had barely turned at the end of the street when Salem skittered around the corner, all arched back and puffed up fur, the trademark of an indignant cat. Dogs have the market cornered on soulful looks while cats do a mean withering stare.

Ducking behind another bank of shrubbery bordering the front porch, Salem proved he could deliver a dirty look in both his native forms. He took a seat on the wicker love seat, and I joined him.

"Why didn't you tell me?" Salem growled. "This witch/familiar thing only works if you put in the effort. Keeping something this epic from me is...well, it's mortifying to start with. I'm not some pet you can leave food out for when you go away and get unconditional love when you finally return. Doesn't our history together mean anything to you?"

He was mad, and I didn't blame him, but I'd underestimated how much pain I had caused.

"I'm sorry, Salem. Truly. I didn't want you to let something slip to Terra or one of the others before I had a chance to tell them myself."

"And how did that work out for you?" You have not experienced sarcasm until it has been delivered by a cat/man hybrid and I snatched back the hand that had reached out to pet him on the arm. Judging by his expression, my finger would probably freeze if I touched him. I'd better add a new batch of kitty toys to my shopping list.

"You have no idea what I've been through since you left. They've gone right off the deep end." His tone changed. "One wrong move and they're going to top the Faefern Decimation of '09, and I'm not sure if you going in there is going to make it better or worse."

The Faefern Decimation was the faerie meltdown all subsequent meltdowns had been measured against. Soleil, hopped up on Twinkleberry wine, had been juggling fireballs, lost control and burned down Terra's patch of tender ferns that only germinated every third century.

Terra, also an entire factory full of sheets to the wind, had retaliated by opening up a shaft, sending her sister deep underground, and closing the hole behind her. Next thing we knew, the soil started to heat up, and a mini volcano erupted in the backyard. Soleil was tossed back to the surface along with a lot of pyrotechnic debris. Evian had to climb up on the roof and dump about an ocean's worth of water to douse the flames. Fog blanketed the town for days.

Today had the potential to make that experience look like a blip unless I handled the situation with tact.

"I owe them an explanation, and I owe you an apology."

"You owe me at least a week of groveling." Salem stood, whirled to present his back to me and said without turning around, "And don't think I didn't notice you smell like dark magic." He left me there to contemplate his last words and went inside, probably to warn the faeries of my impending arrival. Or maybe to hide.

Had I really performed dark magic? Now that I'd calmed down I didn't think so, but I didn't entirely trust my own ability to judge. The image of Serena standing next to the fallen tree I'd obliterated clung to the back of my eyelids, but I shook it away. As a witch, I'm about as green as it gets and this wasn't the time for an existential crisis. There was a real enough one waiting for me inside, and I needed to stop procrastinating.

Steeling myself for whatever waited on the other side, I got up and opened the door to face Faerie Apocalypse #877.

Have you ever pictured your own personal hell? What I walked into that day was mine. Over the years, I'd witnessed the results of faeries using the elements as fodder when fighting with each other. This was different; this was directed at me.

Eyes. A thousand at least, fixed and staring at me from creepily lifelike porcelain faces. Dolls. I hate dolls. Give me spiders or snakes any day of the week. I mean, one doll isn't so bad, you know, all by itself. In a group with their creepy eyes and tiny hands reaching out toward me....shudder.

I pressed my back to the door and tried to watch them all

at once. If one moved, so much as a blink or the slightest flutter, I'd probably make a Lexi shaped hole in the door on my way out, and my screams would be heard in the next town over.

Dolls are evil and should be burned. Every. Single. One.

My skin crawled the entire time, but I ran the gauntlet anyway. Down the hallway and past the stairs to my rooms.

"Salem, where did you go?"

It was too quiet for the type of reaction Salem had led me to expect. Not comforting.

"Anyone?" Crickets. I headed for the kitchen, the room where the godmothers spent the most time. Nothing to see there, until I looked out the sliding glass doors. One glance at the backyard and I knew I'd found ground zero and that I'd jumped to a mistaken conclusion earlier. I was not the only target of wrath. From here, it looked like a three-on-one situation, not surprisingly, with Vaeta the lone defender.

After a half second of wondering why, I realized they'd come to the same conclusion I had about who had let Sylvana out of her prison and Vaeta was taking the brunt of the punishment.

The sleepless night wanted to drag my eyes closed, to force me to give in to the craving for a minute of solace before wading into the fray. I wouldn't change a thing about them, even if my family isn't in the same zip code as normal and I deserved whatever they had in store for me today.

Under any other circumstances, earth, fire, and water clashing with air would fool the uninitiated into thinking they'd stumbled into a festive occasion. Vaeta danced out her vengeance in graceful steps, bending like a willow in the wind as she directed with elegant hands.

In contrast, Evian's motions seemed sharper, tighter. Water fountained from every fingertip. If not for the snarl—and how unfair is it that even snarling she was breathtakingly beautiful—on her face, she might be mistaken for a statue carved by artist's hands.

Soleil left showers of sparks behind as she flitted from place to place like a firefly. Flame-colored hair atop a slim body gave her the appearance of a candle burning against the sun.

My true godmother, Terra, had shed her Earth Mother persona to embrace another side of her personality—that of avenging fury. Eschewing an aerial attack, she directed the ground below Vaeta to suck and pull at her feet. Vaeta nimbly avoided being caught.

How had I never realized the breadth of her strength before today? To hold her own against all three irate sisters made Vaeta a formidable force.

Scorch marks traced black and sooty across a wide swath of lawn leaving behind a boulder slagged from a burst of intense heat and two trees burning like torches. A little more destructive than Soleil normally got, I thought, until the shadow of a dragon rippled across the grass, and a burst of flame set another tree alight.

The moment of admiration over, my hand closed over the sliding door handle, but before I could pull it open Sylvana, a ball of magic forming between her hands, strode across the lawn to turn a mere apocalypse into an all-out nuclear war. The next ten seconds blurred and then I was standing between Sylvana and the four faeries as if my presence might be enough to diffuse the situation. For a second, I'd forgotten the faeries were mad at me. A crucial error.

You could have heard a mouse fart in the moment of shocked silence.

"I thought I told you to let me handle this," I said between clenched teeth.

Sylvana gave me a look meant to quell any further outburst, which I returned with one eerily similar. "Go away, you're not needed here." A tiny flinch betrayed her emotions.

"Well, I thought it was high time I met your benefactresses. I owe them a great deal for standing in for me during my unfortunate incarceration. Really, ladies, I can't thank you enough for all you've done for my Lexi."

Terra's eyes narrowed at the slight emphasis on the word *my*. She dismissed Sylvana with a sniff and rounded on me.

"There's a dragon burning down the yard," I pointed out before Terra could work up a full head of steam. "Someone should probably send it back to wherever it came from." Or maybe, given the current state of her carefully tended gardens, Terra no longer cared. An acre of lush plantings had died a black and greasy death and was now studded with bits of rotting fruits and vegetables.

Fury-filled eyes trained on mine, Terra flicked a hand over her shoulder, and the dragon went poof, though his sulfurous odor remained to torment the nose.

"Lies and betrayal. After all our time together, this is what you offer us." It was a speech worthy of a Godfather movie in both tone and content.

"I didn't..." To my consternation, I teared up. Hurting the

godmothers had not been my intent. "It's been crazy since right before Beltane. Finally going through my Awakening, then that business with Kin and the enchanted guitar, and Jett dropping the God bomb on me. I was overwhelmed, and when I figured out Athena was Sylvana, it was a shock, and I needed time to process before I was ready to talk about it. I'm sorry for making you think I didn't care about how you would feel, sorrier than words can say, but I won't apologize for handling this in my own way."

Terra's mouth softened just the tiniest bit, and I knew she wouldn't hold a grudge. Against me, anyway. My mother was on her own.

My mother. Saying those two words together and having them apply to a living, breathing human filled a yawning cavern inside me and opened up another that I hoped wouldn't swallow me whole. That's what would happen if it came down to trading her for the godmothers. Talk about an impossible choice. I owed my loyalty to the three Fae. Terra chose to raise me and even when the job was done, she and her sisters wanted to stay. Sylvana had been released from her underworld nexus for more than six months before she made contact with me. That kind of math is hard to ignore.

But family isn't about the math. Or the logic. It's about the things people do to and for each other in the name of love. The good, the bad, the sublime, the ugly.

All my life I had loved the version of my mother that I'd built in my head. She was a valiant figure of a woman who had lost her life defending herself—and possibly me— against wickedness. The version of Sylvana I pictured would have fought anything in her path to get back to me, and when she did, she wouldn't have lied about her identity.

From the moment she'd stepped between Delta and me, I'd flipped between wanting her to stay and wanting her to go away and even now, standing between her and the women who had taken her place, I still didn't know which I wanted most.

Well, other than not wanting to watch either faction commit murder.

"I don't need you to defend me, Lexi." Sylvana cautioned. "I'm just here to make sure you're safe."

"From us?" Terra's bland expression might have fooled my mother, but it wasn't fooling me. She was so close to the edge her toes were hanging over.

Pointedly, Sylvana turned to survey the plainly visible evidence of faerie fury.

"Come, Lexi. You'll stay with me for a few days, let your... roommates get control over their emotions."

A jet of water shot past me and took Sylvana in the chest, and she not only went down, but she also rolled a few feet from the force of it. When she came up, spitting, her eyes glowed with green fire, and things got ugly.

Four elements and a ball of witchfire whizzed around the yard in a whirlwind tempest while I watched with disgust. Sylvana moved quicker than a flash, and each time one of her spells got close enough to make purchase, the faeries would swap into their mini forms and zip out of the way. Back and forth the fury raged, and I figured half the block would be peeking through the bushes if it got any further out of control.

I'm telling you, all I meant to do was diffuse the situation when I planted my feet firmly on the first paving stone of the road where good intentions lead and plotted my course straight to hell.

Heated fury turned me inside out, burned off the husk of calm that was all I had left in me. It had been a long day followed by a long night, and I'd had enough, so I let it out. All of it. The pent up pain from being abandoned, the shrieking void where my magic had lain dormant for ten long years, the fatigue of refereeing yet another elemental bout of childishness.

My fists clenched so hard blood oozed from the divots formed by my fingernails, my eyes squinched up tight, and I set the magic free. Every last ounce of angst that I'd carried for so long rushed out of me like a wall of force and when it had passed, the ground was littered with an annoyed witch, four shocked faeries, and one poor familiar who got caught up when he came out to see if he could help.

Essentially, I'd just thrown my first, and possibly last, magical temper tantrum and it felt good. After surveying the damage for a moment, I turned and walked away.

Once again, I fled for the comfort of a safe haven at Kin's house, and this time I simply walked through the door and dropped my purse on his foyer floor with a thump.

"Honey, I'm home," I called, my attempt at cliched humor not quite carrying. Instead, it came out mournful and just plain sad.

"What's happened now?" Kin's voice was slightly guarded, and it occurred to me—not for the first time—that the constant state of upheaval of my life might take a toll on anyone close to me. Specifically, anyone human.

I brushed the thought aside and allowed Kin to wrap his arms around me. "I'm sorry; I've hardly seen you in days, and now that we're together I'm a mess again." I murmured an apology into his neck.

"Don't apologize; I'm just worried about you." Kin's unflappable calm was one of the things I loved most about him. It was such a stark contrast to the way I'd been brought up, where emotions were considered as normal as the catastrophes they often triggered. It felt like night and day with Kin, and I wondered for the millionth time how long he'd want to deal with my so-called crazy life.

"Well, I followed Sylvana into the Fringe, then got into it with Jett and Serena, and finally had to deal with four angry faeries and a ticked off kitty." I left out the part where I'd blasted them all. "Basically, all hell is breaking loose." Something about my tone seemed a bit too jovial, and Kin definitely noticed.

He cut me off. "We'll come back to whatever the Fringe is in a minute. You got attacked by Jett again? Are you sure you're all right? You really don't seem like yourself right now." Shrewd assessment.

He wasn't wrong; I didn't feel like myself—I felt better. I could still feel the power thrumming in my ears; still felt energy crackling at my fingertips. And it felt good.

"I'm fine," I tried to brush past the awkward moment, "I'm a little keyed up, given all that's happened in the last few hours. The bigger issue is that Jett now knows Sylvana is alive, and he's royally ticked off." I explained the rest of my encounter and the confrontation with my godmothers wrapped protectively in Kin's arms.

"So I just left them all to do whatever they're going to do and hightailed it over here. I know my mom was trying to protect me, but getting into a magic fight with four elemental faeries isn't a good idea, especially when they have an emotional investment in the topic of conversation."

"She's got some nerve, I'll give her that. What do you suppose she thought she'd accomplish?" He voiced the same question I'd been wondering about myself.

"I have no idea, but I doubt anything good or helpful. Just add it to the list of questions I need answers to. The one I'm concerned with at this very moment is: what do I do about keeping the peace between them?"

"Do you want my opinion?" Kin asked lightly.

"Of course." I rubbed my thumb gently against the back of his arm, enjoying the warmth he always exuded. I was starting to wish I was normal and could spend my life here, have babies, and die at what most would consider a ripe old age. Never gonna happen; I was a Fate Weaver, with all the responsibilities that entailed, and I'd do my level best to live up to the name.

"Well, I come from a big family. You know I have six brothers and sisters; I'm the middle child, and my parents have been married for thirty-five years. They were high school sweethearts, and I believe they are soul mates. Maybe you can tell me when you meet them." The thought of meeting Kin's family was both terrifying and exhilarating at the same time. At my age, the fact that Kin was my first real boyfriend was, frankly, a bit pathetic.

"Anyway, we've had our share of ups and downs, and sometimes they do things that make me completely crazy. Did I tell you about the time I had to go pay off a bookie that my younger brother had stiffed for two thousand dollars? The only reason I made it out of there without a serious beating is because the guy recognized my voice from the radio and made me arrange to play his favorite song every day during his lunch break for a month. I know it's not in the same universe as what you're dealing with, but the bottom line is, she's family. Whether that makes me comfortable or not."

I was silent for a long moment trying to come up with the right words. "I think I've always had this image of a perfect mother; if she had been here, none of the bad in my life would have happened. She would have protected me. But I realize that it's possible I wouldn't have any of things I love if she had stuck around. I'd probably have even bigger problems, judging by what I've experienced in the short time she's been back."

Kin stroked my hand in a comforting gesture, "It's something you can't change, no matter how much you wish you could. Think of the butterfly effect; or your power of threes. Everything has a flip side, comes with a price, or could have been different *if only*. You'll never know, and you'll drive yourself crazy considering all the outcomes. All you can do is move forward. You don't know the whole story yet; you couldn't possibly. At the very least, you deserve more of an explanation. Either to open yourself to the possibility of a relationship, or just for closure. I don't see you walking away without bothering to try. Whether it turns out good or bad, you owe it to yourself to find out."

Kin's words struck a chord; no, it wasn't like me to just give up. The double meaning of his words didn't escape me either. He could have been talking about our burgeoning relationship, and he didn't even realize it.

"Doesn't it scare you that I've got all of this baggage? Have you really thought about the repercussions of being with me?" I waited for his response with bated breath.

"Where did that come from? And yes, of course, I've thought about it. But I also know we're meant to be together, so it's all worth it." He squeezed me tighter, and I let out the sigh I'd been holding in.

"Jett went after you once already. Aren't you concerned that he'll try again? I can't keep you safe all the time; he's human, at least partially, and he's out there every day just waiting for his opportunity."

Kin brushed off my concerns with far too much confidence in my ability to protect him, and that worried me further. It felt like I was taking a swim in shark-infested waters; I'd been nipped, but my limbs were still intact. How much longer that would last, I couldn't be sure. I knew I wouldn't walk away from Kin unless there was no other choice.

Was it possible our union wasn't fated to bring good into the world? What I had learned from Jett's attempts to sabotage my matches was that there was more than one path a couple could follow. Delta had even suggested that some couples needed to be ripped apart for the good of the world, but she couldn't possibly have meant fated couples, could she?

I spent the rest of the night contemplating intentions: Jett's, Sylvana's, Delta's, and even my own.

Perhaps Jett had been planting kernels of doubt in my mind on purpose, like some hippie throwing wildflower seeds onto highway medians; no actual planned outcome in mind, just hoping to incite general chaos. Maybe he was counting on me being too good a person to let someone I cared about remain in danger, thinking I'd suffer in silence as long as Kin was safe as houses.

If so, he wasn't wrong, because I'd leave Kin and never look back if it came down to him leading a long and happy life or being snuffed out as a result of the insanity I called my life. Regardless, the seeds had grown roots and were firmly implanted in the soil of my consciousness. It irritated me to no end that I could see snippets of any other couples' future except my own.

What can I say; I was young and inexperienced, and it never occurred to me that my inability to foresee my own fate was more of a blessing than a curse. If Back to the Future had taught me anything, it's that nobody should know too much about their own destiny. I guess Doc Brown really was as smart as Marty McFly thought.

# FIFTEEN

Perched on the padded seat of the bay window in my room, I hugged my knees to my chest and watched Salem dart across the tender new grass in the front yard. Terra must have marshaled Soleil and Evian to help with repairing the damage because the gardens appeared almost normal again.

Hightailing it from somewhere near the clearing where Clara stood immortalized in stone, Salem was little more than a black streak moving across the green. According to the terse note he'd left on my desk the night before, he'd taken himself off to wherever it is familiars congregate for some well-deserved R&R.

Shadows moved a fair distance across the grass before I heard his feet on the stairs.

Apparently, he was still angry with me for, as he put it, *dumping my problems off on him and leaving him stuck in the middle* of the whole godmothers vs. birth mother debacle. Then there was the unfortunate incident at the end. I hadn't meant for him to get caught up in the tantrum. Then again, I hadn't meant to throw one at all. Twenty-five is a little too old for such juvenile behavior.

Surprisingly, when I crept back into the house the next morning, the incident had gone unmentioned, and the faeries treated me with slightly more respect. Acting like a great big jerk is how they seem to define family, and I'd apparently risen a notch in their eyes—and probably dropped one in Salem's.

I suppose I couldn't really blame him. Hence, the seafood chowder in the refrigerator, as promised. When he finally slunk into my bedroom, all dreamy-eyed and smelling of fish, it took everything I had not to pounce on him (pardon the expression) and beg forgiveness.

"You're not completely off the hook, Missy, but keep up with the brown-nosing, and you might just get back in my good graces."

By brown-nosing, he meant letting him drag me back to the workshop for another round of witch classes.

We holed up in the sanctum, which was turning into just that for me. The ancient couches were padded with throw blankets and pillows in a variety of vibrant colors to brighten up the space, and I had hung a few tapestries on the walls and dusted off some hand-woven rugs I'd found rolled in a cobweb-covered corner. I'd stocked the alchemy station with an assortment of teas I favored, and a variation of Terra's clean charm kept the dust at bay.

"Let's start with scrying since I've already seen you do it once." When Kin's soul was in jeopardy, I had used the skill to figure out where Jett was holed up; as it turned out, he had been close by at the home of the one and only Serena Snodgrass.

It was entirely possible that the close proximity had more to do with my success than latent skill. Turns out, I was due for some good karma.

I laid the necessary materials out in front of me: a map; a teardrop-shaped clear quartz crystal on a silver chain; several candles; a cup of water; and a mugwort infusion. When everything was ready, I called to the goddesses of the east and dipped my fingers in the water before asking the pendulum to show me where FootSwept Matchmaking was located. The tip of the pendulum whirled a couple times, then slapped down on the map with a thump.

"Score. A direct hit." I joked, but Salem didn't seem to get the movie reference.

"That was easy. Now let's try something farther away." He nodded in approval.

Four more times I scryed, testing my capabilities, until finally, it became apparent my power stretched halfway across the globe, at least.

The pendulum showed me the current location of a displayed Monet painting (which I double-checked on the Internet), the tomb where Elvis's body is buried (he's dead, people, deal with it), and confirmed that Kin was, in fact, at the local radio station where he composed commercial jingles during the day (right where he was supposed to be).

I tried sneaking a peek at where Sylvana was spending her time but came up with nothing. She probably had some sort of cloaking spell cast around herself for exactly this reason. My heart sank at the thought because it probably meant Cupid's bow was similarly protected. I checked anyway, brushing away Salem's protests, only to have my suspicions confirmed.

"I think you've proved yourself; we can move on to tarot cards or the crystal ball if you'd like." Salem suggested.

"Crystal ball. Let's try that."

We moved further into the recesses of the sanctum, to a small round table with two comfortable wingback chairs. In the center of an ornately-carved wooden pedestal rested a transparent sphere of quartz crystal about the size of a cantaloupe. I could tell from the energy vibrating off the stone that it was made of ancient, authentic quartz and not one of those new-age hunks of glass you find in most magic shops these days. It must have been worth a small fortune; not that I would ever consider selling even one piece of my family history.

"Gazing requires a high level of concentration and discipline, as well as the ability to interpret what you See. Also, you must remember that nothing is set in stone; whatever you See can and probably will change based on the choices you make. Or, it's possible that you'll make choices in an attempt to change the outcome, and wind up causing the very problem you were trying to avoid. It's not to be taken lightly."

I nodded, barely hearing what Salem was prattling on about. I had my own goal in mind, and nothing would sway me from making it a reality.

"Now," Salem instructed while lighting a cone of my favorite sandalwood incense, "gaze into the crystal, keep your eyes relaxed and your thoughts on what you are trying to See. Focus your mind, and take deep breaths, in and out."

He continued to speak in slow, soothing tones, lulling me into an almost trance-like state while I channeled all of my intent into being shown how to find the Bow of Destiny. Just when the thought that perhaps I wouldn't be able to See a blasted thing flitted across my mind, the cloud of incense smoke began to coalesce, rotating into a miniature wind tunnel, and then rushing into the quartz sphere. The cloud reformed into a blurry image, and as I bent forward to get a better look it solidified into a scene so real I could have been watching a tiny movie screen.

It was me; I recognized the back of my own head, dark tendrils of unkempt hair cascading down my back. A nearly identical figure marched beside me through a dense forest, her shoulders tense with either worry or excitement. The forest itself wasn't familiar to me, but it reeked of magic. The smell hit me so hard and unexpectedly it made my nostrils flare, and that's when I realized that I was no longer just watching; I was actually inside my body, inside the crystal ball, but as a passenger, unable to control my limbs or affect the situation.

I watched Sylvana follow me and quickly understood it was excitement and a deep desire that drove her forward. Not only was I able to sense the Bow of Destiny, but I could also feel the familiar sensation of being guided by my LPS.

Only this time, I wasn't searching for matches—I was searching for an item of power with the power to beckon *me* and I could tell it wanted nothing more than to be wielded by a Fate Weaver. And, even better, I felt confident and in control; not nauseated or weak in the knees as I had the last few times I'd been compelled. It was as if both sides of my psyche were working together rather than fighting one another for top billing. In the vision, I felt like a Fate Weaver; not two separate sides of the same coin.

Just as quickly as the vision had taken hold, it evaporated. Perhaps it was my excitement that made me pull focus, but I have a sneaking suspicion Salem was the responsible party and the vague pain in my knee had something to do with a strategically-placed kitty claw.

Now, he was staring at me with a concerned expression. "Are you all right? I was starting to get worried."

"I got what I needed." Well, maybe not exactly, but at least now I knew there was a key to the lock I'd been desperately trying to pick ever since realizing I was more than just a witch. All that was left to do was find it.

CHAPTER
# SIXTEEN

As much as I'd have liked to focus solely on my personal life, I was beginning to realize that its ever-closer proximity to my work made it nearly impossible to separate the two. Mona was itching to get her mother paired up with a nice new man, and it was time to put my plan into action.

"But I don't want to go to the vet," Salem whined the next morning when I explained what was in store for the day. "He'll probably try to give me a shot."

"I know, and I'm sorry, but everything is all set, and I need you to help me pull this off, so you're going to follow me, and when we're close, you'll get into the cat carrier. Act like you're sick when we get there and I promise I'll make it up to you later. Don't you want to help Mona's mom make a love connection?"

"I ought to make you carry me the whole way." Salem grumbled.

"Try it, and I'll strap you backward on Pinky, and by the time we get there, you really will be sick." My patience was wearing thin.

"None of my other witches treated me like this."

"And how many of them bought you gourmet salmon mousse?" I retorted.

"Fine, I'll do it, but if I end up having to get a shot, you're buying me a whole rotisserie chicken."

"Getting sick of seafood?" I couldn't fathom such a thing. "If you pull this off, it's a deal."

"You doubt my acting skills? I had you fooled for ten years." Salem said smugly.

"What do you want? An Academy Award? You acted like a cat, you are a cat. How much acting skill did it take? Please, do this for me. Mona's mother deserves a happy ending. Did I tell you she's a widow?"

Resigned, Salem morphed and followed me out the door.

When Mona and her mother turned the corner near Dr. Cooper's vet clinic, we were ready.

"Look, there's Lexi." Mona chirped and made a beeline for where I stood. "Oh dear, what's the matter." Her acting skills were better than Salem's, not that I would say that in front of him.

Affecting a panicked expression, I gestured with the cat carrier. "It's my cat. I think something is horribly wrong with my Salem. I don't know what I would do without him." Playing my own role to the hilt, I let my hand tremble and my voice quaver with tears. "I'm so scared, do you think you could come in with me, you know, just in case..."

"Of course we can, right Mom? Lexi shouldn't be alone at a time like this."

Vivienne surreptitiously glanced at her watch but gave in gracefully. I mean, really, who wants to sit in a vet's office comforting someone they barely know over a sick cat? Worse, I dragged the two of them right into the examining room with me. Mona gave me a subtle elbow to the rib when Dr. Cooper stepped through the door.

Tall and soft-spoken, Levi Cooper walked like he spent time in a saddle. Tanned skin and sun-streaked hair that probably ran darker in winter added to the cowboy appeal of his chiseled face, now frowning in concern. Salem acted his part to perfection by sprawling on the cold metal table as though too weak to hold up his head, and I felt a pang over playing such a deception on someone so deeply committed to his job.

Still, he hadn't spared more than a glance for Vivienne and Salem wasn't really sick, so I needed to do something to get the ball rolling. Normally, when I arrange the first meeting between two matches, one of the pair has secured my services and puts a little effort into showing interest in the other. Staging a chance encounter like this wasn't my thing.

"These are my friends Mona and Vivienne. I dragged them in here for moral support because I'm so worried about Salem." In return, Dr. Cooper asked me a question about Salem's bathroom habits. What was I supposed to say? He scoops his own litter pan these days.

Salem's acting was so convincing that he kept Dr. Cooper's focus away from the attractive woman standing next to me, and so—even knowing it was going to cost me later, I waited for my moment and pinched his tail.

Narcolepsy boy took the hint and bounced up off the table like his butt was on fire, and his belly was a powder keg. That he managed to stripe my hand in the process, I'm sure, was a bonus, but bless him, he did the right thing. Two steps and he took a flying leap at Vivienne's chest. Out of reflex, her arms came up to catch him, and Levi Cooper finally took a good look at the beautiful woman holding the inky cat.

The man blushed. I mean, couldn't you just die? How cute is that? Vivienne's lips curved in that way a woman's do when she knows a man finds her intriguing and Mona looked like she was attempting to suppress a squeal. The excitement leaked out in the form of an elbow in my ribs.

Putting together couples of a certain age can be tricky because they require more work. Initial proximity isn't always enough to guarantee a solid connection for those who are used to a slower, subtle pace to their rhythm. Levi chatted with Vivienne about Salem's possible ailments as though she had been the one to bring him in, but there was nothing of a personal nature in their conversation.

"It seems our patient has undergone a spontaneous recovery." Dr. Cooper's tone was as dry as the disinfectant-scented air in his office. Salem's purr filled the close quarters with sound.

He refrained from using the term hypochondriac—I didn't know that was a thing with animals—and suggested running a series of tests, the notion of which wiped Salem clean of any residual smugness. To prove his state of well-being, Salem squirmed out of Vivienne's arms, hit the metal table with a resounding thud, then executed a standing back flip in pursuit of a bug not much bigger than a fruit fly.

Dr. Cooper allowed that testing might be premature, advised more interactive playtime, and encouraged a return visit should symptoms recur. I retrieved my cat and made a great show of putting him in the carrier to give the older couple a little more time. Levi didn't take the bait, so finally, Mona filed out of the examining room ahead of me, her mother following closely behind.

"Oh no. I left my purse back there. Vivienne, since you're closest, could you be a dear and grab it for me?" She was gone for a lot longer than it took to retrieve my handbag and exited the exam room door with a Mona Lisa smile.

If I wasn't mistaken, Vivienne had a date.

CHAPTER
# SEVENTEEN

Why couldn't I have one day free of dealing with mothers in one form or another? If this was some cosmic signal, it would have been nice if it came with a code key because all I could interpret was a scrambled mess of static. That seemed the only kind I was destined to receive from the gods, and I was starting to think that side of my family was a bunch of jerks and I'd skip the reunion if they ever had one.

With the complications of my own family to worry about, I was having mixed feelings about mothers in general. Add in the near-perfect (at least from my perspective) relationship between Mona and Vivienne, and top it off by being forced to meet Kin's mother—okay, forced is probably not the most accurate word to use—and I was done.

But I was also stuck. Swayed by Kin's excitement, I'd said yes to a dinner date. The man could show me his dimples and make me do most anything.

I'd gone from being a loner to having way too many people vying for my time. And I knew I sounded like an ungrateful witch with a capital B. My mother had come back from the dead in a moment worthy of a soap opera. In fact, my whole life was taking on that sort of quality. The only thing missing was the aging matriarch who seemed benign, but was the one pulling all the strings. Unless you counted my stoned grandmother in that capacity.

None of this was any excuse for trying to duck out of meeting Kin's mother. She had to be a lovely woman to have raised such a wonderful man, right? It's just that I'd never had a relationship serious enough to get to the meet-my-mom stage. What if she didn't like me?

This thing with Kin seemed like it was moving way too fast sometimes. Probably came from sharing true love's kiss before he'd even had a chance to see me in my laundry day granny panties. After that, meeting his mother felt a lot like picking out china patterns and I wasn't sure I was ready for all that. On the other hand, Kin had been the Mary Poppins of boyfriends, practically perfect in every way.

Come on, Lexi. How bad could it be? Put on something pretty and meet the nice lady who probably won't be watching you like a hawk for signs you're not the right woman for her precious son. I wagged a mental finger at myself and stepped into the closet at FootSwept Matchmaking.

Yes, there was a closet full of clothes at my place of business. Designer stuff, mostly, donated or discounted from former clients. My matchmaking abilities were not limited to creating couples; if the bottom fell out, I could make a killing as a corporate headhunter.

One aspect of my job involved helping clients feel their best. By the time they landed in front of my desk, most had been through the dating wringer. They staggered into my office a raw and bloody mess. What I gave them wasn't strictly what you'd call a makeover so much as emotional triage.

I hit the street a minute late, but confident I could make up the time by taking one of my shortcuts. What I didn't count on was the dark wave of compulsion that was becoming increasingly familiar to me.

The need to follow the tug in my gut fought against my desire not to disappoint Kin and won. Reaching for my phone to let him know I would be late, I realized it was still sitting on my desk at FootSwept. Then I forgot all about the phone and Kin as my LPS chattered to screaming life. I could no more ignore its directing presence than I could stop the incoming tide and I let compulsion carry me away. Like Calgon, only without the warm bath and soft skin.

Voices raised in anger cut the air like knives.

"You're scum."

"Are you high? I'm not cheating on you with that woman, I've never seen her before in my life."

"No, I'm not high, you jerk, and I'm not blind either. You think I can't see the way you're looking at her."

My attention homed in, not on the fighting couple taking advantage of the outdoor café seating, but the one avidly watching the spectacle from across the street. Jett and Serena.

I should have known.

Under other circumstances, I'd have relished the opportunity to ask my half-brother a couple of pointed questions about our family traits—and when I say pointed, I mean with something sharp staring him in the face while he answered. However, since our sibling relationship was already based on an intense dislike, and since I'd nearly killed his girlfriend during our last encounter, I doubted even threats would force the truth out of him.

Too bad the Cupid half of my life didn't come with a user's manual.

After a mental game of eenie-meenie-miney-mo, I sat down at the table next to the fighting couple and, pinning Jett with a *na-na boo-boo* look (I was feeling very juvenile around him for some reason), cast a shield over our two tables. The look on Jett's face when the fight ended was almost enough reward for missing dinner and the inevitable discussion I would be having with Kin later. Almost.

I also made a mental note to talk to Salem about creating a batch of protection charms against my brother's influence. Something small and innocuous might work. I could be the Johnny Appleseed of love, sprinkling magical protection over the city. Don't mock; I have a vivid imagination.

With the immediate danger over, the compulsion faded, and I had to make a choice: go back to the restaurant and salvage things with Kin and his mother, or confront Jett and Serena in a public setting and hope things didn't turn ugly.

I'm ashamed to say I went with option two.

As confrontations go, it was a bit of a non-starter. Jett tossed a tired repetition of how he'd made it his mission in life to undo my every good deed. He attempted to appeal to my softer side with a lament about how I had my mother back, but he'd never see his again. I called Serena a few names, and we traded insults until a group of tourists showed up, and I revisited my options.

No one was going to give me a medal for being an ideal girlfriend, but at least I skipped stopping in at the office to grab my cell phone on the way back to the restaurant. Too bad I arrived just in time to see Kin and his mother walking out the door with Delta.

Delta.

And Kin.

Bells, warning whistles, and an air raid siren went off in my head, which didn't explode, but not for lack of trying. I ducked into the nearest recessed doorway for cover and watched Delta—minus the biker-babe makeup and clothes —lay a scarlet-tipped hand on Kin's arm. You read about people saying their blood boiled, but until it happens to you, the whole concept is just a piece of purple prose.

The woman could get to my man, and right in front of me. Was she simply driving home the message that anything less than my full cooperation would not be tolerated, or was she letting me know she didn't trust me any more than I trusted her? That if I stepped out of line, my boyfriend would pay the price? This was exactly the type of situation I'd been tossing and turning over every night. Kin would probably be better off alone with a broken heart than with me.

It occurred to me a moment too late that I could have cast a spell to overhear the conversation instead of watching it speculatively. I ducked back when Kin's head turned my way, and when I felt it was safe enough to look again, he and his mother had gone, and Delta was walking toward my hiding place.

Triumph flared to life inside me. Our game of cat and mouse with alternating roles was about to end and with me being the cat for once. I'd grab her as she passed by, then drag the confrontation out into the street. That wicked blade of hers was bound to stay sheathed in a public setting. She said she wanted to talk; well, I was finally ready to listen, so I waited.

I waited for longer than it should have taken her to get to where I stood, and then the ookie-spookies set in. Was she right there waiting for me to stick my head out? Or had she simply poofed? She was a supernatural hunter, which meant poofing was a possibility.

No spell for seeing around corners came to mind, and since I wasn't carrying my purse, I couldn't try the old mirror technique, so my only option was to stick my neck out. Assuming I'd be less of a target, I crouched and gingerly poked my head around the corner.

Known to the locals as café ally, Pearl Street ran through the heart of a city beautification project initiated some twenty years ago. The once sterile brick and mortar canyon sported a line of trees dotted with wrought-iron street lamps, and benches. There was no sign of Delta.

It took forty-five minutes to thoroughly check every place of business between where I'd hidden and where I'd last seen her, so when she stepped out of a recessed doorway and blocked my path, I was a bit taken aback; the mouse again, despite my best efforts.

"What do you think you're doing, talking to my boyfriend? I'm going to make this very clear; stay away from me; stay away from my mother; and stay far, far away from my boyfriend."

Delta raised an eyebrow and fixed me with the kind of

condescending stare adults use on jealous teenagers. "It got your attention, didn't it? You need to listen to me, or you're going to be sorry."

"What's the big deal? I'm looking for the blasted bow, what more do you want?"

You'd think I'd be used to that breathless moment when an otherworldly being shows its true face, but Delta's was scarier than a Stephen King book. Thankfully she caught herself and put it away before anyone else got a good look at her.

"There's a target on your back and you don't even have the sense to stop putting yourself in danger. I'm beginning to doubt the sanity of the gods, choosing you to wield the Bow of Destiny." She looked at me with derision and I fiercely wanted to punch her in her smug face.

"I can handle myself." I'd managed pretty well so far, right?

"Then you're colossally stupid. I've been instructed to—" Delta froze again, and I felt Sylvana's presence at my back. Only a few seconds passed before Delta unfroze this time, and she was spitting nails when she came back to vibrant life.

"I learned my lesson last—" Frozen again, Delta stopped mid-sentence. Each time she shook off the spell a little bit faster, and as she closed in on us, reaching for her rapier and reminding me of a flip book, Sylvana grabbed my hand. I felt my power grow, funneling the energy into her palm until Delta was immobilized.

"Come on, let's get out of here."

I dropped my mother off at her apartment and declined

her invitation to dinner. My nerves were raw, my head felt like it was about to lift off into the air, and I could tell I was keyed up by the gnawing feeling in the pit of my stomach. Or maybe my gut was simply reiterating that I was in for a fight with Kin. And rightfully so.

# EIGHTEEN

I tiptoed through Kin's unlocked front door several hours later than originally planned. It seemed to be turning into a theme; I couldn't remember the last time I had seen his face up close during daylight hours.

The place was dead silent, and I knew that didn't bode well for me. Not only had I simply not shown up to dinner, but I had also been unable to return any of Kin's calls or text messages, and now I was going to have to pay the piper.

He was sitting on the couch in the living room, hunched forward with his elbows on his knees. The room was shrouded in complete darkness. I flipped on a lamp as I sat down beside him, illuminating the hard, set lines of his jaw and face.

"Kin, I'm so, so sorry. I know you're angry with me, but I couldn't help it—"

"Stop. I know what you're about to say. Something important came up; someone needed you; a relationship more important than ours was in peril! I get it. There's always something more important when you've got magical powers. Who was it this time? Sylvana? Flix? Your damned cat? Or one of your four frickin' faerie godmothers?"

"It was Jett and Serena. And I couldn't just let them loose

after what they did last time." I saw his eyes flash with concern at my mention of Jett, but he let it go.

"See, what am I supposed to say to that? I'm mad, and I can't even be mad because you've always got a good reason. But I can't help if it makes me wonder whether or not I'm ever going to fit into your life. Are you all right? You're all shaky again, like last time." He couldn't help but add.

"I'm fine," I waved his concerns away, but it irked me to no end that he noticed and insisted on pointing out my heightened energy levels every time I did a lot of magic. "But they nearly broke up a pair of soul mates, and then I saw you talking to Delta, and I freaked out. Can you blame me?"

"Delta? What?" He looked genuinely confused, and a little freaked out.

"That was her, the woman you were speaking to outside the restaurant. What did she say to you?"

Kin held up his hands in surrender, "Nothing, she asked for directions, that's all. And she seemed perfectly nice."

"Right, because people intending to do you bodily harm always tell you what they're up to first. She cornered me afterward and," It occurred to me that I might not want to tell him exactly what Delta said. "Pushed me to find the bow faster."

Kin nodded, but refused to ask the questions that would satisfy his curiosity. "Do you have any idea how embarrassed I was, sitting in that restaurant, assuring my mom that you'd be along at any moment even though you were completely MIA, and then finally having to admit that you weren't coming after all? I'm pretty sure she thinks I made you up to get her off my case."

The shine was surely off the relationship. We'd gone from my never seeing Kin angry to him being annoyed with me twice in a short period of time. Every new development in our relationship was a new development for me. I had no frame of reference for what happens after true love's kiss—my clients rarely bothered me with whatever inevitable relationship issues they faced down the road.

Most of my ideas of the *ever* part of happily ever after came from romantic comedies and not personal examples.

"I'm sorry," I repeated. "I know it was important to you, and I tried my best. Was I just supposed to leave another unsuspecting couple at Jett and Serena's mercy—stand by while they were ripped apart for no good reason when I was fully capable of preventing it? You can't ask me to do that; I won't."

"I'm not asking you to do anything, Lexi," Kin's voice turned cold, "but I'm disappointed that you couldn't have taken two seconds to let me know what was going on."

"Don't you think I would have if I could have? I'm sure your mother will understand that something vitally important came up; I'll meet her next time. In fact, I'll probably make a better impression than I would have today. Don't you want me to be comfortable and in the right frame of mind?" Even to me, it sounded like a lame excuse.

"If you didn't want to meet her, then why did you agree to dinner?" Of course Kin zeroed in on the one thing I had hoped not to let slip—my reluctance to take our relationship to the next level.

It didn't matter that my trepidation had more to do with the uncertainty I felt about my future, let alone anyone who tried to hitch a ride on my wagon than it did about my commitment to him. Had I not been quite so big an idiot, I would have realized that Kin had insecurities as well, but all I felt was a surge of irritation and self-righteous indignation.

And that's when I finally snapped. "It's not about not wanting to meet your mom, but do you have any idea how much maternal baggage I'm dragging around right now? We've only been dating for a few weeks, and meeting your mother is kind of a big deal! There's no way she's going to like me when I'm so preoccupied I can't hold a conversation, and I don't want to screw it up. Why can't we just wait a little longer, see what happens, and then I can meet her when we know more about where this is going?"

"Where this is going, Lexi? We had true love's kiss, remember? We're soul mates. You know it; I know it; apparently, the gods know it. So what's the problem? That isn't enough for you? Or is all this power going to your head? Because it sure seems like it has to me." Kin looked so hurt and angry all I wanted to do was comfort him. Except I couldn't bring myself to do it.

Now, this conversation had gone down a path I hadn't foreseen, even with magical divination skills. I was beginning to wonder if I should consult the crystal ball every time I left the house. Perhaps I should start carrying it around with me, like some witchy version of a magic 8-ball to let me know whether *signs point to yes* or *outlook not so good*.

"It's not about how I feel or what I want. I'm not the master of my destiny; I can't see our future any clearer than you can. But I won't turn my back on my heritage, either. Not for you; not for anyone. You need to decide whether or not you can deal with that—and if you can't, we might need to rethink exactly what true love's kiss meant in the first place. Call me when you've made your choice."

And with that, I slipped back through the front door, choking back a sob as I stumbled down the porch stairs.

I rushed out of Kin's yard and around the corner, slowing my pace only when I was beyond his line of sight; not that I thought he was going to follow me anyway. The still night air calmed my rattled nerves, and I felt a sudden, overwhelming urge to sink my toes into the earth—to ground myself and release the flood of pent-up adrenaline and anger from my battered body and soul.

I pulled the sandals off my feet and felt cool, dewy grass tickle my heels just before the soft soil below squished up through my toes in a satisfying, nostalgic slurp. Hoping old Mrs. Chatterly wasn't watching me through the lace curtains in her upstairs bedroom, I skipped barefoot on her front lawn. And if she was watching, maybe she was in a good enough mood to simply yell at me rather than falling back on her custom of calling the police whenever something happened around the neighborhood that she considered inappropriate.

Just as that thought flitted through my mind, I saw one of the curtains twitch, and Bigfoot, her fat yellow tiger cat, hopped up onto the windowsill to stare fixedly in my direction. By the time I realized it wasn't Mrs. Chatterly herself, I was halfway down the block and at my own front door.

That's when something caught my eye from across the street.

Light sparkling off the quartz and mica embedded in the granite form of my grandmother was not a new phenomenon, except for it was happening in the dead of night. Not even a sliver of moon lit the darkness, much less the statue.

The glints drew me to her; roiling emotion sent me to a seated position in the damp grass at her feet.

Ignoring the futility of yelling at an unresponsive hunk of rock I cut loose.

"Who did you kill to end up like this? And what were you thinking? It's not that hard to do the right thing. I do it all the time. Is it too much to ask that my family have at least some semblance of decency? What I need is a role model and look at you, you stone cold witch."

I rose, gave her skirts a solid, toe-damaging kick, then limped home.

My toe still hurt two days later when Mona's call woke me from a sound sleep and she asked me to meet her at the gym for some early morning cardio-yoga, the newest mystifying, oxymoronic fitness craze to crop up on the net, I figured I'd take the cosmic hint and get some of my aggression out in a productive way. I grabbed a pair of leggings and a fitted tank top from the closet and fished my nearly forgotten running shoes from the pile, and headed downtown.

Mona had already found me a mat and was seated on a matching one three feet to its right, her knees bent butterfly-style, her head pressed snugly against the floor between them. She looked like a human pretzel, and my regret-o-meter starting clanging like a klaxon. What had I signed up for?

"Isn't this a beginner class?" I asked, settling onto my mat and attempting to copy Mona's posture. I made it about halfway and noticed her sink even lower as she exhaled a deep breath.

"No, it's an advanced class. I thought you were a yogi—I mean, you've always got that Zen kind of calm thing going on...I mean, you've been a bit, uh, preoccupied lately, so I thought you could use a little detox. Do you want to leave? There's a spin class going on next door." Mona offered.

And walk away from a challenge? "No, this is good, I'll follow along."

Before I could start questioning her about how I seemed, *uh, preoccupied lately* (not that I could argue, but if I've got people questioning my sanity, I'd like a heads up before being involuntarily committed), a woman clad head-to-toe in Lululemon tiptoed in and dimmed the lights. A hush spread over the group, and before the giggle I was already preparing to squelch could bubble out of my throat, the drill sergeant-cum-yoga instructor began running us through a series of poses created, I could only imagine, as some form of medieval torture method.

"Get taller on the inhale; lift up through the top of your head, elongating your spine...and as you exhale, lean even deeper into the twist." She intoned.

Yeah, because that's doable when you're standing on one leg, bent over with your palms together in prayer pose, twisting to look up at the ceiling. The fact that everyone around me wore serene expressions—eyes lightly closed, tiny, smug smiles on their relaxed faces, while I huffed and puffed, trying not to make too much noise and wobbling all over the place—only made me want to try harder.

I concentrated on each word Lululemon uttered as she wandered through the crowd, occasionally placing her hands on a back or a neck or a waist and making tiny adjustments, and poured all of my will and intention into not making a complete fool out of myself. My breathing steadied, and I stopped shaking convulsively through every balance pose, avoided tumbling over and taking Mona down with me—and, I hoped, finished the session with a sense of accomplishment.

"Good job, Lexi." Mona's smile didn't quite meet her eyes when the lights finally came back on, but she was too nice to hurt my feelings.

As we made our way to the weight room and got in the long line for a post-workout smoothie (brilliant idea, kudos to whoever decided to put smoothie bars in gyms), Mona gave me the details of Vivianne and Levi's relationship.

"She's like a whole new woman, Lexi! I can't tell you how grateful I am to you. First, you found me Mark, and now my mom is happier than she has been in years. God, I hope she doesn't try to talk me into a double wedding! Wouldn't that be just the worst? She's been shopping; I haven't seen the woman doll herself up in years, and suddenly she's buying cocktail dresses and dangerously high heels! It's fantastic, and I think my dad would be really happy for her."

Mona prattled on, and I realized that either I had gained more from the yoga class than I thought, or I had simply been in more dire need of a girlfriend than I'd realized. I enjoyed the duality of Mona: on the one hand, she was driven, focused, and attentive to the tiniest detail in her work; and on the other, she was frantic and appeared to suffer from an inability to focus on one thing at a time— both in equal measure.

At least my job was done; one more successful match, and this time the personal connection made the pro-bono work even more worth it.

While an impossibly petite and perfectly-toned girl

whizzed up a mixed berry smoothie with a vitamin shot, I surveyed the equipment room and noticed a crowd forming near the bank of free weights lined up along the wall to our left. Several women were practically falling off their treadmills; their necks were craned so far in that direction.

Mona and I exchanged a puzzled look and wandered over to see what all the fuss was about; lo and behold, there was Flix, bench pressing about twice his body weight as half the people in the place watched in fascination.

"49...50..." He pretended to struggle but I'd seen Flix pick up the front end of a Lincoln Continental with his pinky finger, so I knew he was milking the situation for all it was worth. He was shirtless, of course, his chiseled pectoral muscles tightening in faux exertion, glowing skin a perfect sun-kissed gold.

I shook my head, and that's when my gaze landed on none other than Kin. He stood there, clad in his usual gym attire and speaking out of the side of his mouth to a nondescript man in track shorts and a t-shirt with the sleeves cut off who was ogling Flix with even more lust in his eyes than any of the women in the building.

I raised one eyebrow at Mona, who had already waved my almost-ex-boyfriend over with an exuberant hop and a friendly smile.

"Hey Kin, how's it going—did you know Lexi and I were going to be here?" She asked innocently.

"Uh, no, I didn't, but I'm glad to see you both." Kin reached for me tentatively and deposited a stiff kiss on my forehead when I returned his grasp on my fingers with a gentle squeeze. The man almost literally turned my bones to jelly, making it extremely difficult to stay angry with him. Even when I knew I was right.

"Lexi, this is Carl." Kin gestured to the man with the track pants he had been talking to, and for a moment all thoughts of my troubled relationship were forgotten. First of all, I was insatiably curious about this man with whom Flix had been spending all of his time—especially since he was usually so forthcoming about his conquests, but had been annoyingly silent when it came to all things Carl-related. And second, of all, I was angrier than a wet hen sitting on a cold egg because Kin met him first.

And since when did Kin and Flix go to the gym together, anyway? I wasn't aware they were friends for any reason other than having me in common, and now I felt like I was the one out of the loop. I chose to ignore the fact that I'd been in my own little bubble lately, too, and Flix's behavior wasn't exactly something to condemn him for.

To adhere to the rules of basic etiquette, I tamped down my hurt feelings and smiled brightly at Carl.

"I'm Lexi; it's nice to finally meet you."

The easy smile Carl had been broadcasting before my arrival widened even further. "Lexi, I've heard so much about you." A friendly hug and a kiss on my cheek later, I could see why Flix was so enamored.

Even though there wasn't anything particularly out of the ordinary about Carl's features at first glance (I'd sorted him quickly into the *nothing special* category), after a few moments in his presence, I could feel the tug of his charisma.

Curiosity overwhelmed indifference and my instincts began

to scream. I gathered all of my energy together and reached out with my witchy senses, searching for any supernatural energy signature that might be radiating off Carl. He was clean, but he looked straight into my eyes like he could tell exactly what I was doing, and his smile drooped for a fraction of a second.

There was a story here, of that I was sure. Right now, I was too discombobulated from Kin's presence, and slightly irritated that I hadn't known he and Flix had become friends to follow through with Carl.

"Lexi. Hey." Flix, finally having extricated himself from his adoring public, greeted me without fully meeting my gaze.

"Are you quite finished?" I kept my voice genial, ribbing on Flix like I normally would, even knowing he could feel every ounce of my jealousy and irritation. "And what are you doing, stealing my boyfriend?" Or taking his side in this stupid fight, I added, silently and using only my eyes to communicate.

"We've both been going to this gym since before the two of you met. Remember when you and I signed up together back in January? I've actually used my membership, and now Kin and I meet up to work out. What's the problem?" *Relax* he mimed back.

Mona's nervous giggle pierced the tension my stare-down with Flix was creating, and we all broke away from the group. Mona and I headed in one direction while Flix and Carl begged off to hit some flea market on the other side of town, and Kin sauntered toward the locker room after promising to call me later.

"What on earth was that all about?" Mona chirped as we gathered our things.

"You got me." All of the accomplishment I had been enjoying after the excruciating yoga class had evaporated, and I just wanted to go home. I vowed to deal with Flix and Kin later when I was calmer, and was already planning an afternoon spent indoors, in my pajamas when I remembered that my mother would be picking me up in half an hour.

Sylvana's mood swings were the last thing I wanted to deal with when I was already feeling mood-swingy myself, and I'm only a little ashamed to admit I whined internally about it all the way back home.

I tried to put the Kin and Flix situation out of my mind, and jumped headfirst into obsessing over the prospect of an afternoon with Sylvana. Nervous anticipation and my lifelong-cultivated ability to reign in my own expectations batted down the hope that kept trying to well up inside me.

I flip-flopped between daring to imagine a relationship with my mother that resembled the one I'd always dreamed of, and then rejecting the notion as a childhood fantasy I should have retired long ago. Finally, I decided to take each moment as it came, and ignore the voices in my head. As if that were an option.

We headed out of the city on Route 11, windows open and our dark hair blowing in the wind. If I closed my eyes and tried really hard to forget everything else, it would have felt like a real mother-daughter moment. Or even just a regular day in a regular life I'd never had a chance to lead.

Unfortunately, the intimacy Sylvana and I had experienced the night we'd gone to see the Mudwitch had evaporated in the bright light of the morning, to be replaced with awkward silence. I felt like I'd had a one night stand with someone who'd have preferred I exit quietly through the open bathroom window. Instead, I expected a cuddle and some breakfast in bed—not Sylvana's style, that much was clear.

Or maybe she just wasn't a morning person. 11 AM counts as morning, at least in my book.

"Where are we going again?" I said.

"To the first place I should have looked, actually. Honestly, I don't know what I was thinking. Shadow Hold is the most logical place to put an item you wanted to hide away from all the worlds."

"Shadow Hold. That sounds dangerous, should I be worried?"

Sylvana shot me a fierce, one-sided smile along with a sideways glance.

"Safe as houses."

It wasn't houses I was worried about because I wasn't a fictional witch who needed to watch the skies for the flying variety.

Shadow Hold sounded intimidating. "Once we get through the portal," Sylvana qualified.

*There it is*, I thought, *the kink in the plan*. Getting into the nexus where I'd inadvertently freed Sylvana had taken the combined efforts of several members of the group I was with at the time, myself included. Portals cannot be created by one entity alone. Otherwise, they'd crop up everywhere like quicksand traps, and people would disappear all the time. Opening a portal requires a group similar in persuasion to the one who created it.

The portal leading to Shadow Hold would probably take more.

"Doesn't it usually take a minimum of three different

types of people to open a nexus?" I asked, immediately regretting the question because it seemed pretty clear I shouldn't have the first idea of what it might take to open one. I still didn't want my mother to know I'd had a hand in letting her out of her prison.

"Different kind of portal, you'll see." I needn't have worried. Sylvana didn't know me well enough yet for the thought to have occurred to her. Or, she was just that distracted.

"Besides, we're only here to make sure we have the right location. Trust me. It'll only take a few minutes for you to verify if we're on the right track and then we're out of there."

Sylvana parked the land yacht of a car next to a highway sign promising a scenic overlook.

Overlook meant heights, right? Not as high as dolls on my list of fears, but definitely in the top five. Oh, goody. We'd probably be climbing, and after my morning at the gym with Mona, I wasn't sure my thighs were up for it.

The familiar black pack slung over her shoulder, Sylvana crossed the street to take a path I'd missed seeing when we parked. It looked like we'd be going down, not up. My calves promptly informed me downhill wouldn't be any picnic, either. I could almost hear them shrieking, which brought up a mental image of tiny mouths on the backs of my lower legs. Totally creepy.

On a day less fraught with pain and danger, I'd have enjoyed the hike as we skirted down along the edge of a stream to get to the valley floor. Air cooled by rushing water felt good against skin heated by the effort of picking our way along the marked trail.

"It's pretty here." Sylvana threw a funny look over her shoulder at my comment.

"Your grandmother loved this spot. There's a waterfall at the bottom," I could already hear the rush and thunder beginning to grow, "It's right in a junction where leylines cross. She'd channel that energy and turn the waterfall into a rainbow for me. When I was six or seven, I thought she was the most powerful witch in the world."

As tough as she wanted to seem, the slight droop of my mother's shoulders and the stiffness in her neck suggested a sense of wistfulness over the outings with her mother. It wasn't bad memories she was trying to ward off, but good ones.

"What happened between you and Grandmother? It sounds like you had a better relationship at one time."

"Let it go, please. There's no happy ending to the story. I suppose we both had a hand in shaping our history. Telling you every sordid detail won't alter the past." Was that regret I heard in her voice? The hint of vulnerability drew me to her more than any of her posturing had done thus far.

"Could you show me? When we get there?" Sylvana's chin dropped toward her chest as she took a breath that squared her shoulders.

"Come on." We descended the last twenty yards in a rush and came out into a clearing at the base of the waterfall. I'm a city girl, born and bred and I've always preferred concrete to mossy rocks, but in this place, I could sense the elemental connection to nature that marked most witches.

I felt the pull of stronger forces in the movement of the water; smelled it in the earthy scents, and heard it in the tree songs played by the wind. A bird sang a two-tone of notes that arrowed right to my gut and lodged there with an exquisite beauty that was close to painful.

If this was how Terra felt all the time, I'd underestimated everything she'd given up to spend years in an urban environment while raising me. Her gardens made a lot more sense to me now, and I realized how much I owed her—all of them—for their generosity.

"Sit right here," Sylvana directed me to a flat rock with the best view of the waterfall, and I felt something click into place inside me. This simple re-creation from her past formed a link between us that up until now I'd only felt in hints of possibility for a close bond. Oddly enough, I also felt my grandmother there, or I thought I did, a shadow of a larger presence that didn't feel evil or benign—just incredibly *there*. Glancing at the angle of the sun and back at the waterfall, Sylvana seemed to be waiting for just the right moment.

The spell, when Sylvana raised her arms and performed it, reinforced the sense of being joined by an act in the present to an unsuspected past. There was so much I didn't know.

Sunlight swept through the clearing, climbed the waterfall to touch the first threads of color as they spilled down over the edge. The forest held its breath around me during the sparkling seconds before the magic of light, water, color, and Sylvana thundered into the waiting basin.

Using her hands like she was directing an orchestra, Sylvana wove bands of color into swirls and braided them together while I wept silent tears for the little girl she'd been and for the mother who would play conductor to bring such beauty to her daughter. That was the moment I finally felt like I was part of a family with traditions and a heritage that wasn't only about power.

Even wicked witches sometimes make good magic.

Five or six minutes was all it lasted until the angle of the sun dissipated the spell. Still enchanted, I sat still another few seconds, closed my eyes, and imprinted this moment on my memory.

"Thank you, Mother. That was lovely." My voice was husky with tears, and when Sylvana replied, I was surprised to find hers sounded the same.

"I love you, Lexi. Whatever else happens, you should know that I do."

Leaping off the rock, I launched into her arms and finally experienced the shining feeling I'd been waiting for ever since I could remember. My mother's arms folded around me, and I clung to her embrace while a shiver ran through us both.

How long we stood there, I couldn't say, but when we finally parted, the raw, empty places I'd spent a lifetime covering with a veneer were now solid and true and filled. No matter what happened from here, I'd had this moment, and nothing could take it from me.

Aching calves forgotten, fear of the errand pushed to the back of my mind, I followed my mother deeper into the forest with a spring in my step and a lightness in my heart.

That feeling lasted for half an hour—right up until we turned off the marked trail and into a section of close underbrush that pulled at my clothes and hair.

"Are you sure you know where you're going?" The prospect of spending a night lost in the woods killed all those lovely communing-with-nature thoughts I'd been enjoying a short time before.

"Trust me." The family catch phrase didn't inspire me to any great lengths of confidence. "Follow, it'll be better in a minute." Another twenty feet of hard slog and Sylvana stopped to scan the trees around her. "I know it's right here somewhere." All I saw were more trees, but I gave her the benefit of the doubt.

"Right there, that's it." She strode over to a birch tree with shimmering leaves and laid her hand against a knot that was just above eye level. "Tree grew since I was here last." Sylvana gave the knot a press, and a path opened up like magic. No, not like magic, it *was* magic.

Trees moved out of the way, rocks too. Damn, sometimes it's fun being a witch.

Still, following my mother down wooded trails with uncertain ends was becoming an unsettling habit.

Unlike the path to the Mudwitch's house, this one branched off multiple times, and Sylvana paused at each crossroads to get her bearings. Only twice we turned wrong and had to backtrack when the path ended abruptly or meandered into heavily-thorned brush.

"She probably expected me to follow in her footsteps," Sylvana commented out of the blue.

"What do you mean?" I knew she was referring to Clara.

"Judge and jury. She and her cronies made a mission out of collecting powerful items and hiding them away to hoard the strongest magic for themselves—and then never using any of it." Bitter words. "What's the point of having power if you don't use it to shape the world to your desire?"

A chill stole over me. That sounded a lot like using magic for personal gain—something the faeries did without a second thought, but then again, they suffered fewer consequences. Direct personal gain and witchcraft went together like oil and water, unlike incidental personal benefit, which was harder to define.

Where's the line, you ask? Well, it can be a fine one, but basically, if a witch does a spell for purely selfish reasons, that spell is considered taboo, and the witch has earned a few wicked points. If the same spell is cast to benefit another person and the witch somehow gets something out of it, well, that's okay. You see what I mean about how hard it can be to find the line.

I'd begun to think of my mother as more misunderstood than willful but her statement made me wonder. If wickedness was in our blood, maybe she felt the lure sometimes, too. Something to wonder about.

Not for long, though, because I started to recognize my surroundings.

"Wait. This is it." I recounted what I'd seen in the crystal ball that day with Salem, "I remember this row of trees and the sun flashing off a stained glass window in that distant clearing. But in the vision, I was being drawn toward the bow; I could tell which direction to go. Now, I feel nothing. Why isn't this working? Do you think someone got here first?"

Running forward, I stopped just before pitching down the gentle slope leading to the cluster of buildings and took it all in. Built using large cobblestones, the round structure in the center towered over a series of shorter rectangles circling it like the rays of the sun. Thatched roofs and narrow windows lent a medieval feel to the tableau. From the top of the hill, I could see a second, similar grouping some distance away.

Sylvana sighed and paced back and forth. "Unlikely with so few being aware of this place at all. Do you know what spell you were using to locate it in the vision? At least we know it *was* here, but *here* covers a couple hundred acres and a dozen buildings with stained glass windows."

"The vision picked up with me already feeling the pull—I didn't see what happened first. But it felt an awful lot like the same thing that guides me toward a match—my intuition, I used to call it before...before I knew about the whole Fate Weaver thing."

Something—some cosmic knowledge or maybe some part of my power buried deep down inside me—clicked in my brain. It wasn't *like* the internal GPS that I'd been using for years; it *was* the same thing. And I knew, without a doubt, that I could unlock it. Don't ask me how; maybe because I had already seen myself using it in the vision, or maybe some other facet of my birthright had kicked in. Regardless, I wasn't going to question it, I was going to act.

Minutes passed.

Or maybe I was going to stand here looking stupid in the middle of the woods. In the past, it had always taken proximity to a client's desire for true love to trigger the tracking side of the equation. Well, until I started having those compulsions, but there again, they came from outside; I had never used my own force of will to get the process started. I wasn't sure how to begin, so I squinched up my face and tried to feel something.

I probably looked like a little kid attempting to hold it when she had to go potty.

Nothing happened, so I tried again.

"It's not working."

"How do you know you're a witch?" Sylvana asked a question that sounded ridiculous.

"Because it's my birthright and I've been awakened." Finally.

"That's in your head, how do you know in your gut?" She prodded.

"Oh." I thought about it for a few seconds. "I feel the well of power deep in my bones."

"How do you know you're a Child of Cupid?"

I answered quickly, "Because Jett told me and you confirmed it and because I have such good instincts for putting matches together."

"And what does your gut say about that?"

"Not a lot, and only when it feels like talking. I've never been able to access the side of me that tracks matches on my own. It only comes when it wants to." I explained.

"The only thing that's different is your perspective. Being a witch has been part of your identity from the beginning. I think all you need to do is accept the other side of your heritage as fact. You're not a witch with fancy extras. You're Alexis Balefire. There is no other like you. Find your true self, and you'll know what to do." My mother instructed.

"You think it's really that simple?"

Sylvana shrugged, "Nothing is ever simple, it's just necessary."

I looked around, found a mossy rock to sit on, and moved my body into Lotus position to meditate. "Stop staring at me, mother. This might take some time." I felt her presence withdraw, cracked open one eye, and saw her sitting with her back against a tree several yards away.

Who am I? Aside from a passing visual of Anthony Michael Hall in The Breakfast Club—and I was pretty sure I wasn't a walrus—nothing but a few disjointed adjectives came to mind.

Get serious, Lexi.

With an effort, I moved deeper into a meditative state, letting images come as they would. I saw myself as my clients must see me; slightly mysterious, unconventional in my methods. I saw myself as the faeries regarded me; a child. Less than, if you're comparing chronology to chronology. I saw myself as Kin probably did; exciting and maybe a little dangerous. And I saw me as I must appear from Jett's perspective; a rival for his father's affections and the cause of every bad thing in his life.

Through the bits and pieces of other's perceptions, I looked for the truth of my own. At first, all I saw were flaws. Late to gain my magic, bumbling in the dark, emotionally blocked at times. But these were limits I placed on myself— bits of the facade we all present to the world.

When the meditation took on the same quality as the visions I'd begun having, I knew I was onto something and followed the path of them deeper and deeper. If I'd ever had any question of whether my soul was ripe for wicked dealings, those questions fell away the closer I came to what I needed to see.

Images of myself helping clients, doing things for the faeries, being a friend to Flix, even fighting with Serena crowded my vision like a *this is your life* montage. Each one showing something true, whether that truth was good or bad. I saw and felt every ounce of joy I'd brought to people, and also the pain I'd caused as I moved ever inward.

Light streamed from the center, my epicenter. Light so bright it dazzled my eyes.

The final two images shown were silhouettes. The one on the left had me decked out in full witch regalia. Okay, it was cliched regalia—a peaked hat and pointy-toed shoes, but I got the message. The one on the right was me holding a bow and arrow. *The* bow and arrow, I assumed.

I knew what I had to do. Embracing both silhouettes, I merged them into one. A witch with a peaked hat, pointy shoes, and a bow and arrow. Ladies and gentlemen, meet Lexi Balefire, Fate Weaver.

My eyes popped open and my internal GPS revved into overdrive. The bow was close by, I felt the pull of it stronger than anything I'd ever felt before.

"Sylv...Mom. It's here, follow me."

We hurried toward the cluster of thatched-roofed, stone structures, and I unerringly led her to the round building that formed the center.

"This one."

"You're sure?" The feral gleam in her eye must have been a trick of the light, because the next second, she pulled me into a hug and danced me around in a circle. "I knew you could do it, I just knew you could."

Once the hilarity was over, Sylvana contemplated the door for several seconds. "Now the fun starts. This whole place is a giant magical booby trap. We reset the first trap just by making the path appear. That was the easy part, but I've been here before, and I think I remember what to do." Reaching out a tentative finger, she pressed a spot on the door frame, and we heard a quiet click. The next two hidden buttons, Sylvana danced fingers over confidently, and then a third.

A bolt of blue lightning shot out of the door and hit my mother in the chest. Helpless, I watched her fly fifteen feet like she weighed less than a rag doll to be dashed against the stone wall of the next building over. Her crumpled form crashed to the ground with a heavy thud and lay unmoving. My heart thundered in my chest as I rushed to her side with dread pulling at my feet. She couldn't be dead just when I'd finally started to get to know her.

Dark eyelashes rested on a cheek made paler by the contrast of a scarlet trickle that traced a path from temple to chin. A flutter of a pulse beat at her throat, and I swallowed hard to clear the lump in my own.

Not dead. Okay, Lexi, now what?

Healing spells hadn't topped my priority list or Salem's, so I relied on what little I remembered from a couple of Red Cross courses I'd taken at the Y and a hastily spoken spell to stabilize her neck and spine. A rising lump on her head, bruises blooming darkly across her skin, and out cold, I needed to figure out what to do for my mother, and we were in the middle of nowhere. In fact, I think we'd taken a right at the boonies and just kept going.

Trusting my spell work to keep her stable, I lifted Sylvana in a fireman's carry and thanked my mother for passing along her sturdy genes. Getting her balanced was awkward and I was sweating by the time I felt ready to start the walk back to the main trail.

"I've got you, Mom. It's going to be okay." I didn't know if she could hear me, but I needed the words to be said so that I would believe them during the long walk back. She almost slid off my shoulders when I pressed the knot that closed the trail behind me, and I made it all the way to the waterfall before I remembered the laborious climb back to the car.

One look at the steep angle and I knew I couldn't do it. Not because my heart wasn't in it, but because I'd need both hands to hold her steady and another pair to do the same for myself. Carefully, I laid her on the softest moss I could find and sat beside Sylvana to think. Few options presented themselves.

Taking her to a medical center meant questions and paperwork that I instinctively knew she wouldn't welcome. Calling Kin would bring his help and his sturdy back, but it would also invite questions.

That left calling one of the godmothers. Or all of them, as was often the case. Given a choice, I'd have opted for Vaeta. Something told me she, alone of the four, would be most sympathetic and her wind power most helpful. She'd probably blow Sylvana back to the car—in a nice way, of course. The problem was that I hadn't known her long enough to be able to call to her in that way. Our connection was too tenuous, which left me with three worsening choices.

Soleil's heat and life-giving sun had healing properties, but her attitude toward Sylvana was the most negative. She might refuse to help. Evian's water could lift, but it could also unintentionally drown an unconscious woman. And Terra. Terra could move mountains, so one tiny body posed no problem, and in deference to me, she would never harm my mother. It would be her response to me, to my being here in the first place and the reproach in her eyes that I wanted to avoid.

The sun slipping over the ridge cast the glade into shadow, and I knew I was running out of time. Full dark was still hours away, but I needed to decide now. Before I ended up spending the night here because of my own indecision.

"Terra, I need you!" When it came down to brass tacks, Terra was my faerie godmother, and she loved me. That was never in doubt. "Please."

"What? Are you all right?" Blood stained my clothes, and Sylvana rested far enough away that Terra only saw me when she popped in. "Where are you hurt?"

"It's not me. Leave off." I pushed away the gentle hands searching my body for broken bones and damage. "Over here. Can you help her?" Pulling Terra, I knelt beside my mother.

One elegantly raised eyebrow was followed by a narrow-eyed frown, but Terra did as I asked and gave Sylvana her attention.

"Smells like burned magic. You know I can't reverse spell

damage. I can strengthen her physical body, but she'll have to deal with the magical repercussions on her own."

"Do what you can." My arm went around Terra's waist, and I huddled in tight. She had always been my rock. Even when she rolled over me in what she termed to be my best interests. "For me."

"Very well." Terra laid hands on Sylvana and chanted in her mother tongue while Sylvana lay quiet under her ministrations. The chanting lasted several minutes while white fire flickered from her fingertips to be absorbed into my mother's skin. When it all was over, Sylvana remained in a stupor while Terra appeared visibly tired from her efforts. "She'll live."

My gratitude leaked onto my cheeks along with tears of relief. "Can you get her back to the car so I can drive her home?"

"I'll drive. My license came today."

At that point, I would have let her take me on a magic carpet ride to Timbuktu by way of Peoria, so I agreed.

Long before we reached the outskirts of the city, I envied Sylvana's state of consciousness. Her face might be pale, but my dash-gripping knuckles were just as white. The only other thing I can say about Terra's driving is that it pushed fear for my mother out of my head to make room for fear for my own life. Oh, and that I'd probably better increase the personal liability rates on my insurance.

Sylvana came to with a start as the car rocked to a halt in our driveway. Terra threw her an enigmatic look, treated me to another, and exited the car without another word. It could have been worse. Way worse.

We didn't talk at all during the ride back to my mother's apartment, or even as I got her settled into bed. Between the physical toll she'd taken, and the assault on her pride at having to be saved by my faerie godmother, Sylvana was spent. If I'm being honest, I didn't have a clue what I would have said to her, anyway.

I spent the night alternating between checking on her and tossing and turning on the sofa. By morning, her color had returned and as soon as I heard her hit the shower, I bailed.

CHAPTER

# TWENTY-ONE

"Lexi, sit down, please. There's something we'd like to discuss with you." Terra beckoned to me the moment I stepped into the foyer the next night after work. All four godmothers, plus Kin perched on the edges of various pieces of furniture, each with their shoulders set in determination. Salem, in cat form, blinked at me from the back of the sofa and I stuck my tongue out at him in return for his equally childish behavior.

"You'll have to change back to your human form at some point." I spit at him under my breath as I crossed my arms over my chest and took a seat.

"Soleil, you go first," Terra hissed, passing the buck she obviously felt uncomfortable carrying.

"No, it's Evian's turn." She retorted.

Kin sighed and rose to his feet. "I'll go. Lexi, we're worried about you. You're obsessed with the idea of finding this bow, but do you even know what to do with it if you get it? You haven't been acting like yourself lately: you never tell anyone where you're going; you keep disappearing with Sylvana, and when you come back you're different. Amped up, like you drank a pot of espresso and then ran a marathon. It's scary, and we're afraid you might be in over your head. Are you into something dangerous?"

Like what? Did they think I was doing drugs or something?

Apparently, they did.

The godmothers had not watched a sufficient amount of cable television to be familiar with the show *Intervention*, and it was apparent they had absolutely no idea how to conduct one. But it's the only word that could be used to describe what I unknowingly had walked into.

There was tea, and petit fours lavishly arranged on paper doilies laid out on the parlor coffee table, and streamers hung across all the windows and doors. Streamers. That's what tipped me off to the fact that the godmothers had set up this shenanigan themselves. Absolutely zero understanding of proper human etiquette, those faeries.

"No, I'm not." Or not intentionally, anyway. It's not like I asked for any of this. A bounty hunter, my resurrected mother, my birthright to find, and stupid Jett meddling in my affairs.

"See, you say no, but I can tell you're thinking about it, so you really mean yes." Kin pressed.

I ran my hands through my hair and pulled a little at the roots; the sharp pain kept the top of my head from blowing off when my blood pressure hit critical mass. All I had been trying to do was help people and keep everyone safe.

And maybe learn some stronger magic than Salem, the King of over-protective, wanted to teach.

"We're worried about you." Soleil finally did take her turn. "We think your...Sylvana is a bad influence. She might not have your best interests at heart. Too much power, too fast, can lead to, well, consequences."

Terra interjected, "I saw what happened last night, and I know for sure she has no respect for the rule of threes. If dark magic is the fastest way from point A to point B, she'll use it. None of us want you caught in the crossfire. Maybe this bow isn't worth the price you'll be asked to pay to get it."

Me nearly blasting Serena to little bits flashed through my head, and I pushed the memory away just as quickly as it came. That had been a one-time thing. A momentary loss of control.

*It felt good, though, didn't it?* The devil on my shoulder insisted.

*It will never happen again.* The angel replied.

*They're jealous of Sylvana.* The devil sneered.

The devil won.

"You're just jealous because you've had me all to yourselves for years and now that she's back, I'd like to get to know my mother, and that makes you feel threatened, so you're lashing out at me."

"If that's all it was, I wouldn't be here, Lexi," Kin spoke quietly. "It's more than that. It's the look in your eyes when you come home from spending time wherever it is you go with her. I'm scared because you're acting like you're hooked on the magic. Salem said it's a possibility."

Salem should have exploded into a singed furball based on the look I scorched him with.

"Compared to what Sylvana has taught me, Salem is a glorified pet who should mind his own business. I'm an adult, not a fourteen-year-old novice witch. I have more control and skill than a teenager, and you," I pinned the cat with a gimlet-eyed glare, "should have the sense to let me fly."

Terra's firm voice cut through the silence. "Are you quite finished?"

Maybe I was, maybe I wasn't, but the respect I owed her stilled any retort I might have made and she cut into me using her most formal tones. The ones I knew she only used when she was clinging to the fine edge of her temper.

"You're right, you're not a child, but you *are* a novice witch, whether you want to believe it or not, and there is a danger of getting too strong too quickly. You would be wise to listen to Salem's council, and the way you're treating him is not exemplary of how we raised you. Are you going to go to Flix's house and call him a half-breed while you're at it? As to the matter of jealousy..."

Fear chilled me briefly when Terra's beautiful facade slipped just enough to show the vengeful faerie underneath. I'd seen her mad enough times to know this was a whole other level of emotion.

"...you're my charge regardless of any other relationship we have forged between us. That is a bond I cannot alter. It is not, however, a bond that my sisters are required to share, nor does it require the extra consideration you've enjoyed thus far. I've looked on you as my own, and I don't mind saying I'm worried about you. There are things you lack the experience to understand and an addiction to dark magic is one of them. Be mindful of the rule of threes. What you send out will come home to roost."

"I'm fine. None of you are witches, and you have no idea

what you're talking about. I'm not practicing black magic and I can stop anytime I want." Couldn't I? I was sure I could. Tossing my head, I strode out of the room. The one thing I couldn't do was handle being around any of them any longer.

# TWENTY-TWO

Kicking Pinky up to top speed, I roared off down the street.

How dare they accuse me of embracing the darkness when it had already cost me my family? The legacy of wickedness passed down from Clara through Sylvana would end with me. Not that my mother was wicked, and how dare they suggest she might be?

She wasn't the one standing like a granite effigy to evil. If she cut a few corners to get the job done, what was the harm in that? No one had been hurt, and my spell-casting skills were exponentially better, so what was with the intervention? For as long as I could remember, I'd regularly stopped Terra from doing worse things to Soleil than I'd ever done. What a bunch of hypocrites.

Serena's face swam through my head, but I pushed it away. I was the one who had had to use one of Terra's poultices to help heal the damage from that confrontation and she'd walked away without a scratch. Call me wicked? Please.

I ignored the fact that none of them had actually used that word.

What I wouldn't give to run into Delta right now; I was in the mood for a good fight, and I'd had just about enough of her skulking around. I was so used to Terra looking in on me I didn't even notice her attention anymore, but I'd been feeling like Delta's eyes were on my back every time I left the house. The sensation made me twitchy and self-conscious.

The bulk of my life I'd been powerless, Unawakened. It had become a habit to look to someone else for supernatural protection whenever I thought I needed it. Before Sylvana came back, I could have used some witchy self-help tapes to play at night.

*I'm a strong, confident witch. My spells always work, and I can take care of myself.*

Salem would have hated it.

Righteous anger carried me to my dealer for a fix. Sinclair Fuller wasn't a supernatural, but you couldn't prove it by the magic he made with chocolate. I hit the front door of his shop so hard his little warning bell made an angry sound. Sinclair took one look at my face and pulled out a large box with his Sinful logo scrawled over the top.

"Don't tell me; it's a twelve." We have a system of evaluating how bad a day I've had based on the number of chocolates it will take to cheer me up. I consider myself a happy person, so a twelve was as rare as a tie-dyed unicorn.

Picking through a tray of confections, Sinclair started loading the box without asking for my input. That was okay by me; I trusted his judgment.

"You don't know the half of it. Make it a double."

Sinclair's eyes went wide with shock, but he pulled out a second box and leaned toward me conspiratorially, "I've got something in the back I've been experimenting with, you want?"

"Hit me."

"You sure? This is some hard-core stuff. The centers are half a shot of cinnamon liqueur in a hard chocolate shell, and then I roll the whole thing in a thick layer of truffle."

"Hit me," I repeated and motioned for him to run along and load me up with the goods. I juggled the heavy boxes into my bag while he rang me up—with the friends and family discount, of course.

"You'll tell me how you like them later?" Sinclair sounded concerned, and I gave him a thumbs-up over my shoulder.

Dark chocolate cravings could wait until I found a place to settle for the night. I pulled out my phone and called Flix.

"You up for some chocolate, a bad '80's movie, and some good conversation?" I asked when he picked up on the fifth ring.

When he didn't answer right away, I guessed what he was going to say, and was right on target. "I wish I could, but I'm going to have to take a rain check. Carl's here," he whispered conspiratorially.

I wasn't in the mood for false intimacy. I'd wanted to vent, and selfishly wished Flix was still single and available at my beck and call. I needed my best friend. Unfortunately, it didn't look as though tonight was going to be my night.

"I get it. Call me when you can." I hung up, wishing for about the billionth time that you could slam a cell phone. Maybe he knew about Kin's little coup d'etat.

Fine, if that's the way they all wanted to play it. There was one person I knew who wouldn't shame me for using magic; one person who might understand what I was going through. The spoiled brat inside me knew it was a vindictive thing to do, running to Sylvana when my faerie godmothers would prefer I keep my distance—but the brat didn't care.

Besides, I wanted to check up on her after her unfortunate experience the night before, and now I could at least spread the calories around to someone who probably needed chocolate therapy as much as I did.

"Can I come in?" Leaning sideways a little, I tried to see past Sylvana to the interior of her place. "I've got high-end chocolates, a bottle of Twinkleberry wine, and I need a place to sleep tonight. It's okay if you say no; I can go stay at my office. I thought you might still be feeling under the weather."

"I'm fine," Sylvana mumbled something about healing potions and averted her gaze to step aside and let me in. In the light of day, I noted things I hadn't the night before. Like all the spaces inhabited by someone in possession of magical abilities, it was much nicer on the inside than it appeared on the outside.

It must have been a witch who coined the phrase *never judge a book by its cover*. Fresh paint covered the walls; the floors were sparkling clean, and the décor possessed a bohemian vibe that fit my mother's appearance and temperament to a T.

"Did anyone follow you here? Are you in serious trouble?" I couldn't tell from her tone whether she was more concerned for herself or me.

I'd had a really, *really* bad day, and I wanted my Mommy. Except, I couldn't say that because we didn't have that kind of relationship, and I wasn't sure we ever would.

"No. I... never mind." I turned to leave.

"Wait. I'm sorry for sounding paranoid. Please don't go. I'd like us to get past this awkward phase. Of course, you're welcome to stay the night, and if you don't want to talk about what happened, that's okay, too." A pause, "did you say Twinkleberry wine?"

"From Terra's private stash. Don't be fooled by the name; it's potent stuff. But maybe you shouldn't, after last night."

"Oh, my Goddess, Lexi, I'm *fine*. And it's been twenty-five years since I had a taste of faerie wine—far too long." Sylvana's eyes were sparkling as she nipped the bottle out of my bag. Who needs a corkscrew when you have magic? The cork flew into the corner, and she took a long gulp of the dangerous brew, right out of the bottle.

Several sips in, Sylvana was more relaxed than I'd ever seen her, and I sensed her defenses were down, as were my own inhibitions. I figured I'd start the questioning off at a slow pace, with a fairly innocuous query that I probably could have learned from the books in my sanctum if I'd taken the time to look.

"Explain to me how the aging thing works. How old was Grandmother?"

Sylvana sighed, "It pains me that you have to ask; didn't one of the other witches ever tell you anything? Cleo, Beatrix, not even Listora? And what about your faerie godmothers? We're talking Witch 101 here."

"I don't know any of those people. Really, I don't know any other witches save for Serena Snodgrass, and she wouldn't pee on me if I were on fire—she'd sooner douse me in gasoline. As for my godmothers, I'm not entirely sure why they do the things they do. Considering none of us thought I'd ever come into my magic, I'm guessing they figured giving me a lot of details that were never going to apply to me was cruel and unusual punishment on top of insult to injury."

I still felt a nagging need to defend them, even though I'd have loved to curse the lot of them with butt boils at that particular moment.

Sylvana's eyes narrowed as she began to do mental math. "Well, Clara was 225 when she had me; but I was only 25 when she imprisoned me in the nexus. My grandmother died at least a hundred years before I was born, and I don't know much about her."

"Why not?" I asked with curiosity.

"Mother would never talk much about what happened; said it was too painful and she'd explain it to me when I was older. I don't think she'd have ever considered me an adult, but that's probably the way of all parents." Sylvana's tone turned bitter.

I could understand the feeling perfectly, having complained about the godmothers treating me with kid gloves more times than I could count. Hearing the sentiment come out of Sylvana's mouth, though, and in a bitter tone, made me wonder if I had also sounded like a petulant child.

"Probably," I replied lightly, not wanting to break our camaraderie with an argument.

"Except, we're witches, and youth is not merely tied to appearance with us," she continued, "age is measured in experience and power commanded. You'd think the latter would have earned me at least a measure of respect, considering how evenly my magic matched hers, even taking into account her age."

"So that's why even in the pictures I've seen she looks more like my sister than my grandmother?" My mind raced with the implications, even as I tried to block out the most concerning one—the one involving Kin, and the differences in our expected lifespans.

"Yes, but I think most of those were taken before I was born. Having children speeds the process—at least until the child comes of age. I think that's part of why she treated me with such contempt. Your grandmother was vain and resented the fact that as I grew older, she aged as well. A decade doesn't seem like much, but when you've become accustomed to the same appearance in the mirror for more than two centuries, it stings. Especially when you're a Balefire."

"Why would that matter?"

I thought I heard her mutter something about "damnable faeries" and "own story," but chose to let it slide just this once, in order to get the answers I craved.

"Balefire witches have been Keepers of the Flame for thousands of years—since the beginning of time, some say; few know the real story—and there has never been another family line. We are descendants of the original Balefire clan. Had you allowed the flame to extinguish, one of the Messengers would have been tapped to take your place—but she wouldn't have been a true Balefire."

The look of bewilderment on my face must have clued her in that she'd lost me again, and with a sigh, Sylvana continued in further detail, "The Messengers? The witches who come to take the flame. How do you think it gets from our tiny little city to every corner of the earth?"

I'd rather be turned into a warty toad than answer that question, but before she could launch into the story, I needed more than chocolates to soak up some of the wine buzzing through my system. After a short debate, we settled on burgers and fries from the diner downstairs. Handy, that.

Sitting across from me at a vintage kitchen table, one of those fifties jobs with a patterned Formica top in red with flowers on each end and chrome legs that had probably come with the apartment, Sylvana doctored her burger with a dollop of horseradish sauce and started talking.

"We witches have always kept our secrets close to our hearts, and what I'm about to tell you is one of our most highly guarded. Thousands of years ago, the Fae were in the throes of a civil war. One contingent, the Black Court, or Unseelie, hated all non-Fae and forbade all faeries from consorting with other beings—humans and witches being at the top of the list."

I reached for the ketchup just as my mother did, and our hands brushed with an almost electric result that I did my best to ignore. She upended the bottle over a small plate, then added a liberal squirt of mustard on top of that, followed by, to my utter horror, a small heap of mayo.

"The Seelie, or White Court, resented being told who they could mate with and banded together; some had no interest in mixing but fought against the decree on principle alone," I heard her say faintly over the ick noises in my head when she dragged a fry through the condiments and popped it into her mouth.

"The first Balefire witch, Esmerelda, was the wife of a great wizard. He had a half-Fae sister, who he died protecting, leaving Esmerelda and their young daughter alone and vulnerable. Oberon, the Unseelie prince, came looking for them, but fell in love with Esmerelda at first sight and refused to harm to her or her daughter."

Refusing the offer when Sylvana pushed the condiment mixture to the middle of the table, I stuck with just ketchup and made the first comment that came to mind. "Sounds like the Hatfields and McCoys."

"Something like that. Oberon turned to the light, made Esmerelda immortal so she could be with him forever, and then she convinced her brother and sister witches to join the fight against the Unseelie."

The diner made fabulous fries, I'd have to remember that for the future, and the burger was juicy on the inside, with a crisp exterior. Just the way I like them, on a homemade bun no less.

Between bites, Sylvana continued, "Our side won by a slim margin—many say we did so only because the prince betrayed his family—but that's not all there was to it. According to Balefire lore, Esmerelda crafted a special flame to protect against the Black Court—and we struck an accord with the Seelie: we would keep the flame alive, and in return, the Fae would serve as protectors to our kind while in our realm."

"What happened to Esmerelda and the Prince, then, if they were immortal?"

"You know time works differently in Faerie, right? Well, they both made a promise to return; the prince was now a king, and Esmerelda his queen—they left four Seelie princesses in charge in their absence—a mere year in Fae time—and stayed on earth for a hundred years."

You know when you smell something truly nasty and feel that urge to share with others? That's sort of how I felt about the ketchup/mustard/mayo combo. Maybe it was the wine, or maybe it was morbid curiosity, but I finally gave in and dipped a fry into the concoction.

"The newly anointed king," I heard my mother say, "bestowed the power of prolonged life unto Esmerelda's daughter, who by then had married a human and had no wish to be immortal. She agreed to tend the flame and pass it on as long as the King extended his gift to all witchkind, ensuring the Unseelie would be unable to reenter our realm even if the Balefire line died out."

Spicy tomato mingled with sharp mustard and the creamy mayonnaise provided a balance between them. It wouldn't be my go-to choice, but I had to admit, it wasn't as bad as I'd expected. There might have been a lesson in that if I'd taken the time to think it through.

"What happened to them after that?"

"Unfortunately, the ban included King Oberon and Esmerelda by extension. They're still there, ruling over the Faelands."

It was a lot of history to take in, especially with my brain slightly buzzed on Twinkleberry wine, so I let the story lie while I moved on to other topics.

I wanted to hear about my father, so I asked her to tell me about him.

It was a classic tale of boy meets girl. Sylvana glossed

right over the fact that she'd had to sneak out of the house, cloud the mind of the bouncer outside a club she was too young to be in, and had been well-lubed on Long Island iced teas when my father spotted her doing her best impression of a stripper. That's not exactly how she described it, but my imagination filled in the blanks well enough.

"Our eyes met, and I knew. You believe in love at first sight, right?" A safe assumption given my choice of profession. "He was perfect and beautiful and intense. Sexy as sin and twice as confident."

As she talked, I could picture it in my head. My half-brother, Jett, had shown me a memory of our father and I could see why Sylvana had fallen so fast and so hard. Neither baby nor winged child carrying a bow and arrow as portrayed on the top of Valentine chocolate boxes, Cupid's earthly incarnation could have gone by the name Hunky McHunkerson. Chiseled jawline, piercing eyes, lips that begged for kisses. And *eww*, that's my father I'm talking about here. Still, it was hard to have any daughterly feelings for a man I'd probably never meet. From what I'd seen, he and my mother would have made a striking couple, though.

Sylvana described the developing relationship in glowing, romantic terms, but what it boiled down to was that once she set her sights on him, my mother pursued Cupid with all the tender mercy of a lioness stalking her prey. God of love or not, my father never stood a chance.

"Do you have any idea where he is?" I asked, not sure if I wanted to know the answer.

Sylvana sighed, "I have plenty of ideas, but nothing concrete." That's all she would say on the subject, save to toast our second glass of Twinkleberry wine in his honor. By the time I'd drained my cup to the dregs once more, my tongue was looser than usual, and Sylvana had blithely turned the conversation toward my upbringing. All faerie insults aside, for once, it was as if she understood the hurt and anger I was feeling would subside eventually and I would forgive the godmothers. Or maybe that was giving her too much credit, and she just didn't want to chance ticking me off again.

"Terra once charmed a boy in my class and his nose grew like Pinocchio's whenever he lied. It was a foot long and covered in purple spots by the time the janitor found him crying in a restroom stall. Then she refused to lift the curse, and finally, Evian had to wipe both his and the janitor's memory to keep the poor kid out of the loony bin!" I wiped tears of laughter from my eyes.

"That's nothing; Clara performed a similar spell on one of my boyfriends from high school; except a little further south than his nose! He said it took him all night to get rid of it and then refused to speak to me for the rest of the year."

I could barely breathe but managed to choke out, "Magical Viagra, that's hilarious," only to be met with a blank look from Sylvana. Oh, yeah, she'd been gone so long she had no idea what I was talking about.

We traded stories until the sun and moon had swapped places, long after any normal person's bedtime. I'd always been a night owl, and Sylvana showed no signs of falling asleep anytime soon, making me wonder if late hours were the norm for her also.

"...he can't handle it when a bird flies through the backyard, even in human form." I giggled, recounting some of Salem's more ridiculous antics.

"Endora never liked them either; I think it's just a cat thing, regardless of the form."

"Endora, like from Bewitched?" I hedged a guess.

"Yes, exactly," my mother said brightly. I smiled knowing we had both named our familiars after characters from television shows about witches.

"What happened to her anyway? I mean, you're not dead..."

"I might as well have been. She couldn't track me down there, and I have a feeling whatever kept her rooted to this mortal coil let her go when I disappeared." Sylvana appeared saddened by the thought. "However, I was only her fourth witch, so I guess she's out there somewhere."

She watched me intently while I debated asking her another loaded question.

"How did you know I needed help Awakening? That's why you set up the magic shop and pretended to be Athena, right?"

"Of course. I knew there was no way you could have ascended without the Stone of Blood, and since I'd had it on me all those years—rotting away in the nexus where its power was nullified—I guessed you required my assistance."

Well, that made sense, but it wasn't something I hadn't deduced on my own.

"Right, but how did you know I'd happen to pass by that particular location. Sinful—the candy store I was visiting that night—is considered a hidden gem in the city; that area of town isn't heavily traveled, so how did you know where to put your little pop-up shop?"

I already knew the answer—there was no other explanation—but I wanted to hear it straight from her lips.

"I followed you," Sylvana admitted, her cheeks turning a delicate pink in the first blush I'd seen cross her face, "those six months were among the worst in my life. Coming out of that Nexus to find out how many years had passed—I sort of lost track of time, you know—I can't tell you how that felt. Not that I need to," she added hastily, "you've dealt with enough pain of your own, I'm sure you can commiserate.

"Anyway, I realized I had missed all of it—your entire life—and I'd never get it back. I could tell the Balefire had been reduced to coals, but when I tried to approach the house, I got knocked clear off the front steps by a burst of faerie magic. That drained what was left of my power reserve, and I knew the only time I'd be allowed through the door was on Beltane." The information bubbled out of Sylvana in such a way that I was nearly positive she'd rehearsed this speech many times in preparation for the opportunity to explain herself.

"Of course, you know that if I'd waited for Beltane, the Balefire would have gone out and you'd have turned into an ordinary human. I certainly wasn't about to let that happen, so I spent some time searching for your father, and when that didn't pan out, I called in an old debt and forged an unbreakable glamour."

"But why?" I interrupted, driving at the answer I wanted most of all, "just because you couldn't come in through the front door didn't mean you couldn't approach me on neutral ground—my office, for example, or you could have used one of those secret entrances to the house...” The pain showed on my face, and I got the distinct impression my mother desperately wanted to avoid coming clean.

My mother began to pace the room while she talked, and I was once again stricken by the resemblance between us. “Because I was scared, Alexis. Is that so hard to understand? Forget about the worry that you’d have some preconceived notion of who I was; it was possible you’d been poisoned against me years ago, or that you’d just be angry like you were when I froze Delta, and refuse to talk to me at all. The more immediate concern was your family. I realize you are used to being surrounded by Fae magic, but traditionally faerie godmothers don’t make their presence known to the witches they protect.

“What Terra,” I could tell just speaking the name was difficult for Sylvana, but she kept her tone neutral, “has done for you is quite unusual—I’m not sure you understand just how unusual. Their purpose, as I have always understood it, is to guide us from harm when they can. The ability to do so requires powerful magic, and I believe part of the reason they stay hidden is that it doesn’t always mix well with our own. You mentioned having had a hard time with spells lately—I wonder if your proximity to your godmothers is part of the reason.”

I wasn’t about to tell her that I’d flat-out lied about my spells going wonky because I’d needed Salem to inform said faeries of Sylvana’s unexpected presence in my bedroom. I already knew that different types of magic didn’t always work well together, but I was living proof that striking the right balance made the whole stronger than the two separate halves. I was different; I was special—maybe that meant whatever implications mixing Fae and witch magic carried didn't apply to me.

"I hope you can understand why I acted the way I did, and that you believe me when I say I came to you as soon as I possibly could."

"I believe that you believe that. And that's enough for me. People make mistakes, and they deserve to be forgiven and allowed to move on. I won't hold it against you anymore. But if you ever disappear on me again, don't bother coming back." I warned.

"Understood."

# CHAPTER
# TWENTY-THREE

Sylvana was still snoozing when I woke up the next day wishing for coffee in an IV, and one of Vaeta's faerie wine hangover tonics. Given the state of our relationship at the moment, she might have spiked it with Drano if I asked.

I knotted my hair into a messy bun, scrubbed my face with some handmade cleanser on the counter in the bathroom (that made my cheeks feel like a baby's butt, by the way), and headed out for provisions. The bright early afternoon sunlight had me digging into the depths of my massive purse for a pair of sunglasses, though they did nothing whatsoever to relieve the pounding headache settling into that sensitive spot right between my eyes.

Three blocks down from where Sylvana slept, blissfully ignorant of my departure or destination, I felt the hairs on the back of my neck stand at attention just before something hit me in the shoulder, hard, knocking me into a narrow space between two buildings and out of sight. Before I had a chance to counter, everything turned black.

I couldn't have been unconscious for more than a few minutes. The sun was still in approximately the same place in the sky as it was when I exited Sylvana's apartment, and I was only a handful of steps away from where I'd been ambushed, propped up against the brick exterior of the coffee shop next door. People walked back and forth past the mouth of the alley, within feet of where I sat, but none of them seemed to take notice. A thick layer of magic clung to the sides of the building like plastic wrap, concealing us in plain sight.

Yeah, us. I wasn't alone. Delta the Fiach was facing me, squatting on her heels and holding the same giant rapier in both of her hands, the blade resting on the ground between my knees. *Son of a witch.*

Obviously, I was supposed to sit still, what with Delta's clearly implied ability to put me out of commission with a few well-timed flicks of her sword, but I panicked anyway and tried to raise my hands to defend myself—except I couldn't. My wrists were wrapped together in my lap, wound round and round with a thin silver chain that glowed sapphire blue against my skin. Magical handcuffs. With them clamped tight, I couldn't even light a candle, much less find a way of defending myself.

"Terra!" I screamed as loud as I could. For the first time in my life, she didn't show up at my side instantly.

"She can't hear you. It's a barrier. Very simple magic really; if the faeries knew of its existence, they could break it in an instant. I've gone to great trouble to make sure they don't. Now, first things first. I'm not going to hurt you." Delta sheathed the sword and sat across from me, intentionally keeping her empty hands visible as she spoke.

"But you *are* going to listen to me this time, you slippery little witch. I'm done chasing you and trying to circumvent your mother's little repelling spell. You know she's got you warded into oblivion? Tracked, too. I've never met a Fate Weaver who was a bigger puppet on a string."

I glared across the meager three feet between us and straight into Delta's eyes. Sure, she said she wouldn't hurt me, but what kind of fool would I have to be to believe that? "Well, maybe you could put down the...what's the name for the little wooden thingy?"

"I'm trying to help you here. You followed the trails of bread crumbs I left, so you can't be completely daft, and yet you refuse to think past your own desires. You need to step up your game so that when the bow comes to you, you will have a shot at using it."

"Do you think I give a hot damn about that bow?" I asked in a dry, sarcastic, downright snotty tone. "It's just one more piece of family drama, if you ask me."

The look on her face almost cut through my fury. "You'd turn your back on a gift from the gods?"

"They weren't around to help me when I needed it, and something tells me this thing isn't going to come with instructions, just like all the rest of my powers. But no, I won't turn my back, it was my father's, and I want it. Just what do you think I'm trying to do, anyway? And what bread crumbs?"

It took me a minute to circle back around, but I wanted an answer.

"All those matches at the Port Day Festival. You didn't believe that was a coincidence, did you? I was trying to draw you out of the woodwork. Put a face to the name. But then you came tripping along and I thought you were your mother, and you know the rest." The look she gave me reminded me of the one Sylvana used when she thought I was being particularly daft. "But you're the one wasting time with family drama while your enemies grow in strength."

So Jett *wasn't* responsible for my experience that night. While Delta had been serving me matches on a silver platter, Jett had been playing in the minor leagues. Maybe he was overstating—or overestimating—the decimation he was causing. Tiny man, big head. A nuisance I would be more than happy to dispatch; I'd have blown him and Serena halfway to the moon if I thought they wouldn't come crawling back like cockroaches.

"Enemies? You mean Jett and Serena? Small time." I tried to dismiss them with a wave of my hand, but couldn't so I had to use my head instead.

"So you've attacked me for no other reason than to tell me to hurry up? That seems productive. I know where it is, but I'm not going to go screaming in there unprepared. You'll all just have to wait until I'm ready."

"I wasn't attacking you; I was merely trying to get you to listen to me without being interrupted and interred in a block of ice. Jett and Serena are the least of your problems, there's another foe, but you need to talk to your mother about that one." Delta fiddled in her pockets and refused to meet my gaze.

Goody, more people I didn't even know who had decided not to like me. "Thanks for the sketchy details. Really helpful."

Delta ignored my sarcasm, "And I've been trying to give you something; something that will help you in your search."

Finding what she'd been searching for, she handed me a box, and I sent up a prayer that this wasn't some kind of trick. The silver chain made it difficult to pop the lid, but after a short struggle, I managed it and found a gold compass on an intricately woven chain nestled inside. On the back was an etching of the Bow of Destiny, complete with a heart-tipped arrow.

"Thank you," I said lamely, the words sounding more like a question than a statement. A resounding thud drew my attention to the saran wrap barrier. There, on the other side stood Sylvana, the palm of her hand pressed against the center of it, the power emanating from her fingertips causing its surface to shimmer and shake until it came crashing down in a shatter of glass shards that disappeared before they hit the ground.

Two things happened at once. First, Delta backed away, looked up, shot into the air faster than a rocket, and disappeared. Second, all four of my godmothers appeared just in time to see Sylvana send a tower of sparks into the air from her index fingertip, even though Delta was long gone.

"Did she hurt you, are you okay?" Soleil demanded as all five of them rushed to my side. The bindings fell away from my wrists at Terra's delicate touch. At first, I thought she was referring to my mother, but the next words out of Soleil's mouth clarified things, "this is your fault, isn't it?"

"Enough, it's not her fault. I'm perfectly safe, thank you for showing up." My eyes spoke the apology I would give voice to later when we were alone. It wasn't a conversation I wanted my mother privy to.

"Can you guys give us a minute?" I knew they would

hear every word I spoke to Sylvana, but it couldn't be helped. I was starting to feel like a child of divorce walking the line between two parents who didn't get along and had major jealousy issues.

"We'll be right over there." Vaeta huffed, throwing a pointed look at Sylvana as if she was the one who had yanked me off the street and into oblivion. Would the tug of war ever end?

"How did you find me? Delta said you wouldn't be able to sense I was in danger. She also said you're tracking me six ways to Sunday. Is that true?"

"I wish I *could* say I sensed you were in trouble, but that damnable Fiach somehow managed to block me." She looked a bit sheepish, and I could tell it wasn't settling well that Delta had been able to get the upper hand.

"I was going for a cup of coffee when I saw you. Barriers are simple; if the caster is fast enough, they can fool even the best witch for a time. She knew she only had moments anyway. A barrier is just an illusion; this one was powerful, but I'm gifted with the ability to pierce illusions. I can teach you if you like." A shadow of vulnerability passed my mother's face as she helped me onto my feet.

"Yes, I'd like that very much." I'm sure I blushed.

"I'll let you get back to...them...now. I'm sure your *family* is worried sick. You know where to find me."

For a second I thought she was going to hug me, but instead, she turned awkwardly and walked away, skirting Terra, Evian, Soleil, and Vaeta to squeeze out of the alley. The second she was gone, they descended upon me, checking me over like I was a child who had fallen down the stairs. I have to admit; it felt nice to be doted on after all the arguing and fighting we'd been doing lately.

"Stop. I have something I need to say."

"Don't be silly, dear. We love you too." Evian shushed me, placed her hand on the small of my back, and refused to let me get another word until we were safely back home.

CHAPTER

# TWENTY-FOUR

Unfortunately, I never got the opportunity to apologize sufficiently, because I was waylaid at the door and after that, well, I was in no shape to converse about *anything*.

"Lexi?" Kin's voice swelled over the sound of the evening breeze, and I could see the outline of his body against the row of shrubbery bordering my yard with Mrs. Chatterly's. Of all the times for him to show up unexpectedly, this was one of the worst possible scenarios. I was still shaking from the feeling of vulnerability at being rendered magic-less, and I was sure my hastened breath betrayed every tingling nerve.

The godmothers entered the house quietly so we could have a private minute.

"You're shaking, and you look like you've been doing too much magic again."

"What do you want, Kin?" I snapped. "Surely you didn't just come over here to berate me about doing what I was born to do. I'm a witch. Magic sort of comes with the territory." I wasn't about to explain myself to him; he'd already jumped to a conclusion, made his bed, and now he could jump on it if he wanted to continue acting like a child.

"I thought I made it pretty clear I wasn't in the mood to talk after you convinced my family to turn against me."

"You're exaggerating a little bit, don't you think? We all love you and care about you. I know I'm the one who said to give her a chance, but I don't trust your mother, and I don't think you should, either. Is that where you've been?" Fear colored his voice; whether he was worried about me running to Sylvana or simply walking away from him, I couldn't be sure. Probably a little bit of both.

The worst part was, he was right about me exaggerating. I had forgiven the faeries, but for some reason, this felt different. They knew me better than anyone, and I could forgive them anything because I trusted them. Kin and I were still too new, and it felt like he was asking me to be someone I wasn't. Maybe true love's kiss was wrong; maybe I had been wrong to reveal myself to him. Maybe I had made more mistakes than I was willing to admit.

Ultimately, I didn't know if Sylvana was trustworthy yet either, but you know how it's fine to make fun of your own family, and then if someone else breathes a negative word about them—look out? Well, this was one of those times. "She's my *mother*, Kin, who I thought was *dead*. So far, she hasn't done anything to hurt me, and she had a good reason for not telling me who she was. She's not perfect, but neither are any of us." I stopped, sighed, and looked around. The trees and shrubs could have eyes, and the last thing I needed was to have this conversation broadcast to any of my enemies.

"Look, this is not the place to discuss this. Follow me."

I led Kin around the side of the house and into the back-yard. From any outside angle it looked completely ordinary, but if you crossed the threshold and were on Terra's "nice" list, a faerie wonderland appeared. Instead of a fence, towering sequoia trees lined the perimeter of the nearly twenty acres magically crammed inside our average-sized city lot.

Each of the godmothers had taken over a different portion of the space—save for Vaeta, the newest member of the household, whose element of air gave her dominion over the atmosphere itself, as evidenced by the perfect temperature and humidity levels we usually enjoyed. Moments before, I had been sweating in the midsummer night's heat, and now, without even needing a wish to make it so, the air turned cool as a cucumber.

Magically tuned to your comfort. That's what the ad would read if Vaeta could have bottled this perfection and sold it to homeowners everywhere. Long past their normal growing season, lilacs perfumed the air with their heady scent.

Because they were my favorite, Terra kept them blooming right up until winter slammed us with snow and she finally let the gardens go fallow for the season. Or most of them, anyway. Her winter gardens were something to see. A faerie wonderland of crystal roses.

Deeper into the woods I dragged Kin, whipping the branches out of our way with a flick of my hand, creating a path that finally ended in front of something out of a fantasy movie. Terra once told me that before she found me, the sisters didn't live together. I think she was trying to explain why they bickered so much; they weren't used to such close quarters.

Evian's grotto beneath the harbor was where she felt

safest, while Soleil retreated to a cave along the equator when she needed recharging. Of the three, Terra's mud hut was my favorite.

A cross between a hobbit hole and a gingerbread house, the little cottage's windows flickered with soft candlelight, and as we entered the oven door opened with the pinging of an invisible timer, and out popped a pan of chocolate chip cookies, the edges toasted to a light golden brown. Terra was nothing if not a gracious hostess.

Too bad neither one of us was in the mood to eat.

We settled onto two cushy toadstools in the corner. I sat as far away from Kin as I could manage, perched on the edge while he gave it a funny look, then plopped right down in the center of the fungus. Spores wafted out into the air and twittered out through an open window. He scooted forward to mimic my posture and waited expectantly for me to begin speaking.

"Kin, I know you're worried about me, but you need to understand that I'm a big girl, and I can make my own decisions. Why don't you trust me? I've been around magic all my life; I think I would know if my choices were about to lead me down a dangerous road."

Making that statement while sitting where we were seemed ironic, but since that word is miscued all the time, I might have been wrong.

"It's not just me who worries about you, Lexi. If your godmothers are concerned, don't you think you owe them a little bit of understanding?"

Kin's words—specifically the part about me owing the faeries—struck a chord. I could only imagine what Terra,

Evian, and Soleil had gone through, caring for me with absolutely no frame of reference for raising human children. Still, I was an adult now, and it was time for some independence. I wouldn't let anyone own me, and I would never be able to live with myself if I didn't explore a relationship with my birth mother while I had the chance. He had no idea what it felt like to be missing so many pieces of family history. Mine had, up until now, consisted of what little information I could glean from a handful of old photographs, a few love letters, and a statue so scary it made little kids cry.

"This isn't about the faeries; that I can deal with. I'm used to them meddling in my life, and I can't see it ever changing. But if you doubt me, you doubt us. And I can't deal with that. We've been dating for a couple of months; don't you think it's a bit early to be having these kinds of problems?"

All I wanted him to say was that he trusted me implicitly; that he'd put his faith in me and be content to allow me to live my own life. I realize now, of course, that my question regarding how early it was in our relationship turned out to be fairly ironic considering what I expected in return, but at the time it seemed reasonable. Hindsight has a nasty way of revealing colossal errors in judgment.

"So I have to trust you, but you don't have to trust me when I say that the way you've been acting is concerning? How is that fair?"

It wasn't, but I pushed forward anyway.

"How is it fair that I have to fit into whatever little box makes you feel more comfortable? You knew who I was and what I was before things got serious."

"You said you were a witch, Lexi; a good one. But lately, I'm beginning to wonder if you were right to worry about turning out wicked!"

That comment was what undid me, "So now you're going to throw in my face something I said to you in confidence? Wow, Kin, just...wow."

I watched the dissolution of our union in stop-action. I watched us pull the pin on our relationship. I watched it go up like the holy hand grenade. I watched his face turn harder and colder, and finally, I watched Kin step over the threshold of the hut and then counted to a hundred while keeping my tears in check. When I was sure he'd exited the yard, the torrential downpour began, and that's all I remember. Except for the sound of my heart shattering into a million tiny pieces.

CHAPTER

# TWENTY-FIVE

I'm not sure if it was Salem who alerted the troops to my near-catatonic state, or if the godmothers had been keeping tabs on me from the second Kin had shown up—but I cracked an eye open the next morning to find three of the faeries and Salem crowded around my bed.

Vaeta looked increasingly uncomfortable as her rear end sunk deeper and deeper in Salem's favorite furry polka-dotted beanbag chair.

I closed my eye and pretended to be asleep.

"Lexi, that's enough. You've got to eat something and take a shower. This is getting out of hand." I could hear Soleil's voice carrying through the hallway and could tell when she rounded the corner and stood in my bedroom doorway, even with my eyes squeezed tightly shut.

"I know you can hear me, dear. Now get up. It's been two days, and this madness has got to stop."

I sat up and opened my eyes. "Two days? Really?" It felt like two hours; or a dozen years, if I thought about it too much. Kin and I were over. I had only just found him and had already lost my soul mate. A bit dramatic, I know, but cut me some slack. Kin was my first real boyfriend. Ever. I knew it was pathetic, but that's just the way things were.

Evian shoved Soleil out of the way and sat down on the

edge of my bed. Soleil opened her mouth to utter some kind of counter, but Terra kicked her in the shin and pointed her index finger, mom-style until Soleil backed down.

"Dear, you were crying so loudly the family of pixies who lives in the back yard came to my window to complain about your howling. I had to give them an entire quart of honey to get them to agree not to torture Mrs. Chatterly's Pekingese, and then we carried you inside. You were pretty out of it." Evian said as gently as she could manage.

The sensation of her comforting aura surrounded me like a soothing bath, and I reached out with my own power to touch the warm heat offered by Soleil, the calming breeze contributed by Vaeta and the grounding force of Terra's steadfast love.

Feeling a tad shameful, I clambered out of bed and slunk into the bathroom, casting an apologetic glance behind me. When I'd scrubbed my hair and skin several times, blown out my thick mane of hair, and reassembled myself into a respectable adult, I ventured downstairs to find them all seated around the dining room table, chattering away.

"Mona is on her way to pick you up," Salem informed me. "I texted her. She's going to take you shopping. You're welcome."

"Am I?" In truth, the second Salem had said Mona's name my spirits lifted. A little shot of normal might just suit me today. What did bother me was his willingness to meddle, and this wasn't the first time. He was the one who had lured Kin into our yard the night we met. This whole thing was *his* fault, as far as I was concerned. I'd tell him it was his turn to provide the sucking up gifts, but I'm not a fan of tuna tartare.

I parked my butt on the passenger side of Mona's periwinkle blue Volkswagon Beetle and was pressed into the back of the seat when she gunned the engine and took off with more gusto than I would have suspected the little car had.

"Sorry," she muttered, looking not the least bit apologetic, "how are you? Do you want to talk about it?"

"No." I softened my tone, "not yet. Still processing. How are your mom and Levi?"

Mona's eyes turned dark and stormy. "Actually, it didn't work out."

"What?" My own eyes narrowed to slits, "What happened? Why didn't you call me?"

"I knew you had your hands full, and I didn't want to bug you. I'm not sure exactly what went down; Mother wouldn't tell me the details, just that it was sudden and unexpected. She's been burying herself in work, and when I stopped by yesterday, it looked like she was in the middle of a monster spring cleaning project."

Jett. There was no other explanation. I had seen the happiness in store for their future with my own eyes, and while I was willing to accept that circumstances could change the course of history, I just couldn't swallow the idea that it had happened to such a solid match.

"I'll see what I can do," I promised and accepted Mona's desperate thanks as we headed out of the city to spend our money at a decaying, near-forgotten relic. While it's all well and good to traipse around the quaint streets of Port Harbor, meandering from store to store, the high temperatures outdoors had Mona and me fleeing for the air conditioned, Cinnabon-scented halls of South Port Mall, located on the outskirts of town.

"I doubt this place will even be standing in a few more years. It's a shame; I practically grew up inside these walls—I think I lived off Orange Julius' and soft pretzels during junior high. See that bench over there—the one behind that big potted fern—that's where I had my first kiss. It's practically a ghost town now. Where do the kids hang out these days?" Mona asked, savoring the last few licks of her Dairy Queen chocolate dip cone and juggling several shopping bags with her free hand.

I giggled, my mood lightening significantly, "Anywhere shiny and new that has free Wi-Fi."

"True story. Hey, isn't that Flix over there? Mona pointed toward Hunters, a big sporting goods store. "And Carl." She added, prompting a groan of irritation from me. The last time I had tried to get in touch with my best friend, he'd been knee-deep in new boyfriend quicksand, and I wondered if I'd ever get him back.

Flix looked up and blanched at the sight of me. Literally blanched. It's not easy to catch a Fae off guard. What the hell was going on? "Hey Lexi," he greeted me with a kiss on both cheeks, having reassembled his face into a welcoming smile.

"Hey," I kept my voice light and devoid of emotion, "Hello, Carl." The poor guy looked like he thought I might bite his head off. I knew it wasn't fair to take my irritation out on him, but I was too caught up in my own drama to care.

"Can I speak to you for a minute? It's about work." I raised an eyebrow in Flix's direction, knowing he could smell a lie just as easily as I could spit one out.

"Sure. Be right back," He nodded to Carl, who chatted conversationally with Mona and waved us away with a nervous smile.

"What is going on? Don't you know Kin and I broke up? I needed you, and you weren't there. Why?" I pleaded for answers, sick to death of trying to coerce people into telling me the truth—especially people I considered family.

Flix sighed, his eyes darting to where Carl and Mona were giggling conspiratorially, "I'm sorry about you and Kin. I know how hard this must be for you, and I know you've been going through a lot. I'm sorry I haven't been as available as I normally am. But I've got a life, too. Can you understand that? I'm happy for the first time in more years than I want to count. I've never been angry with you when your life has taken you away from me, and I'd hoped you could be happy for me."

I didn't know if I softened because he'd willed me to, or if I just knew in my heart, he was right. "I do get it, and I'm not really mad at you for being preoccupied. I'm more worried you're taking Kin's side. And I'd like to get to know Carl if he's this important to you. I feel like you've been keeping him away from me on purpose. Does he not like me or something?" I might have pouted a tiny bit.

"Stop worrying; I've told him so many good things about you, I think he's more worried you won't like him. We're in a bubble right now and I'm not ready to leave it yet. I need you to trust that I'm always there for you and that it'll all be okay in the end. Can you do that?"

What was I supposed to say to that? The weight of my own expectations felt heavy on my shoulders, and I knew Flix deserved to be cut some slack.

"Okay, then." I avoided meeting his gaze until Flix wrapped his arms around me in a tight hug.

"If you need me again, just call."

I let it go at that, retrieved Mona, and continued our shopping excursion while pretending not to think about how badly I wanted to drive to Kin's and tell him I'd do anything he wanted if he'd just take me back. Watching Flix and Carl saunter off hand-in-hand had driven a knife right through my heart. I wanted to go back to my own bubble.

I was just too stubborn to admit I was wrong.

CHAPTER

# TWENTY-SIX

Attending an engagement party that had ballooned into gala proportions wasn't high on my priority list for several reasons. First, Kin was slated to play for the happy couple. Second, I hadn't had a hand in uniting the lovebirds. And third, Kin was slated to play for the happy couple. Okay, it was only the two reasons, and the fact that the faeries put the event together wasn't enough to overcome either of them.

When I let Sylvana into the sanctum, it felt like I was sneaking around behind their backs even though this was my house and my sanctum now; I tended the Balefire flame. How my mother felt about having been passed over for the gig hadn't been discussed, but I felt the conversation looming like a dark cloud, just waiting to dump another torrential downpour in my lap.

For now, we had to find a way to unlock the door to Shadow Hold that had so vehemently rejected Sylvana's touch. Clara's stash of ingredients and information was at the ready, and it seemed likely if she had left any clue at all, it would be here.

"The place hasn't changed much." Sylvana surveyed the room with cool, assessing eyes.

"Did you spend a lot of time here when you were

young?" Exploring all the nooks and crannies also hadn't been on my priority list, much to Salem's disapproval, though I had been making more of an effort in the days since the split with Kin—mainly to stay busy during the unprecedented downtime at work. I'd also been looking for information on Shadow Hold.

Though I didn't believe a word of it, Sylvana vehemently denied that she was any worse for the wear after our first attempt to storm the castle, as I'd taken to calling it. It certainly looked like one, all stone outbuildings and turrets. I was surprised there was no dragon-filled moat surrounding the place, but that didn't mean I had forgotten the dangers we were slated to face.

"Enough to know where all the skeletons are—or were," came the terse reply.

"There are skeletons?" Silly me, for a split second I thought she meant the kind made of bones.

"And the closets they're stuck in, but that's not what we're here for right now, and as much as I appreciate Terra's willingness to heal me one time, we'd better make sure there's no need for it again." It sounded to me as though her appreciation went about as deep as a layer of makeup, but I was no longer willing to choose sides in a battle between the people I loved. All that got me was one less boyfriend and a whole lot of hassle.

"I've looked through Clara's journals," I earned a mild sideways glance for using my grandmother's given name. "Came up empty. Maybe you'll have better luck since you're more familiar with the sanctum, or we could just figure out a way to hack the system."

"Hack the system? What an odd turn of phrase." I keep forgetting Sylvana had been living out of the loop. Way out.

"It means using non-magical methods of figuring out how to get inside." This whole operation reminded me of those heist movies that were big a few years back. "Maybe we could use something like fingerprint dust on the door to find where hands have touched it most recently."

"Fingerprint dust? Interesting idea."

"Assuming the powder sticks in the natural oils from skin and leaves a mark, that would give us the areas, but maybe not the order. What happens once we're inside? You said the place was full of booby traps." I almost didn't want to know what kind.

"First step is to get inside, once we're in, everything from that point on is meant to test your resolve." Sylvana muttered.

"I'm not sure I understand your meaning. If I've never met any of the keepers, how would they know anything about my personality or resolve?"

Sylvana strolled around the room picking up things, looking at them, then putting them back down. What she was searching for, I couldn't imagine. "It's pretty standard stuff. A magical obstacle course, if you will. I went through it with Clara a few times, and it was always the same. Piece of cake. All we need to do is get inside."

Somehow her blithe assurance fell flat against the memory of the sound of her body hitting solid stone with a hollow thud.

"Let's talk more about the dust thing. What made you think of it?" She asked.

"Forensic shows are a big thing these days. They practically teach a person how to get away with a crime."

"What's it made from?"

"I'll show you. I just need a couple of things." A sliver of charcoal went into the mortar, and then I used a heavy stone to pound the wood off a bit of pencil. The graphite joined the charcoal to be ground into powder with a few bashes of the pestle. Finally, I selected a soft brush from a drawer full of odds and ends. "Pick up that glass beaker." Sylvana complied. "Set it back down."

I fluffed the charcoal over the glass to bring out her fingerprints.

"Didn't you ever watch any cop shows back in the day? This is an old staple."

She gave me a quirk of a smile. "Not much. Television was never my thing, save for a few sitcoms. Some people watch, some people do things worth watching."

"Oh." A little cocky.

The fireplace groaned, and the wall around it cracked open. Salem rose up on his hind legs, morphing into human form as he stalked toward me. I'd forgotten about him when I'd invited Sylvana into the sanctum. Honestly, was it too much to ask that the people in my life get along—at least a little bit?

"What are you doing?" His tone reflected innocent curiosity, but I wasn't fooled.

"If I tell you, you can't rat me out to the faeries."

"If you don't tell me, I'll just follow you and find out for myself. No deal. My job is to keep you safe." He cast a glare at

Sylvana that plainly said her priorities needed sorting out. "And what is she doing here?"

"Salem!" I exclaimed, "That's enough!"

"Lexi is safe with me." It must have been a testament to how badly she wanted to get on with the task at hand; I had yet to see Sylvana back down from a confrontation.

"Yeah? Where's your familiar, then?"

Sylvana's eyes refused to meet Salem's, and she changed the subject abruptly. She wasn't about to tell him anything more personal than her name, and I had my doubts she'd have even given that up willingly.

"I think we could adapt your fingerprint powder to something that detects the traces of where magic touched the door." I explained.

"What door?" Salem insisted on being filled in, so I told him what door and his eyes nearly fell out of his head.

"Shadow Hold? Are you serious? You can't go there; I forbid it."

"There's no choice; I'm meant to retrieve the Bow of Destiny, and that's where it's being kept. Sylvana's helping me and you can do the same or I'll lock you in here until I get back. It's not up for discussion." I held up a hand to stop him from protesting further. "I have to do this, Salem, and I don't think you have the power to forbid me from doing it."

What I didn't say was that this destiny was one I felt I could embrace. Well, depending on how that bow actually worked. I know witches are supposed to be comfortable around blood; we use it in spells when we have to because that's where the magic lies, but I'm not a *guts and gore* kind of gal. If pelting people with love's arrows turned into that type of pursuit, I'd have to rethink my options.

Sylvana held up the beaker with the fingerprints, "It won't matter if we can't retrieve the bow, so maybe you should pay a bit more attention to your spellwork and potion making than placating your little helper." The sharp edge to the words sparked a flare of rebellion that I quickly tamped back down. My mother was here to help, and I should listen to her.

"Now we need to add the magic component. What can we bind the charcoal with?" I asked, routing the conversation back to what was really important.

"Nothing incendiary," both Sylvana and Salem chorused, shooting each other narrow-eyed glares before quickly looking away.

"Let's start with salt; it's a basic ingredient for most divination spells, and the sodium should have a grounding effect on the charcoal. The problem is, we don't have any way to test it."

"I can take care of that." Sylvana disappeared behind a row of shelves. We quickly followed the sound of something creaking open and turned the corner just in time to find her rooting around in a trunk tucked into a recess I hadn't yet discovered. "Remember what I said about skeletons? This one happens to be one of mine."

She pulled a silver plated chest about the size of a shoe box out of the trunk and brought it over to the alchemy table. "I was about thirteen when I cast the protection spell on this box; there's nothing more than childhood trinkets inside, and the hex wouldn't have been potent enough to harm anyone after all this time. Still, it's a similar spell to what my darling mother would have used on the door. We should be able to fashion something usable with it."

I was more than curious to see what trinkets my mother would have considered worth protecting as a young girl. The chest was old; probably a priceless antique, though taking into account what else was housed under the sanctum roof, its worth probably paled in comparison. Sometimes I felt like Clara's ghost resided in this space; I could see her flitting from shelf to shelf, preparing potions, standing in the center of the large casting circle while performing great and powerful (and possibly unspeakably evil) spells.

Now, the ghost of my mother's past had joined her, running through the stacks and picking up discarded baubles to keep in her treasure box. The bigger my world got, the smaller and more inconsequential I felt, as if the childhood I'd been mourning had never been mine to begin with. Maybe, someday, all the pieces of the puzzle would click into place, and I'd finally feel like I knew where I belonged.

"Okay, it's time," we all crowded around the box, and I dusted a thin layer of the mixture over the entire surface, watching as several fingerprints appeared.

I tentatively reached out to touch one, willing the box to open as my fingertip caressed the lid. A blast of red sparks shot from the clasp, and I deftly whipped my head out of the way. Crimson fire ricocheted off the shiny surface of a recently-polished silver tray hanging on the wall behind me and landed on Salem, who immediately sprouted a pair of bird wings and began to lift off the floor. Images of Charlie and Grandpa Joe flashed through my mind as Salem floated toward the domed ceiling above the sanctum, panic turning his ebony skin to a greenish color as he flapped in an attempt to ground himself. Burping probably wouldn't be useful in this particular situation.

"Lexi, help!" He squealed while Sylvana doubled over in a fit of laughter. She flicked a finger and Salem thudded to the floor, landing on his feet in his cat form before launching himself at Sylvana's face, claws unsheathed and fighting for purchase.

"Enough, both of you. And you think I'm the one acting like a child." I admonished, forcing a mumbled I'm sorry from each of them. "We're missing something. All we're getting is regular prints, and who knows how many times this thing's been touched by non-magic hands."

"You're right; we need a catalyst."

"The mugwort infusion worked pretty well when we were scrying," I plucked a vial of powdered mugwort from one of the chock-full shelves and turned to my mother expectantly.

Sylvana nodded, "Mugwort is probably the best choice; it's got hallucinogenic properties and might reveal the magical residue along with the prints. Good job, Alexis."

"Add one part of that, and one part consecrated salt and grind it as fine as you can." I nodded silently at Salem's instructions, still internally soaring from Sylvana's praise, and did as I was told.

Again I brushed the mixture, which was now vibrating at a low frequency, onto the lid. Tiny curling lines and swirls began to appear, finally coalescing into identifiable fingerprints—of a sort—that glowed with a blue-white iridescence.

Salem took a big step back as I reached out once more. This time, a couple of taps caused the clasp to flip open, and the lid to slowly rise. Sylvana snatched the box away before I could take a look inside.

"That's all we need to know about that." Her tone warned I shouldn't press the matter, so I respected her boundaries and decided to let it go. "Let's gather the rest of what we need; a magical grab bag, if you will, just in case."

A half hour later, we'd raided the supply cache for a few basics, loaded two backpacks with provisions, and dressed appropriately for a stealth mission. I'd fastened my father's compass around my neck and tucked it beneath my shirt for protection. I had a feeling I'd need it.

"There's just one more question I want to be answered." Well, that was an understatement and a half; I had an infinite number of questions I'd have loved to pelt her with, but only one that had been gnawing at me for the past few days. "Delta said you know something about a new enemy who might be after me."

Sylvana shot me a narrow-eyed look, "That's not a question and why would you believe her, anyway. Not only has she followed you, harassed you, kidnapped you, and tied you down in an alley, but she's also drawn a sword on you and threatened me. Why would you take anything she says seriously? She's just trying to motivate you to find the bow, and if you seriously think she's planning on letting you keep it, you're just being naïve."

Wow, tell me how you really feel, Mom.

# TWENTY-SEVEN

Gray skies wept a light drizzle over the drive to Shadow Hold, which I hoped was not a harbinger of worse to come. "Got any umbrellas in the back of this boat?"

"Afraid not." Sylvana replied dryly. "I've got a tent, but I don't think that's going to do the trick."

"It would if you could put legs on it."

"A walking tent? What kind of crackpot magic do they practice around here these days?" Sylvana took an extra-long look in the rear view mirror, and I wondered if she thought we were being followed. Twisting in my seat, I saw nothing suspicious behind us.

"Forget it, but I don't think the powder is going to work on a wet surface. Shouldn't we just wait for a dry day?" I pressed, suddenly willing to rethink the whole plan now that the time for action was upon us.

"You know that's not an option." Now she thought I was nervous or something. Can't imagine why. "Between Delta and Jett, we're playing beat the clock already."

"I'm just not a fan of my toes going all pruney," I ignored the flutter of nervous energy in my gut and muttered under my breath. Not for a moment would I admit that I was scared of getting zapped by something wicked my grand-mother cooked up.

"Then put a spell on your shoes to make them water-proof." She shot back.

"Can't. Goes against the rules."

"What rules? You mean personal gain? Don't get me started." Sylvana rolled her eyes. "Consider it for my benefit, then. I don't want to hear you complaining the whole way." When she put it like that, what choice did I have? While I was at it, I spelled my clothes, too. And my hair. After all, I shouldn't go to my possible death looking wet and bedrag-gled; a girl needs to look her best during times of crisis. Not that this was a crisis exactly, but it certainly was stressful.

Whether deliberate or not, I felt like Sylvana was holding something back. She'd been jumpy and cranky all day, and there had been none of the closeness we'd begun to share.

We pulled into the turnoff leading to the waterfall, and she killed the purring engine with a twist of her wrist. "Just remember, once we go through the door, the only way back is forward. We're prepared, and your magic is stronger than you give yourself credit for."

After that, we spoke little as we gathered matching black packs from the trunk and, dressed identically in black jeans and hoodies, made our way down the slippery hill toward the bottom of the waterfall. There would be no rainbow today.

The soft echo of a breaking branch reached my ears, but I could see nothing behind us save for a squirrel racing from tree to tree. Pearled mist muted and distorted the sounds of the forest, and we slogged through rain-soaked foliage toward the spot where Sylvana pressed the knot and revealed the hidden trail. She took the lead, her back straight, looking neither left nor right and I wondered if she was battling the memory of that blue flash from our last visit.

Time plays tricks on your mind, stretching and winding back on itself during times of duress. This was one of those times. The minutes felt like hours and also like mere seconds as we approached the compound and our first test of the day. Sylvana pulled the powder out of her bag and motioned toward the door, kept dry by a thatched overhang. "Here we go. Let's see if forensics and magic can work together."

Starting with the locations she'd touched last time, my mother applied the powder with one of my old blush brushes. She must have lied about never watching crime shows on TV because her hands moved in an expert motion that spread the lightest layer of powder over the largest amount of surface area. Once the colored dust coated the door, she turned her attention to the frame.

"If memory serves, there should be five touch points."

"Six if you count the bad one from last time. You remember where it was, right?" Every time the scene replayed in my mind, I cringed.

"Trust me; I'm not likely to forget."

"Shouldn't it be glowing by now?" I strained to see any evidence our spelled powder was working. "Maybe it's not dark enough." I lifted my arms and stretched the material of my sweatshirt to block as much of the misty gray light as I could.

"There, do you see it?" Sylvana leaned closer to the door.

"It's working." As her breath fell on the powder, the effect became more pronounced, and I could see five separate areas of glowing green taking shape.

"Blow on them. Just lightly." I ordered and watched each small fiery brand flare to life. "Do you think it makes a difference which order you touch them in?"

"Deosil to raise energy, widdershins to banish. That's how it works. Are you ready?"

Holding my breath, I nodded, and Sylvana pressed a finger to the first lighted spot. Then the next and clockwise navigated the pattern, skipping the mark that had sent her flying last time. My hands were shaking. Hers were solid as a rock, and I admired her level of courage.

For the space between one breath and another, nothing happened. Then the door simply clicked open, and my knees turned weak. It was time to go and find my birthright. The Stone of Blood hung heavy and channeled a bit of the Balefire heat where it rested in the valley between my breasts, its chain and its essence both mingling with that of the golden compass around my neck.

Would the stone protect me or condemn me for going against my grandmother's wishes and retrieving what was rightfully mine? Had she truly hoped to keep it from me in the first place, and if so, why? I discovered I didn't much care; I wouldn't waste an ounce of my time trying to answer those questions until I had the bow safely in my possession.

Providing I survived the experience, of course. The pull from the bow was stronger than anything I'd ever felt before. Standing still under its influence was not an option, and I wondered whether, if I tried it, my feet would skid helplessly along the floor as it dragged me closer.

"It's straight ahead." My voice sounded loud though I'd spoken the words softly into air made heavy by magic. "And close." Arms reach if I could trust my senses. Sylvana's hand clamped on my shoulder. We'd agreed that maintaining constant contact would be the wisest course of action, but I'd already almost forgotten she was there in my haste to answer the call of the Bow of Destiny. I felt it there, close by and aware, like a living thing, speaking to my soul and beckoning me forward.

It couldn't be this easy, could it?

I managed two steps deeper into the hold and got my answer when I ceased to exist. My body lost touch with its senses, leaving nothing to anchor my mind to the physical plane. Was this what it felt like to die? I screamed into the void and kept screaming until it started to seem a little silly. First, since I had no ears, I couldn't hear myself anyway, and then, what was the point? This must be one of the tests Sylvana had warned me about—the testing of body, mind, and soul.

Clearly, this was the test of my mind, meant for me to think my way through the problem. But how? A spell? No. According to Salem, my magic came from my blood and was merely directed by my conscious mind, which was all that was left to me now.

Panic tried to rise again, but I ruthlessly stuffed it back inside. Logic and hysteria cannot occupy the same space, and only one of those two things would help me now. I did what I always do when I'm uncertain. I made a list. Flix would be laughing at me right now if he knew.

What did I have to work with? My thoughts, memories, and imagination. Not a lot, but better than nothing. The pool of my magic had gone with my body—I knew even before I tried reaching for it—but it's better to explore all options. Magic would not be added to the list.

With nothing more to help me, I explored the only option I could conjure into my head. Maybe I could remember my body back into being.

Starting with my toes, I imagined them in the tiniest detail. The texture of the skin, the curving sharpness of nail, the cracking sound the big one on the right makes when I bend it just so. Memories locked into my cells flooded forth. The feel of mud squishing between my toes, the heat of sand on the delicate arches, the heels down motion of riding a bike.

Ankles, calves, knees and thighs—I traced the path across the body I had taken for granted, examining each glimpse of the past and building the flesh anew, inch by solid inch. Even the elbows I've always thought were too bony got my focused attention.

I can't tell you how long it took, other than that it seemed like eons before I finished experiencing my body in a way I'd never imagined—until it felt settled and whole and fully mine in a way it never had before. As tests go, this had been an unexpectedly positive one given that it had been thought up by a wicked witch.

Sylvana's hand clutched my shoulder painfully, and I

welcomed the sensation until I heard her labored breathing. Turning, I caught her as she fell and cradled her to the floor.

"I'm okay. I just need a minute." Faint and wheezy, her voice shook, and her eyes fluttered closed. Stroking sweat-tangled hair from her damp forehead, I held her until the tremors slowed and finally stopped, then rummaged around in my pack for a bottle of water.

Her lips, when I raised the bottle to them, were darker than their typical red—so dark they seemed almost black against skin so pale it was nearly translucent. She brushed off my questions about what had happened to her and scrambled to her feet.

"We'll talk about it later. After this is all over."

If the bow hadn't been filling my head with its persistent call, I would have recognized the lie for what it was.

"Are you ready to move forward?" Power sparked through my body, renewed and enhanced with an electric flare of energy. I felt like I could take on the world while Sylvana still looked a little shaky. "Stay close; I'll protect you." Not too shaky to shoot me a glare that burned.

With her hand again on my shoulder, we kept walking, and I got my first good look at the Hold proper. I'd come in here expecting to encounter a museum-like space—something cataloged, organized—with shelves or cases to store the magical items deemed too dangerous to be left in the free world. The reality was quite different. It looked like a trash dump. Magical items had been tossed hither and yon with no thought for where they landed on the dirt floors. Who knew there were so many dangerous things that needed to be isolated from the world? What evil could old Legos accomplish? Or had someone banished them here to keep from stepping on them with bare feet in the dark of night?

I reached to brush a harmless twig off of a shining golden halo, and Sylvana pulled my hand back. "Don't touch that. It's all that's left of a tree known as Job's Tears. The wood is full of tiny slivers, and if one of them pierces your skin, you will have to face seven deadly trials. Very dangerous. Epically so." She used the water bottle she still carried to nudge the bit of wood deeper into the pile where an unwary hand would be less likely to make contact.

"It should have been sealed in an urn and buried. This place has gone to the dogs since I was here last. Clara would be unamused." I found the statement odd, but didn't have time to think more about it when Sylvana asked, "Which way?"

Everywhere. That's how it felt to me. How was I supposed to pinpoint a single direction when the bow crowded my senses?

The sixty-four-thousand-dollar question. Which, of course, I had the answer to tied around my neck. "The compass!" I pulled the gold chain from beneath my shirt and tried to orient on the bow. "Dead ahead. No, we've passed it." Beads of sweat dampened my brow as I concentrated. The hands of the compass spun around in circles. "Lot of help that was. It's everywhere at once. Should we just keep going and hope I can figure it out when we get closer?" There was only one path through the mess, so forward was our only option. If I ever got the chance, I'd ask Delta why she bothered giving me so useless a tool.

"Lead on," Sylvana said, and at the same time, I thought I heard my name called from a great distance.

"Did you hear that?" I stopped to listen.

"Hear what?"

"It must have been an echo." Moving on, I tried not to get distracted by the volume of stuff or the fact that my fingers itched to tidy up the mess.

The second trial hit as unexpectedly as the first and came in the form of an attack of conscience. I felt my eyelashes fluttering against my cheek, but didn't remember closing my eyes as a wave of memories flooded past my shuttered lids. Not my memories, I realized quickly, but those of my friends and family—and along with the memories I felt their emotional reactions to things I had done or said, starting with the most painful.

"I hate you." Terra's heart had broken when I tossed the words at her in a moment of youthful rebellion, and now her pain broke mine as well. To me, it had been a passing fit of pique; to her a knife in the gut thrown by a careless hand. The parade of pain lasted long enough to send me to my knees with the agony of regret for the hurt that returned to me and was now burned into my soul. A black mark, a stain branding me with one word.

Wicked.

That was me. Wicked to the bone because I'd been born that way. The best thing I could do would be to lay down here and die before I hurt more people just by being in their lives. Look what I had done to Kin. We'd shared true love's kiss, and then I'd pushed him away until he finally got the message. I was damaged goods, a liability, and I should have never tangled myself up with him in the first place. He deserved so much more than my withered, black heart had to give. Letting him push me away had been my gift to him.

Tears burned acid tracks down my cheeks, across my throat, and into the valley where the Stone of Blood rested against my skin. Salty wetness seeped along the setting to charge the bloodstone with the essence of my sorrow and pull from it that which gives my family purpose. The life-affirming spark of the Balefire that lives within its keepers.

Those who are truly wicked never experience regret. As the words rang through my head, their truth caused the bloodstone to flare with light and heat and conviction. Floodgates unlocked, I now experienced another spate of memories—ones that showed the joy, love, and compassion I felt for my family and theirs for me.

Kin. I saw inside his heart. A heart open and full of the kind of love that would make a man do stupid and awesome things. I'd hurt him deeply, but the flame and spark remained. There was hope for us yet.

Glowing in the fire cast by the Stone of Blood, I rose to my feet as though lifted by an unseen hand and recognized the universal truth that we prove our potential based on our choices. Life is lived in the balance, not in the extremes, and accepting love is almost as important as giving it.

The vision faded away but left a lingering mark on my soul.

Sylvana huddled beside me, her back hunched against a weight doing its level best to bear her to the ground. Streaks of white threaded through her chestnut hair and veins dark with blood coursed just under her skin.

Whatever vision she'd just seen had clearly been worse than mine, and I knew that if I didn't help her, she might never come back from the place where her mind had strayed.

Reaching down, I lifted her as though she weighed nothing, rested her head against my shoulder, and whispered into her ear. "Don't leave me again, I need you. Come back to me. You saved me. You helped me. I love you. Come back, Mom."

An eternity passed before her body twitched and relaxed into my embrace. She felt frail as a bird in my arms, her heart beating in double time. "That's it now. Listen to my voice and come back." My tears continued to charge the bloodstone as I used it and my words like a beacon to guide her back. No matter what she had done or failed to do in the past, she was mine. My mother, my blood, my family, and I would not let her go.

"I'm okay," Sylvana said. "Don't let me go." She clung to me, and I held her until I felt strength returning to her limbs and gently set her back on her feet. It hurt my heart to see her so diminished.

"I think I should go on alone. This is becoming too much for you."

"I said I'm fine," She snapped at me then her face softened slightly. "Sorry. I don't like being coddled." Stubborn witch. Runs in the family. "We're close now, I can feel it. I said I would help you get the bow and that's what I plan to do."

"It's all around me; I can hear it singing." Pulling out the compass once more, I checked the direction, and this time the needle remained steady. "This way," I pointed to the right where I could see a pale light ahead.

"There, do you see it?" My body hummed with taut energy that strained toward the reason we'd come here. Forgetting Sylvana for the moment, I ran toward the Bow of Destiny.

CHAPTER

# TWENTY-EIGHT

My headlong flight carried me through a door that slammed shut behind us and right up to the edge of a chasm separating an island pillar topped by a stone pedestal from the center of the room. In a pool of pink and golden light—sunset colors—the Bow of Destiny rested on the dais. So close and just out of reach. No more than four feet of echoing space was all that stood between me and the narrow ledge on which the pedestal rested.

With a running start, I could make the leap, right? I gathered myself to try.

"Lexi, no! Wait." Sylvana put out a cautioning hand. "Not yet. There might be wards." She reached down to scrape a scant handful of soil from the dirt floor, which she then tossed toward the stone plinth.

Sure enough, the soil hit an invisible wall before scattering down into the black depths of the chasm. Right where I would have ended up if I'd taken that leap. Relief shuddered over me with a touch of the warm fuzzies and a hint of the wobbly knees. My mom had my back. She'd saved my life. If not for her quick thinking, I'd be falling through inky blackness.

"Now what?" The bow wanted me with a visceral need, a

tug in my bones that I had to strive to ignore. "I can't just walk away; it won't let me."

"I—we didn't come all this way for nothing." Sylvana, seeming more energized now than she had since we walked through the door, pulled the pack off her back, and dropped, cross-legged to the ground. "Sit." She ordered, and I did while she rummaged through the contingency spells we'd packed only hours before.

Nimble fingers delved into the bag's contents, and Sylvana laid out a vial containing a clear vision potion and several of the spell jars we'd hoped not to have to use.

"Bottoms up." She quaffed half the potion and handed the bottle to me. Why couldn't these things ever taste like cherry cola? Was it some kind of rule that a potion had to have the texture and flavor of dismal swamp? I gagged, but kept the liquid down and felt its fetid warmth spread through me. Slowly, my sense of sight intensified and expanded.

"It's working." I know it's uncool to jump up and down in celebration of being a witch, but there are times when I badly want to.

Still seated, we simultaneously turned our gazes toward where the bow rested. "Well, would you look at that?" A curtain of rippling shadow circled the center island to a height slightly above waist-high level. Angled inward at the top, the shimmer formed a conical shield that could be scaled, but only with delicate precision. Had I leaped without looking, the slant of the shield would have funneled me into the deep. As it was, there was no way I could cross the barrier unless I could fly, and I wasn't sure I could. Salem hadn't covered that part of my education yet, and I'd felt the question was too silly to ask. Until now.

"That whole flying on a broomstick thing, that's a myth, right?"

"Irrelevant." Sylvana replied, her eyes still focused on the bow. "This is a physical challenge. The first was mental; the second had to do with matters of the soul, and this one is purely physical. No magical means allowed."

"So I'm supposed to what? Jump across a four-foot void at an upward trajectory and land on a dime? Exactly what in our short history together would lead you to believe I have anything close to that level of athletic ability?"

"There might be another way." Rising with some of her former grace, Sylvana's face glowed white against the darkness around her eyes. Her lips, still almost black, pursed as she strode around the rim of the chasm. I'd hoped that with the return of her vitality, her features would go back to normal; the crazed witch look gave me the creeps.

"What other way?" I scanned the area above the plinth to see if there was a rope to swing on. Playing Tarzan sounded slightly better than the only other possibility that came to mind, and I figured it was a more viable solution than me attempting to pole vault across. A mental image of which made me shudder over the sheer number of ways that could go wrong.

"Remember how we accessed the path to the repository?" Sylvana asked. "There's probably a switch somewhere."

"A switch? How's that supposed to be a physical challenge?"

"I never said it would be easily accessed."

Drat the convoluted mind of a witch.

We searched in a widening arc spanning out from the dais in the center of the room and only found it once we thought to look both high and low. High. It had to be high. Above the door that blocked our way back, my enhanced vision picked out a tiny ray of light falling on a button nestled above the door.

"There, but how do we get to it?" I pointed.

"Classic Clara. Always goes for the obvious. We need more light." As one, we conjured cold flame in our outstretched palms and used the glow to search the area. Appropriately enough, I was the one who found the ordinary bow and arrow leaning against a support post.

"Mom." I held up the weapon. "Do you think...."

"Prove yourself worthy by testing your aim? What a cliché."

"Great. I don't suppose you have any latent skills to bring to the table?"

"Other than the eagle eye potion?" A bitter smile twisted Sylvana's ebony lips.

Picking up the bow, I tested my strength against the string. We'd done archery in PE class the year I turned fourteen, and I'd been so worried about my awakening that I hadn't paid attention. I think I scraped by that year with slightly below average grades in all my classes. Still, my body sort of remembered the motions and the stance. Nocking an arrow to the string, I pulled back experimentally to get a feel for the rising tension and sighted in on the button. With any luck, heredity would kick in and take me from rudimentary to a higher level of skill.

"Here goes nothing." The shot went wide, and Sylvana let out a choked cry. When I turned to see what had caused the strangled noise, I saw her clutching a spot just above her hip.

"Well, that's unexpected. Even though I should have guessed." She moved one hand away from her side and held it out to show the crimson stain.

"How did that happen?" Crossing the space between us, I fell to me knees to examine the wound. "You were behind me; there's no way I could have hit you."

"Consequences. Clara was a big fan. You have to try again." She urged.

"No, what if I miss again, it could be worse the second time."

"That's a given, but if I know my mother, the only way to reverse the consequences is for you to hit that button. Try not to miss, okay?"

"I wasn't trying to miss the first time. Nothing like a little added pressure when I'm playing with pointy objects." Sarcasm, a girl's best friend.

"Breathe into it and don't close your eyes this time." Helpful directions came out with a wince and the pressure of knowing what would happen if I missed sent my heart into a mad gallop. Trembling fingers fumbling against the string, I blinked and shook the hair away from my eyes.

"Quit stalling," came the directive from behind me.

"Why don't you try it then? I'd rather be hit with the arrow than the one doing the damage."

"You're a Balefire, not a wuss," Sylvana practically growled at me, and on that note, I let the second arrow fly.

And missed. The arrow quivered in the post not an inch above the button.

"No. I'm sorry. I'm so sorry." All the blood drained out of my face when Sylvana failed to answer. I whirled to see her slumped over on the ground and I knew what I had to do.

As I cocked my elbow and pulled the third and final arrow back, I let the part of me that belonged to Cupid take over. My chin dropped, my eyes focused in on the button with uncanny precision, and I breathed into the shot.

Thwack. A solid hit and dead on target. The door swung open, and behind me, Sylvana stirred.

"You did him proud."

"Are you all right?" I pushed her hands away from her side to make sure.

"Right as rain."

"Isn't that touching?" Delta's voice ringing out of the darkness jumped me half out of my skin. "A genuine moment. I'd almost believe you, Sylvana. Almost."

"All I'm here to do is help my daughter; you can believe whatever you want. Come, Lexi. It's time." Delta followed us back to the edge of the pit where Sylvana took her place on the opposite side to cheer me on. I checked that the barrier was down and took a moment to gauge the distance. Overshooting my mark could send me into the blackness just as quickly as coming up short when I leaped toward the pedestal.

I'd gathered my nerve and risen to the balls of my feet to start the first running steps when Jett stepped out of the shadows, followed by Serena.

"Where did you come from?"

After that, everything happened so fast it's hard to remember how it all went down.

Kin sprinted through the door with Salem hard on his heels.

"Lexi, Jett's... already here."

"I've come for what's mine. I have more right to that bow than *she* does." Jett tried to dodge around Kin to make the jump before I could, and Kin pushed back. It looked like Serena was going to leap onto Kin's back, but Salem grabbed her before she got close. Fists flew, blows landed, and it was hard to tell who was winning until the two men broke apart.

Kin was too close to the edge. I called to him, but it was too late. Jett charged forward and shoved the heel of one hand against Kin's chest, and he teetered on the edge of the pit.

If he fell, he would take half of my soul with him, and I couldn't let that happen.

Adrenaline shot through me and time folded back on itself. Or, in my moment of need, I might have subconsciously uttered a spell that warped time to suit my needs. My memory is a little hazy on the details. Delta was too far away to help, but Sylvana was close enough to grab Kin before he went over the side leaving me free to get to the bow before Jett could make the leap.

"Mom. Save Kin." She loved me, right? She'd save Kin for that reason alone.

It was a good plan. Too bad it never happened.

Sylvana's expression turned savage and cold, and instead of helping Kin, who was still fighting to regain his balance, she flung herself across the chasm to land heavily next to the pedestal. I made a split second adjustment, dodged in the other direction, and grabbed Kin's shirt just before he plunged over the edge. He almost took me with him, but Salem, dragging Serena along with one hand, planted the other firmly around my arm, and yanked us both to safety.

The biggest surprise of the day happened next. Flix appeared out of nowhere and blasted Jett with some type of faerie magic I didn't even know he could do. A whirling cloud of thunder and lightning swallowed Jett whole while Serena screamed his name.

When I turned back to the place I had last seen my mother, Sylvana was gone, and Delta lay on the ground, a purpling bruise forming on her temple. On her way out, Sylvana must have clocked the Fiach with the handle of the bow. So much for this little mother/daughter bonding exercise. She'd duped me, stolen the bow, and left Kin to die.

I guess I should have listened to Delta.

All I could do at that moment, though, was cling to Kin and let the adrenaline jitter through my body.

"Are you all right?" Kisses rained across my face, and I returned them all.

"We'll just leave you two alone," Salem marshaled a still-wailing Serena toward the door while Flix half carried Delta out of the hold. "So you can play kissy-face in private." His undertone of disgust was clearly an act since he'd been on Kin's side all along.

"I'm so sorry. I shouldn't have doubted you," Kin murmured into my neck as I began to apologize, "I'm the one who is sorry. You were right not to trust her. Can you ever forgive me?"

Cupping my face in his hands, Kin rested his forehead against mine. "If you'll forgive me for walking away. Say you'll take me back, I can't stand it if you don't."

A kiss that left us both tingling answered for me, but I still had one question for him.

"Are you sure? I'm not destined for normal. What if this is the tip of the iceberg?"

Staring into his eyes, I looked for signs of doubt and saw none.

"As long as we're together, I can handle anything. Normal is overrated."

Truth. At least for right now, and that was all I could ask of him.

"We stick together from now on. No matter what happens. I know now that I'm not wicked, and I never will be. What I experienced today; I can't even explain it, but things are clearer now." The words tumbled out and I realized that I truly believed them.

"I'll never leave you again. I love you, Lexi."

"I love you, too, Kin."

It felt good to say the words and mean them.

Pressing close, Kin laid firm lips over mine to seal the deal.

If I had known what was waiting for us outside, I would have cut the kissing a little shorter. As it was, we exited the building and landed in the middle of a strange tableau.

Flix had taken charge of Serena, who sat on a rock about fifteen feet away from the group. I felt the other witch's baleful stare but ignored the mask of hatred. Frankly, she wasn't worth my time.

My four godmothers were there. How had I not known that? Then again, Kin hadn't been concerned with giving me details. I walked up to the circle, which also included Salem, and followed their gazes down to the object that lay on the ground in the center.

The Bow of Destiny. In pieces.

"Well, that's unfortunate," I understated the situation. "You want to tell me how it happened?"

The story came out in dribs and drabs.

On his way to knock on my door and beg forgiveness, Kin had seen me leave with Sylvana. He'd also seen Jett and Serena come skulking out of the woods to follow along behind. Knowing they were up to no good, he'd gone in to warn the faeries, and come with them when they decided it was time to help.

By the time they'd reached the clearing, Sylvana and I were already inside Shadow Hold and so was Delta, who had nipped through the door just behind us. Kin and Salem followed Jett and Serena, but the faeries had been barred access. Probably something to do with being Fae, though it hadn't stopped Flix, who had been drawn to me through our empathetic connection during the first trial when I'd been screaming into nothingness.

Maybe it had been fate or maybe just dumb luck, but when Sylvana shot out the door with the bow in her hands, Terra and her sisters had been waiting. They ambushed her and Evian, who was closest, had snatched the bow right out of her hands.

A few sizzling bushes and some odd looking animals attested to the shortest faerie battle of all time before

Sylvana had taken herself elsewhere in a hurry. My heart ached to do it, but I blocked all thoughts of her betrayal from my mind, put them in my little box, and tucked it away in a dark corner once again. I'd deal with it eventually, but not right now, in front of everyone.

"I don't know what happened. It just...broke." Evian turned stricken eyes on me. "I'm sorry."

"Fae magic confounds that which the Gods have made," Delta shouted at us. "You've just undone all my hard work with a single touch."

Delta looked like she was about to launch herself at Evian, but knew better than to write a check she couldn't cash.

"So that's it? We did all this for nothing?" I whispered.

"I don't know. We're in unprecedented territory."

Delta looked up into the sky as she had that day in the alley, and I expected her to shoot into the air and disappear again. Her eyes lost focus for a few seconds before her gaze fell on me again.

"I have to go back and tell them I failed my mission." She swallowed hard and made me a solemn vow. "I'll scour the earth and beyond for anything that will aid your quest to restore the Bow of Destiny. May I have your promise that you will pursue that goal?"

Terra, Evian, Soleil, and Vaeta each took a step backward and waited for my response. "You told me the truth, even though I didn't want to hear it. You helped me even though I threatened you and chose the wrong side, and you showed up here to ensure the Bow of Destiny ended up in the right hands. You've earned my trust, and I will make that promise."

"Thank you, Lexi Balefire." Delta offered her hand, and when we sealed the agreement, I felt the bond of promise seal our fates together. "If it is the will of the Gods, I will return." With a whoosh, she was gone.

"Terra, take us all home," we were there before I could add the *please*.

# EPILOGUE

Three days crawled past in a morass of faces and conversations, considering everybody insisted I be kept company twenty-four-seven; it was a wonder I was allowed to use the bathroom alone. They all—the faeries, Flix, and of course Kin—seemed to think I was a woman on the razor's edge of a hissy fit or worse in my grief over Sylvana's betrayal. I would never call her Mom again, but she certainly wasn't worth dropping my basket over. Looking back, the clues to her true nature stood out in painful detail and so did the shutters I'd put over my eyes in order to give her the benefit of the doubt. More than once— more than she deserved.

Mercifully, Flix came to my rescue when he shimmered in to let me know things at the office had undergone a sudden turn.

When I demanded an explanation for what had happened to Jett, and what kind of magic Flix had used to banish him, I discovered my friend possessed an affinity for manipulating the space between worlds and he'd blasted Jett into one of the seedier sections of the Faelands.

I didn't feel one pang of remorse when Flix said he might never find his way back.

"Lexi, it seems Jett's forced vacation broke his contact with Serena. Without his energy to fuel them, his curses have been shattering all over the city. We've been getting slammed with calls from people who have been dating their worst enemy for the past few months, and they're all in the market for a healthy relationship. It's getting a bit hairy; you feeling up to coming back?"

I'd immediately begged off another shift with the depression police, though I caught Flix motioning to the faeries that he'd keep a watchful eye on me, and hightailed it to the office. A full pot of coffee later, I'd finally sifted through the messages and set up a solid week of appointments. So when Mona tripped into my office, iced caramel swirls in each hand, part of me wondered if I should decline —but that would have been rude, and besides, caramel swirl.

"Lexi, you're not going to believe it! Dr. Cooper and my mom got back together! Just like that; it was as if he came out of a spell, he said he didn't know what he was thinking, and he begged her to take him back. And I swear I wouldn't be surprised if they end up making it permanent. I know it's crazy, but you should see them together; it's the most adorable thing. I don't know what you did but thank you, thank you, thank you!"

I returned Mona's hug and may have even giggled a little. A very little. "I had nothing to do with it, I swear, but that's wonderful!" Like coming out of a spell, indeed.

My knee must have accidentally tagged the button mounted under my desk because Flix shimmered into view behind Mona. Startled, he rolled his eyes and pretended to have entered through the salon door.

"Flix, I didn't know you were here." Mona's brow furrowed, and she shook her head as if to clear an image. "Did you hear about my mom and Dr. Cooper?" she asked, then followed him through the door and down the hallway, chattering away.

Now, I know it might sound like things were back to normal, but the truth is everything had changed. Yes, I'd been hurt and betrayed; a part of me had died back in that chamber, watching Sylvana choose personal gain over saving someone I loved. But I'd also learned a thing or two about myself. When I wove the threads of my two halves into that bow-wielding witch and tapped into my Fate Weaver essence, I began the process of coming to terms with *who*, or to be more accurate, *what* I was.

And that filled holes that had been eating away at me during my entire life.

Take and give left me somewhere in the middle, riding a wave of acceptance I knew would come crashing into shore eventually.

Out of all the people in my life, the only one who hadn't attempted to wrap me in cotton and put me in a box for my own safety was Salem. As my familiar, he was—pardon the pun—familiar enough with my emotions to gauge them correctly.

"Again," he said later that night, flickering light from the Balefire playing across his features. "And this time, keep your eye on the ball." He whipped the hard rubber ball against the tile floor, and it went ping-ponging through the large space. Eyes tracking its trajectory, I funneled power into my outstretched finger and blasted the bouncy sphere to kingdom come.

"Better." We'd decided to work on my defensive spells, just in case. Who knew when Sylvana might return, and I wanted to be ready. Would I give her a chance to explain? Maybe, and then again, maybe not.

By the time I'd killed fifteen high bounce balls, I was shaking from the effort of using such pinpointed magic and was ready for a hot shower, a pair of comfy yoga pants, a facial, and a cheesy movie.

Oh, and laundry. Judging by the size of the mountain in the corner, it had been weeks. I know some people consider the chore nothing short of drudgery, but I like the way the clothes smell when they come out of the dryer all warm and soft.

I'd scooped up the first pile of darks when something clanked to the floor and rolled under the laundry sink.

The ring. The one Mag had folded into my hand just before Sylvana crashed through the door. What was it she'd told me? The ring had belonged to Clara who would have wanted it to come to me and that I wasn't to show it to anyone.

More drama? I hoped not. I'd had enough drama to last me half a lifetime.

Carrying the ring back to my desk, I held it under the light to get a better look. The simple band of beaten silver felt heavier than its size would suggest, and had a crude design carved or possibly pressed into the rim.

Jewelry in my house fell under two categories; that of the magical heirloom variety or the pricey stuff conjured up by faeries. Mag said this piece belonged to my grandmother, so right away I was expecting the former.

Warmer than my skin, the metal felt alive in my hand, and I swear I intended to put it in a box for safekeeping. Right up until I slipped it onto my finger. It fit like it had been made for me and sent an electric spark dancing across my flesh.

My grandmother had worn this ring, did it still carry her essence? Was it safe to wear?

Fading dusk carried just enough light to see my grandmother's stoned body in her silent clearing. Not for the first time, I wondered what happened the day she ended up looking like one of the Furies.

I sank onto the cushioned window seat and pictured it the way Terra had described the clearing on the day she found me. Scorched earth, stoned witch, and the stench of black magic hanging in the air like smoke.

Unconsciously, I twisted the ring around and around on my finger while I wished for the millionth time for a clue to the events of that day. The ring flared with light.

What on earth?

The world shifted around me so quickly I didn't feel it happen and the next thing I knew, I was surrounded by the chilled air and mist of a damp spring day. Gooseflesh shivered to life along my arms and legs when I heard the sound of my mother screaming.

*You didn't think Lexi's life could get more tangled, did you?
Spoiler alert: it can—and it does.*

Keep reading for a preview of To Spell & Back, where Lexi dives into the past, battles the present, and faces a future that's more complicated than even her faerie godmothers could have predicted!

## QUICK AUTHOR'S NOTE

If you weren't already aware, ReGina and Erin are a mother/daughter writing team, and yes, that means we mix family and work—with all the ups and downs you might expect. It helps that we basically share a single brain most of the time and tend to finish each other's sentences...literally. It also means we sometimes squabble over plot points, but since we're best friends, too, we let that stuff roll right off our backs.

When it came time to write All Spell is Breaking Loose, we knew we had to push Lexi Balefire further into her magical and emotional journey. Love—whether romantic, familial, or the kind you find in your chosen family—is messy, complicated, and sometimes downright magical, and this book gave us the perfect opportunity to explore all of that.

Of course, Sylvana had to make her mark, taking her disruption of Lexi's life to a whole new level. We're always asking ourselves: what's the best way to turn Lexi's world upside down...while giving her (and you) a chance to laugh along the way?

And let's not forget Kin. We both agreed that while finding your soulmate might be the stuff of fairytales, keeping that spark alive in the face of challenges is where the real magic happens. Kin and Lexi's story is a reminder that even when love is fated, it's still a choice you make every day.

But you know Lexi's journey wouldn't be complete without diving deeper into her family's tangled history. In To Spell & Back, Lexi faces the legacy of the Balefire witches head-on as she travels through time to uncover long-buried secrets, confronts Serena's escalating schemes, and discovers that the Bow of Destiny has plans of its own. You won't want to miss this twisty, heartfelt chapter of Lexi's story!

Anyway, if you've come this far with us and not decided we're complete and total whackadoodles...and especially if you have, we're offering a chance to sign up for our newsletters— the best place to get new release updates, sales notifications, and other fun content.

You can sign up for ReGina's newsletter and/or Erin's newsletter, and as a thank-you gift for hanging out with us, you'll also get a FREE novella that isn't available anywhere else. And of course, we promise not to SPAM your inbox!

Love, hugs, and happy reading,
*ReGina & Erin*

P.S. If you enjoyed this book, it would be great if you could leave a review or recommendation at your favorite store, GoodReads, or BookBub.

Your reviews help indie authors sell more books!

# EXCERPT FROM TO SPELL & BACK

## FATE WEAVER - BOOK THREE

"Get away from him." Sylvana's scream cut the air like a knife, her voice edging toward hysterical. "You vicious old witch. Leave him alone."

White fire lanced from her fingertips, arrowed toward her mother's body. Clara batted the sizzling flame away with as much attention as she would have paid a fly buzzing around her ear.

While her daughter raged, Clara's attention remained focused on the man who was at the crux of this fight. Or, technically, the minor deity: Cupid. The one and only god of love who carried a bow and heart-tipped arrows, but was as far from a winged cherub as a donkey is from a goose.

Chiseled perfection from head to toe, there was nothing baby soft about him. It was no wonder Sylvana had fallen for his...charms. Had that been all there was to it, the three of them might never have come to this moment. Or rather, the four of us.

I'm Lexi Balefire, daughter of Sylvana, granddaughter of Clara, and Cupid? Well, he's my dad. I know, it shocked me, too, when I found out.

While the fight raged, I was the squealing infant tucked into a carry basket and left forgotten on the grass. Paradoxically, I was also the time traveling interloper watching the biggest mystery of my past play out before stunned eyes. Not your typical Wednesday, I'll grant you.

This was the pivotal moment that would leave me virtually orphaned, send my mother to hell and my father to who-knows-where. In a few minutes, nothing would be left but a black scar on the ground, my grandmother's body turned to stone, and me; a crying infant who would grow up with the stigma of having hailed from wicked witches.

Or a murdering witch, if you want to get technical. When my faerie godmother found me, she assumed my grandmother had killed my mother—a supposition I recently learned was a total mistake. Now I would find out exactly what happened that fateful day.

I wasn't sure I could watch, but I knew I couldn't look away.

"She doesn't know what you did, does she?" Clara Balefire's wrath curled around Cupid like a living thing that might strangle him if she gave full reign to her temper. "Just how many lies *did* you have to tell to get my daughter to let you put a baby in her belly?"

More white fire arced from Sylvana's direction, to be deflected with a twitch of Clara's finger while my father's burning gaze rested on my grandmother.

"Of course he told me." Looking at my mother at this age gave me a shiver. Peaches and cream complexion, wide green eyes under thick black lashes, and ruby lips. Except for the teased-to-the-max '80's hairdo, we could have been twins. Okay, maybe the hair *and* the clothes.

She wore artfully torn leggings under a ruffled mini—both in black—and a hot pink cropped top. Half a dozen bangles clanked together every time she lobbed another ball of witchfire at her mother. Madonna would have been proud, or maybe dismayed at her effect on my mother's sense of style.

"Didn't you, baby?" Sylvana purred at Cupid, then spat at her mother, "We don't keep secrets."

Cupid declined to comment, and even from a distance, I could see the secrets in his eyes. Blinded by her infatuation with him, my mother would never admit my father's intentions might have been dishonorable even if she'd known truth. Not that I would have expected anything different—he's a god, for freak's sake. They don't play by human rules.

"The child has promise. At the right time, I will teach her how to make the most of her gifts." His voice reminded me of a French horn; tenor with a deeper resonance underneath. His glance strayed toward the baby, and I had trouble wrapping my head around the fact that *she* was *me*.

"This one carries the potential to be the strongest of her kind. I would not allow her to take on that burden without guidance."

"How very noble of you." Clara's sneer turned the words to knives. "Do you even know her name? Or is she just a thing to you? Something to mold and shape."

Cupid's lack of interest deflected the cuts as surely as if he'd worn forged armor.

"You presume too much, Clara Balefire. I protect what is mine and Alexis," he placed emphasis on my name to prove a point, "is mine."

"Like you protected Beatrice and Reginald? Like you would have protected my sister if she'd been stupid enough to let you have your way with her? Alexis would be safer if she never realized that potential. You're willing to put a target on her back out of a sense of inflated ego."

Unwilling to allow my attention to slip from what I was watching, even for a second, I didn't have time to ponder who Beatrice and Reginald were, or that I had a great aunt I'd never met.

"He loves us." Sylvana leaped aside to avoid a spell that boomeranged back on her when Clara, without even looking in her direction, deflected the curse with a single finger. "We're going to make a family together, and we don't need you to be part of it. Just leave him alone and let us go."

"Did he tell you that in so many words? Did he tell you how he's been trying to bed a Balefire woman for centuries? First my mother, then my sister, and now my daughter, and who knows how many before that? And all to make a new and more powerful Fate Weaver."

Sylvana thought about it for half a second.

"Shut up, you old cow. You're wrong about him—he loves us, you'll see." My eyebrows rose toward my hairline at Sylvana's harsh criticism; an old cow isn't at all how I'd have described my grandmother, nor would I have dared to blithely show such disrespect to a family member.

Then again, growing up without my true family had given me a different perspective on its sacred nature.

My mother and I had both inherited our looks from Clara, and I wasn't complaining. The Balefire women carry good genes, and I'd bet Clara had heard the tired line about how she and Sylvana looked like sisters from more middle-aged men than it would take to fill a country club.

Eyes trained on my father, Clara slammed a barrier to close Sylvana out of the conversation. "Are you even capable of love?"

Cupid faced away from me and even leaning sideways I caught nothing more than a glimpse of the curve of one cheek, half covered by the edge of the Bow of Destiny. All gold and shining, the weapon's string chimed soft notes against the light breeze.

"Love is my business." The bow looked like a liquid blur practically leaping into his hands, the strings screaming a tune of willingness. What's more, the compass around my neck shrieked to life. Okay, shriek may not be the best word, but saying it broke into song turns this story into something straight out of a Disney musical, and let me tell you, this was not one of those.

Dark was the bowsong, with honed edges that cut and sliced. I only got a glimmer of it from the echo of the compass, which seemed to be acting as some sort of speaker system; my father is the one who took the brunt of the onslaught coming directly off the weapon in his hand. My instincts told me the bow was warning Cupid against rashly taking action. My head rang with a dizzying sound that turned me weak. How on earth could Clara just stand there like she saw nothing happening?

"My daughter's happiness is mine." Fast as a striking snake, Clara crossed the space and before my father realized her intent, snatched the bow, fitted arrow to string, and took aim. "If your will is what makes this thing work, then my own should remove the blinders and help her see her way clear."

She dropped the barrier and dodged as my father made a grab for her.

Silence fell like a balm when the arrow flew straight and true on a course for Sylvana's heart.

Faster than a human can move, my father covered the distance between himself and Sylvana. Clara's arrow slammed into his backside with a solid sound that made me blanch. Did I mention I'm supposed to wield that same bow as Miss Fancy-ass Fate Weaver, or whatever title it is the gods want me to carry? Was I supposed to shoot people with that thing? Nope. Not on my list of things to do.

Clara's triumphant shout ended in a roar of, "Nooo."

The force of the blow slammed my dad into my mom, and she hit the ground hard enough to knock the wind out of her. Staggering and struggling to regain his footing, Cupid yanked the arrow out of his flesh.

"Stupid witch. Do you have any idea what you've done to me?" He grabbed the bow from Clara and then tossed it away as if the bright gold had turned to searing flame. Whether it burned or not, the bow did something to Cupid he hadn't expected. His face altered from robust perfection to a haunted pallor so quickly it reminded me of watching a movie on fast forward.

By the time he turned and walked away without so much as a backward glance at Sylvana, my father had become a shadow of his former self.

My mother, however, seemed to gain all the strength her lover lost.

"Look what you did." Sylvana practically levitated off the

ground, fury oozing from every pore. Almost absently, her hands formed magic like I'd never seen before.

Black fire ate daylight and grew between her palms to a crackling mass so large she could barely hold it. I'm not sure whether a trick of the light made it seem so, or if her eyes actually turned black, but I knew I had to take action.

"Stop. You have to stop this right now. Look what you're about to do to each other. Look what you're about to do to *me!*" I jumped into the middle and shouted until my throat burned, but it made no difference. Neither of them could see me. There was nothing left to do but watch in horror.

The moment drew out long and pregnant with magic while Sylvana railed and cursed Clara with every filthy name she could pull to her lips.

"Think what you like, I only want you to be happy."

Clara's statement, quietly made and sincere as far as I could tell anyway, sent Sylvana fully over the edge to the dark side. Everything after that happened at high speed.

Sylvana let the seething magic go with all the force she could muster. Clara spoke a few short words, but I could tell she'd reacted a half-second too late.

The Bow of Destiny went up in a cloud of smoke. Knowing where it ended up, I assumed my grandmother had wasted precious seconds ensuring my father's legacy wouldn't be found until I searched it out either twenty-four-odd years in the future or a couple of days ago depending on whether I was counting back from my present or forward from the past I witnessed now.

"Ligabis, Ostium, Carcere." Clara's second spell rippled

through the air and turned to a set of shadowy ropes. A binding spell.

Halfway between the two women, Sylvana's crackling, ebony flame crossed with Clara's spell and I saw something I never thought possible. The two spells—well, mingled isn't exactly the right word, but it's the best one I can find.

Sylvana's witchfire absorbed the binding spell and hit Clara, who tried to throw up a shield but failed. Face fierce, hair floating on the breeze created by the force of Sylvana's intent, I watched the spell bust through the feeble beginnings of a barrier and turn my grandmother to stone. Inch by painful inch.

Sylvana's moment of glee quickly turned sour when the evil she'd sent out bounced off the feet of the stone effigy and returned to her before she had time to duck. A flash, a sizzle, the scent of ozone, and a scorch mark on the earth— I'd heard the story so many times that seeing the aftermath in person felt surreal.

Well, except for the cries coming from the basket.

To Spell & Back is available now, or if you'd rather save money, you can grab the box set of the first three books in the series for a discount. Keep reading for a preview of the free novella you'll get for joining our newsletters.

# A FREE STORY FOR YOU

Enjoyed meeting Lexi? Not ready for her story to end?

Sign up for either or both of our newsletters and you'll receive *A Snowball's Chance in Spell*, a prequel novella featuring characters from the *Mag & Clara Balefire Mysteries*, the *Haunted Everly After Mysteries*, and the *Psychic Seasons* series.

*Christmas is canceled!* Lexi Balefire's faerie godmothers didn't mean to knock Santa Claus and his sleigh out of the sky, but now his reindeer are missing, and it's up to Lexi to find them all before time runs out and Christmas is ruined!

## EXCERPT FROM A SNOWBALL'S CHANCE IN SPELL

~

Lightning flirted in shadows of the dark clouds hovering over my house when I came home from work the afternoon before my twenty-second Christmas Eve. Nothing unusual there. With three elemental faeries living in the house, weird weather happened all the time. Or rather, every time my temperamental godmothers mounted some sort of snit.

The godmothers idled at snit.

Going back to work wasn't an option. I'd cleared the last match of the year—a lovely couple with a shared affection for online gaming—and I was no coward. When it came to diffusing faerie fights, I consider myself an expert, and this one didn't look like it rated more than a two on the volcano scale.

Yes, you heard right. I measure faerie fights on the scale of whether or not a volcano might erupt in my backyard. Living with faeries is never boring. Occasionally dangerous —especially because I have yet to come into the magic that is my birthright, but never boring.

A quick check proved they'd contained the madness to the inside and/or the backyard. The two feet of snow on the front lawn was still there and still white—you try explaining black snow to your neighbors sometime. I didn't see any winged denizens—fae or otherwise—dotting the roof ridge, or hear any ominous sounds. If not for the fact that lightning is rare in Maine during the winter, and rarer still when confined to a single area, I'd have thought it was a quiet day in the household.

In my head, I downgraded the threat to a level one, and went inside.

For the most part, my place looks like an ordinary, New England style home. Built by my great grandparents, it's the oldest house in a neighborhood that grew up around it when the suburbs expanded into what was once a rural area.

Because, I think, the faeries wanted to give me a normal upbringing, they left the house in mostly the same condition it was in when they came to take care of me and only added on a wing for their own use.

I stepped into the front hall expecting...well, just about anything. Did I mention the faeries love holidays? Maybe they don't have them in the faelands, or maybe they do and go overboard there, too. I can't say since I've never been, but I could tell at a glance there were more decorations than there had been when I left.

"Terra!" I yelled, but got no answer. Terra, faerie of earth, held sway over all the flora and fauna found on dry land. She would be the one responsible for the pine boughs twining over anything that held still long enough. Fire faerie, Soleil, contributed by setting sparks of faerie light to twinkle inside the delicate ice bubbles crafted by her sister, Evian, mistress of water. The effect was lovely, but not as lovely as the three women could be when their faces weren't twisted, as they were now, with rage.

I came upon them in their favorite fighting grounds: the kitchen. It looked like I'd caught this one early since there was relatively little damage done so far. Steam rose from a puddle of water at Soleil's feet which I assumed had come from Evian. Vines snaked from between the kitchen tiles to twine around Evian's ankles, and there were a few smoking embers dotting Terra's hair. Nothing more than a minor spat.

Keeping it casual, I asked, "What's going on?" There's no rhyme or reason to what will settle a fight or send one into the red zone.

Terra turned one granite pink eye in my direction. "This doesn't concern you." The fingers of her left hand twitched and the vines slithered from Evian's ankles to her knees.

Retaliating, Evian conjured a gush of water from thin air, and doused the smoking embers. The scent of pine boughs couldn't compete with the stench of burnt hair, or the pungent funk erupting from the flowers that burst into bloom near her feet.

"Now look," I pointed out to Terra before she conjured something worse. "Evian is trying to help."

"Was not." Evian snapped her fingers and turned Terra's wet hair white with frost, except because the vines were now questing higher, she overshot the mark and doused a few of Soleil's decorative sparkles.

That was the moment I lost control.

Oh, who am I kidding? I never had control.

Soleil let out a screech and lobbed a fireball at Evian, who encased it in a ball of water and batted it toward Terra. I felt scoured clean when Terra called all the dirt and dust in the house to form a layer over the bobbing ball of doom which now resembled a small planet whizzing back toward Soleil.

It might have ended better if I'd have kept my mouth shut, but I didn't.

"You're going to put an eye out with that thing."

The ire of three faeries is a potent thing, but not as potent as a flaming mudball. I ducked, rolled, and hit the latch on the patio door in what I'd like to think was a graceful move. Probably looked like a seal rolling off a rock.

The flaming fireball arced over my head, its warm breeze tossing my hair, and rocketed off into the sky.

Crisis averted. Except, it wasn't. I should have known.

**A Snowball's Chance in Spell** is only available by signing
up for one of our newsletters here:
https://reginawelling.com
https://erinlynnwrites.com

# OTHER BOOKS

If you'd like to meet more people who live rent-free in our heads, here's a list of other series we've written. Our books are all set in fictional towns in Maine, and some characters like to flit back and forth between series. The cast of Psychic Seasons hangs out with Everly and also with Lexi Balefire from the Fate Weaver series. Mag and Clara Balefire are Lexi's grandmother and aunt!

*The Psychic Seasons Series*
Four women, four love stories, and a whole lot of supernatural surprises. In the quaint town of Oakville, Maine, psychic visions, ghostly whispers, and fate itself conspire to change lives—and hearts—forever

*The Haunted Everly After Mysteries*
Everly Dupree came home for a fresh start—not a full-time gig solving ghostly murders. But when the dearly departed start demanding justice, what's a reluctant medium to do?

*The Ponderosa Pines Mysteries*
Nothing bad ever happens in the weird little town of Ponderosa Pines...until someone dies. Now it's up to best

friends Chloe and EV to solve the mystery—before the town's secrets bury them too.

*The Mag and Clara Balefire Mysteries*
Sister witches Mag and Clara Balefire move to a sleepy Maine town for a fresh start—only to find themselves conjuring up trouble, solving murders, and keeping their magic under wraps in this charmingly witchy cozy mystery series

*Laurel Haven Witches*
Four witches, destined by blood and magic, must embrace their power, battle a dark legacy, and surrender to the love that could break the curse—or bind them to it forever.

*Nell Page: Accidental Investigator*
Nell Page owns a bookstore, drinks too much coffee, and has a habit of noticing things she probably shouldn't. With warmth, wit, and an accidental talent for investigating, Nell tackles mysteries that don't always involve murder—but always matter.